D0276500

Legacy of Greyladies

By Anna Jacobs

THE GREYLADIES SERIES

Heir to Greyladies

Mistress of Greyladies

Legacy of Greyladies

THE WILTSHIRE GIRLS SERIES

Cherry Tree Lane

Elm Tree Road

Yew Tree Gardens

THE PEPPERCORN STREET SERIES

Peppercorn Street

Cinnamon Gardens

a&b

Legacy of Greyladies

ANNA JACOBS

Allison & Busby Limited
12 Fitzroy Mews
London W1T 6DW
allisonandbusby.com

First published in Great Britain by Allison & Busby in 2015.

A CIP catalogue record for this book is available from the British Library.

First Edition

ISBN 978-0-7490-1422-3

Typeset in 11/16 pt Sabon by
Allison & Busby Ltd.

The paper used for this Allison & Busby publication has been produced from trees that have been legally sourced from well-managed and credibly certified forests.

Printed and bound by
CPI Group (UK) Ltd, Croydon, CR0 4YY

Dear readers,

I often get asked what inspires me to write a story. All sorts of things, to tell you the truth! The way a family greet each other at an airport, weeping for joy. The way ordinary people you see on the TV news deal with major life problems, becoming suddenly magnificent and heroic.

But with the Greyladies series, it was something very specific that started me off: Avebury Manor in Wiltshire and the slightly smaller country houses in similar style that you drive past in the countryside nearby.

If you want to see for yourself, do a search online for 'Avebury Manor' and you'll find photos of a large house with steep roofs and gables. The image of this wonderful old house kept creeping into my dreams and eventually I had to write about a similar house. Who could have built it? What were the original occupiers like? And then the 'grey ladies', nuns in grey clothing, began to walk round the house of my dreams.

I knew about the Dissolution of the Monasteries under Henry VIII – and my little nunnery wouldn't have survived that. So what did my grey ladies do after they were thrown out of their abbey?

Well, of course Anne Latimer, the strong-willed abbess, would have saved them by marrying and bringing up a family in the old house, rather than letting it be destroyed. The villagers called it Greyladies, for obvious reasons.

Anne loved the house so much that her spirit stayed on there to guard it and her descendants. And having seen nuns thrown out on the streets and in great distress, she founded a charity to help other women in trouble.

Finally, since men have done most of the inheriting of stately homes in England, I thought I'd even things up a bit. I decided to let this house pass down the female line.

And away I went, into that magic state where a story forms in my mind and characters inhabit my dreams.

I have loved writing every word of this series. It's set in one of my favourite eras, too, the first two decades of the twentieth century, and includes the Home Front in World War I.

For the time being, Legacy of Greyladies is the third and final book in this set of stories, but if you think I can leave the house behind completely, you're wrong.

I've got another idea forming in my mind . . . a story taking place somewhere nearby. Give me a little time to let it brew, dear readers, and I'll be off again on another exciting adventure.

Happy reading,
Anna

This book is for Teena Raffa Mulligan, who is not only a friend, but a fellow writer and who acts as my assistant, doing a wonderful job.
Everyone should have a friend like Teena!

Chapter One

Wiltshire, December 1915

As soon as she entered the house, Olivia heard Cecily sobbing and her heart sank. She prayed nothing had happened to Donald, who had suddenly been posted to France a few days ago, due to a shortage of officers.

As Olivia entered the sitting room, Cecily raised a swollen, tear-stained face but didn't get up from the sofa. 'My Donald's been wounded. He's going to die, like your Charles did, I know he is! And then what shall I do?' She held out a piece of paper in one trembling hand.

Olivia stiffened at this tactless remark, waited a moment to control her own emotions, then took the letter. It was from a hospital in London and said that Captain Donald Ballam had been shot in the leg, brought back to England and operated on at the hospital. He was as well as could be expected and would be sent home to recuperate, arriving the following Monday afternoon.

'I don't think Donald's life can be in any danger if they're planning to send him home so soon.'

But Cecily ignored that, clasping her hands at her bosom and shedding a few more tears. 'To think that my darling was injured and I never even knew!'

'How could you possibly have known?'

'I should have *sensed* it.'

'Rubbish. And think about the positive side. Your husband will be home for Christmas.'

The tears stopped. 'He will, won't he? Oh, dare I hope?'

Olivia had had enough of this weeping and wailing, so decided to turn Cecily's thoughts to the practical needs of her husband. 'If Donald has been injured in the leg, he may not be able to climb the stairs, at first. We may have to make up a bed for him downstairs . . . in the dining room, perhaps.'

'But where would we eat if we did that?'

'In the kitchen. You and I ought to have our meals there anyway, to make life easier. You only have a daily cleaner now.'

Cecily's voice was faint with shock. '*Eat in the kitchen!* Donald would *never* agree to that! He always insists on maintaining standards.'

'He may have to lower his standards if he can't get up and down the stairs.'

But Cecily didn't seem to hear her. She'd gone over to the mirror and was setting her hair to rights, murmuring, 'Home for Christmas.'

Olivia left her to primp and went into the kitchen, which the daily help had left immaculate, as always. She put the kettle on to boil, thankful for the modern gas cooker. It made such a difference to a woman's life to have instant heat to cook on instead of having to keep a stove fed with coal. And the gaslights here made it so easy to read in the evenings. Well, they would do if Cecily would stop talking and leave her in peace.

She decided they'd make do with sandwiches for their evening meal. It didn't really matter what she cooked, Cecily only picked at her food.

No wonder her cousin's wife was so slim and dainty, eating so little. Donald often commented on how pretty and ladylike his wife was, looking pointedly at his cousin as he spoke.

Olivia had her mother's red hair and was tall and strong like her father's side – like Donald himself. It seemed that strength and red hair were all right for him, but not for her. He had very fixed views about a woman's role in life, but for all his bossy ways, he was the only close family she had left now so she didn't want to fall out with him.

She sighed. Already she was dreading him coming home to convalesce for several weeks. She could put up with his bossy ways for a day or two, but the two of them were bound to quarrel if he was here for weeks. They always did.

Oh, how she missed her husband! She still turned round sometimes, thinking she heard Charles's footsteps, half-expecting him to come bounding into the room like an overgrown puppy. He had been such a cheerful man and *he* had loved her being strong and energetic.

The only sadness in their marriage had been the lack of children. That seemed even worse now. If they'd had children, they would have been a legacy from Charles, a way of carrying on his life, not letting it end so completely. She didn't know whether this lack was her fault or his, but he'd never blamed her, just said more quietly than usual that you had to accept whatever fate handed you, and at least they still had each other.

She put the plate of sandwiches on the table, opened a tin

of peaches and one of evaporated milk and called, 'It's ready.'

Cecily appeared in the doorway to say faintly, 'Do you really want to eat dinner in here?'

'Yes. And it's tea, not dinner from now on. *You* don't seem interested in cooking and without full-time help in the house, we have to make things easier to manage.'

Cecily drifted over to the table and sat down with an aggrieved sigh. 'It's the fault of the government for letting women do men's jobs. I believe some former maids are earning quite scandalously large wages in munitions factories. Two or three times what I used to pay mine.'

'Good for them! How else can the government get the necessary jobs done with so many men away at war? And why should they be paid less than a man?'

But Cecily was pouring herself a cup of tea and didn't answer that question. Her soft, whispery voice meandered on between mouthfuls about the shocking price of coal and the lack of some of her favourite foods in the shops.

'Shipping is being bombed, so some food doesn't get through to Britain,' Olivia protested at one point in exasperation.

'But it's still not right to have so many shortages. The government should *do* something about it.'

Olivia concentrated on her own meal, eating twice as much food as her cousin. She nodded her head from time to time as if she was listening and agreeing, which seemed to satisfy Cecily.

She'd go to bed early and read, she decided. At least Donald had plenty of books in the house. He favoured tales of adventure and heroic deeds. Tales for men, but they were more fun to read than the books his wife favoured. Cecily read magazines and silly tales about ordinary girls falling in love with princes and dukes. As if that could ever happen!

Cecily regularly reread the four books she owned by a lady called Ethel M Dell. She had several times expressed a fervent hope that the war wouldn't stop that author writing more of these wonderful stories.

Olivia had tried one out of curiosity and it was certainly full of passion and love, but also contained a surprising amount of violence. Having known true love with Charles, she didn't find the emotions described in the stories at all realistic. She'd said that to the vicar's wife one day and Mrs Simmons had agreed with her, saying disapprovingly that the books were rather racy, and she was surprised Captain Ballam allowed his wife to read them.

Donald would never notice what his wife was reading!

Olivia realised Cecily had finished her meal and was looking questioningly across the table.

'Sorry. I was thinking about something. What did you say?'

'Shall we clear the table and do the washing-up now?'

What else would you do after a meal? she wondered. Yet Cecily asked the same thing every evening.

It was two long hours before Olivia could escape to her bedroom. Even knitting socks for the troops didn't help the evening pass more quickly. She'd never been fond of knitting. She and Charles had talked – oh, how they'd talked!

This way of life definitely couldn't continue or she'd go mad with boredom.

The following day, Olivia was glad to get away for a few hours. She'd taken on a temporary job helping out in the village shop and it was a lifesaver in many ways. Not because she was desperate to earn money, though she didn't mind adding the extra to her savings, but because it got her out of the house and away from Cecily for several hours.

She was sure she now knew more people from the village than they did, even though the Ballams had lived there for four years, ever since their marriage. Well, Donald would consider it beneath him to chat to common people. He was such a dreadful snob. She didn't know where he got it from. None of their parents had had that attitude to the world.

As she was putting on her outdoor things, she decided her life couldn't go on like this indefinitely. She'd stay until after Christmas, because she couldn't leave Mrs Cummins at the shop in the lurch at this busy time. After that, she'd look for something more worthwhile to do with her life. Only, what?

Carefully she manoeuvred the silver hatpin into the crown of the wide-brimmed, navy felt hat, pushing it through her hair and out again to keep the hat firmly in place. The hat had flowers round the crown and was rather frivolous, but her navy tailor-made suit was very practical, with a hip-length jacket and gored skirt in the new shorter fashion. She liked having a hem several inches above her ankles, not needing to brush dried mud off the hem after wet days and being able to stride out freely.

On her way to work Olivia looked across the street and saw a woman she knew slightly, who had also lost her husband. The other was absolutely draped in black, with a veil on her hat to cover her face. Surely that made you feel worse about your loss?

She hadn't had black clothes made, because when he

volunteered for the army, Charles had forbidden her to go into mourning if he was killed. 'Keep that lovely red hair of yours shining in the sunlight. Never, ever hide it.' He'd emphasised that by planting one of his smacking kisses on each of her cheeks in turn. Oh, she missed those sudden kisses so much!

The worst had indeed happened and her husband had been killed in the second Battle of Ypres at the beginning of May. His commanding officer had written to inform her that Charles had been shot by a sniper and died instantly. She hoped it was the truth, but knew only too well many officers said that to soften the blow. But nothing could soften the news that the man you loved had been killed.

She had only just turned forty and some would say her life was over. Her cousin Donald had told her she should live quietly from now on until the time came for her to join her husband in his grave.

'As if I'd live like that!' she told her reflection fiercely. 'Charles would be horrified if I sat around doing nothing. I may not have a husband, but I can still have an interesting life.' Somehow. Once the war was over.

Mrs Cummins peeped into the room from the shop. 'Did you say something?'

'What? Oh no. Just talking to myself.'

'My mother does that since my father died. Drives me mad. You'll have to watch yourself now you're on your own.' The doorbell of the shop rang and she vanished to serve the customer, calling over her shoulder, 'See you tomorrow, dear.'

Olivia gave a wry smile at Mrs Cummins' tactlessness. The shopkeeper was famous in the village for saying exactly what she felt. Luckily the woman hadn't a nasty bone in her body, so the blunt remarks were never unkind.

She walked briskly home to her cousin's house, today's groceries swinging by her side in a string bag.

It was all the fault of the scarlet fever epidemic, which had broken out in Swindon in November. Her cousin Donald had insisted she move to the safety of his home in the village of Nether Bassett. She'd not even argued, partly because Donald was like a steamroller when he wanted something doing and partly because it'd make a change. She'd desperately needed a change.

She left one of the Belgian refugees she'd taken in a few months ago to look after her house. Madame Vermeulen was a capable woman and could be trusted to see that everything was properly cared for.

To her surprise, Olivia was enjoying some aspects of living in the country, especially the way everyone knew one another. She'd said so one day and remembered how smugly Donald had smiled at her.

'I knew it! You must stay here for the duration of the war, Olivia, and keep an eye on my poor darling for me. It's what your parents would have wanted, if they'd lived, I'm sure. Besides, it's not right, a woman living alone,' he'd added.

She hadn't allowed him to get away with that. 'I was hardly living alone. I had five Belgian refugees staying with me.'

'Foreigners, and two of them men! Highly unsuitable. I can't imagine why you volunteered to take them in. After the war you must find yourself a female companion, another widow perhaps, and take a cottage in our village. You can help out at the church and go shopping with Cecily.'

She was about to say she'd rather die than dwindle into

old age like that when he added, 'And anyway, Swindon is full of soldiers, so you can't go back yet.'

'What's wrong with soldiers? *You* are one.'

He stiffened. 'I'm an officer and gentleman, which is rather different, let me tell you. I've heard the men talking. They consider women on their own easy prey.'

'None of the soldiers I met in the street was anything but civil to me.'

'You were lucky, then. But when you live here after the war I'll be able to keep an eye on you and help you manage your money. You haven't given me the details of what you inherited from Charles yet, by the way. How can I advise you if I don't know anything about your finances?'

'I can manage my own money, thank you.'

'Nonsense! Women don't understand these things. Your husband would want me to look after you. In the meantime it's settled: you will live here with Cecily till the war's over and those Belgians can jolly well pay you some rent.'

It wasn't Donald's arguments but Cecily's unhappiness and getting the temporary job that made Olivia agree to stay for a while longer. But just till after Christmas, when the job would end. She could only take so much of a woman whose conversation consisted mainly of worrying about her husband and wondering what comforts to send him in the next package. Chocolate, Oxo cubes, a cake maybe. She agonised over such decisions for days.

But her decision didn't solve the problem of what she was going to do with her life after she got back to Swindon.

At Greyladies in another Wiltshire village, Phoebe Latimer took a phone call and heard her husband's voice.

'I've got five days' leave for Christmas.'

'Oh, darling, how wonderful!'

'I'll arrive sometime in the middle of the afternoon on the day before Christmas Eve.'

She hung the telephone's earpiece on its hook and watched it swing gently to and fro till it came to rest. That was still a week away, but she was so excited at the thought of it she couldn't settle to anything.

She hadn't seen Corin for over a month and since their marriage in June, she'd spent exactly eight days with him. It was a good thing she had plenty to keep her busy at Greyladies, with her charity work for the trust she managed.

She didn't feel like going back to her mending, so decided to walk into the village and call in at the shop where Mrs Pocock would no doubt have some gossip to share.

As she strolled along, Phoebe found herself humming 'It's a Long Way to Tipperary'. One of the soldiers guarding the internees at Greyladies had a good voice and he'd taught everyone the latest songs, but that one was his favourite. Everywhere she went in the house, someone was bound to be singing, humming or whistling, most often about Tipperary – herself included. Even the German internees knew the words now.

As she strolled across the back garden, a quiet voice said, '*Guten Tag*, Phoebe.'

She turned to greet Herr Stein in his own language, which she spoke slightly. Once, he and his wife had been her employers in a shop making curtains; now they were interned at Greyladies because they were originally from Austria. They'd moved to England years ago because of anti-Jewish feeling in Austria but many people didn't see any difference between foreigners who'd moved their whole lives and loyalty to Britain, and those who were potential spies.

For the time being, the Steins were safer here at Greyladies than out among people. She'd seen for herself their shop reduced to ruin by a mindless mob.

Most of the internees had had similar experiences, but these people had skills and knowledge that were useful in the ongoing struggle against Germany, so they hadn't been sent to the Isle of Man, where most internees were lodged.

At Greyladies they formed a group the War Office could turn to for help. As Corin had said when he was commandant there, wars weren't only won by battles and killing.

'Where's Mrs Stein?' she asked.

'Upstairs, remaking some of your curtains.'

'We're so grateful for her help.'

'Ach! It's I who am grateful to you, Phoebe, for letting her do this. My Trudi misses our shop and enjoys having something useful to do. I fear that after the war we'll be too old to open another shop – even if people will allow us to live freely in this country once again.'

'In that case we'll find you a house to rent near here and you can come to tea every week.' Phoebe patted his arm, knowing he was right about the future. His wife was very vigorous still, but he had a frail look to him these days that worried her. 'At least you've managed to save some of your money for afterwards.'

'*You* saved a lot of our money, my dear, brave girl.' He pulled out his pocket watch and consulted it. 'I have a class to give soon and I see from your basket that you're going shopping in the village.'

At her farewell nod, he gave one of his courtly little bows and went back into the house. He had shown a gift for teaching, and was at present running a German language class for selected officers from a special army unit, men who already had some knowledge of the language. No one ever mentioned why they were doing this, but it wasn't hard to guess.

Phoebe turned at the gate to study the roof of her home and check that the previous day's storm hadn't dislodged any tiles. There was such a large expanse of roof, with several steep gables, and it took her several minutes to look at every part she could see from the front. As current chatelaine of Greyladies, she tried to keep an eye on things, even though the government had requisitioned the newer part of the house at the beginning of the war, and that wasn't considered her responsibility now.

Newer part, she thought with a smile. That meant the front half of the house, built in the early eighteenth century and connected to the rear half by a huge oak door. The really old part dated from the sixteenth century, and for some reason the officers inspecting the premises at the beginning of the war had decided it wouldn't be suitable for the government's needs, so had allowed the previous chatelaine, Harriet Latimer, together with her husband Joseph and their two sons, to stay there.

Then one by one, Joseph's three brothers had been killed in the war and he'd inherited the family estate, something he'd never expected to happen. Harriet had reluctantly given up her position here and handed over the care of the house to Phoebe.

Greyladies was always passed down the female line,

though not necessarily to direct descendants, and was only held in trust, not owned, so it could never be sold. The chatelaine always *knew* instinctively when it was time to leave and who would look after the old house next. The ghost of its founder always appeared briefly when the next chatelaine arrived, as if to demonstrate her approval.

Those who didn't believe in ghosts said it was merely a trick of the light, but Phoebe herself had seen Anne Latimer when she first arrived. The transparent figure in Elizabethan costume wasn't at all frightening and had a lovely smile.

Any husbands of those who inherited took the Latimer name, as Corin had done when he married Phoebe. At the same time he'd even given up his plans to take over his family home and estate near Manchester after the war, something she felt guilty about because he was an only son and loved his home.

Maybe all wasn't lost for him. Some chatelaines spent their whole lives caring for Greyladies; others only a few years. She had a feeling she was one of the latter. She didn't know whether to hope so, for Corin's sake, or to feel sad at the prospect of leaving the home she loved.

It was the house and its legacy which mattered, she always reminded herself, not her own wishes. There was a trust fund and the money was used both to run the house and to help women in distress – any woman who needed it, with no conditions set.

Recently there had been an increase in the numbers of women bearing children out of wedlock, because of their love for men going to the front. If the fathers were killed before they could marry and the women's families didn't help them, that could make things very hard for the young mother and her baby.

Phoebe found her hand going to her own stomach. She had exciting news for Corin and couldn't wait to see him again.

Chapter Two

On the Monday afternoon, soon after Olivia got back from the shop, an ambulance drew up outside the house. Donald was rolled down a ramp in a wheelchair and brought in by two orderlies. His leg wasn't in plaster, but it was heavily bandaged and when the man pushing the chair bumped it against the door frame, the patient winced visibly.

Cecily would have run forward and bumped him again, but Olivia grabbed her arm and pulled her back towards the sitting room. 'Let Donald get into the house. It's hurting him to be moved and you don't want to jar him.'

'She's right, old girl. Hey! Careful, you!'

The orderly moved even more slowly, looking tight-lipped, as if he was finding this patient difficult.

Once the invalid was settled on the sitting room sofa, the orderly put two crutches next to Donald and the other man wheeled the empty chair out. Cecily didn't even attempt to show them to the door because she was holding her husband's hand and gazing adoringly at him.

Olivia did the honours instead. 'Thank you for looking after my cousin.'

'Always glad to do our duty, ma'am.'

Even though it was quite chilly, she stood at the door watching them drive away. She didn't go inside again for a few moments, to give the lovebirds time together.

The sound of the car engine faded quickly. How convenient motor cars were! She missed theirs. At weekends Charles used to drive her out for little picnics in the country or visits to friends.

She chewed on her thumb as an idea occurred to her, not for the first time. Dare she learn to drive? She'd never tried to do it when her husband was alive, but it couldn't be all that difficult because since the war had started other women drove cars and even omnibuses.

She hadn't been able to bring herself to dispose of their vehicle, which was standing useless in the big shed in her back garden in Swindon. Such a waste! She shivered and realised she was still standing at the door staring down the street, so went back inside.

In the hall she paused to look at herself in the mirror and said firmly, 'I'll do it.'

In the sitting room, Donald was patting his wife on the shoulder, looking at her fondly. Cecily moved her foot carelessly as she leant forward to kiss his cheek and he sucked in a painful breath.

'Oh, I'm sorry! Did I hurt you, my darling?'

'Just a little. You must try not to bump my leg, old thing. It's still rather tender. They had to put nearly fifty stitches in it.'

Her face turned white. 'You aren't . . . going to lose it, are you?'

'Of course not. But it'll take time to heal and I mustn't put any weight on it yet. Our kind Dr Pelham will have to come and check it every day or two until the stitches can be taken out.'

Donald seemed to realise suddenly that they were no longer alone and looked across to his cousin. 'Nice to see you again, Olivia, old girl. How good it is that you're here to help Cecily look after me.'

She decided to start as she meant to go on, because it'd take a while to get through his stubbornness. 'For the moment. But as I told you before, I'm going back to Swindon after Christmas. There's nothing like your own home, is there? And I'm missing mine.'

He frowned at her. 'And as *I* told you, you can't possibly leave yet. We don't want you catching scarlet fever, and anyway, I'll be back at the front in a couple of months, so Cecily will need you just as much as ever.'

Olivia shuddered at the mere idea. The war might go on for years yet. Even a few weeks with Cecily had been hard to endure.

'Will you be able to get up and down the stairs to bed?' she asked Donald.

''Fraid not. In fact, they forbade me even to try for a couple of weeks.'

'Then we'll bring a bed down for you. We can put it in the dining room if we push the table right back. Cecily, I can dismantle that single bed frame, but you'll have to help me carry the parts downstairs.'

Donald stared at her as if she had suddenly grown a second head. 'Cecily can't help you carry such heavy pieces! And *you* can't dismantle a bed, either. It requires the use of tools.'

'As it happens, I've done it several times already. I had to when I took in the Belgian refugees.'

'You know I never approved of that,' he said, as he did every time she mentioned them.

She was fed up of going over the same ground again and again. Did he ever listen to her? 'I've found them very pleasant and grateful for my help, and anyway, they have nowhere else to live.'

'And so they should be grateful. You always did like to help lame dogs. But even if you did somehow manage to dismantle the bed base, you can't carry it down on your own.'

'I'll go and ask the neighbour's help, then.'

When she came back with the news that the neighbour would be round in a few minutes, Donald was looking angry.

'Sit down a moment, Olivia, if you please. I want a word with you.'

What on earth was the matter now? she wondered.

'Cecily has just told me about you working in the village shop.'

'Yes. I'm helping Mrs Cummins. With her husband in the army, she can't manage alone and her new helper can't start till after Christmas.'

'Then she should find a village woman. I'm not having *my* cousin doing menial work like that and waiting on the local hoi polloi.'

'There's a war on. Besides, I enjoy the work.'

'But *we* have to live here permanently and it won't look good you working in the shop. You must stop immediately.'

'In that case, I'll return home and your wife can manage your convalescence without my help.'

There was a pregnant silence, then he said, 'We'll talk about it again later.'

She knew what that meant. He'd work out a sneaky way to stop her. But he wasn't going to succeed this time. 'I'll just go and dismantle that bed.'

'If the neighbour's coming in, he can—'

She left the room because it was the only way to manage without an explosive row. It hadn't taken long for the two of them to start bickering, but their disagreements were getting worse. He had been an annoying child, but he was an utterly infuriating adult.

Half an hour later, she and the neighbour carried the single bed frame down from the smallest bedroom and set it up in the dining room, then he brought down the mattress while she carried the feather overlay.

The neighbour, a pleasant middle-aged man, started teasing her about how strong she was for a woman. When he caught sight of Donald's glowering expression, he winked at her and took his leave.

Olivia saw him to the door, grabbed her hat and coat and called, 'Cecily, I'll leave you to make up the bed. I forgot to buy something from the shop and it can't wait. We have a man's appetite to cater for now.'

She was out of the house before either of her cousins could stop her.

During a lull between customers, she explained to Mrs Cummins quite frankly that Captain Ballam would probably try to stop her working there. 'And I'd go mad stuck inside the house all day with D— um, stuck indoors. So don't listen to him.'

Mrs Cummins, who had lost all fear of upsetting a lady like Olivia within an hour of her starting work, said comfortably, 'As long as I know what *you* want, dear.'

'I'd like to work here till after Christmas, as planned.' She laughed. 'Though if my cousin throws me out of his house, I may have to come and camp in the shop.'

'I've got a spare bedroom, but I'm sure it won't come to

that. The captain needs you to look after Mrs Ballam. We all know what she's like. My niece used to work for her.'

She didn't elaborate. She didn't need to.

That evening Donald scowled round as he followed his wife and cousin slowly into the kitchen for his dinner. 'Only in wartime would I put up with eating in here. Are you sure you can't find a proper maid, someone who'll cook our meals and set the table properly, Cecily?'

'I've advertised several times with no luck. They're all working at the railway works or on the trams in Swindon, and they get paid so much more than I'm offering that no one even applies.'

'Shocking! What are things coming to when the gentry can't get proper service?' He stared at the food again. 'What sort of dinner do you call this?'

'We call it tea, not dinner,' Olivia said. 'I didn't have time to cook anything today, so it's cold meat and pickles with nice fresh bread.' If he complained, she'd tip the contents of the plate over his head, she decided. Well, she wouldn't really, but even imagining doing it cheered her up.

He opened his mouth to protest, caught her eye and said instead, 'You always were a hoyden. No sense of your position in the world. No feminine skills. Only a rough diamond like Harbury would have put up with you.'

She slammed her knife and fork down and stood up, covering her plate with another one and putting them in the pantry as the other two gaped at her. 'I'll finish this later, when I can eat my food in peace without someone insulting my husband, *who gave his life in the service of this country*, I will remind you.' She stormed out.

Donald called to her to come back but she didn't. It wasn't dark yet and a short stroll would be just the thing to walk off her annoyance.

She didn't give in to the tears that threatened, but when he talked so slightingly about Charles, she wanted to thump him good and hard.

It was bad enough when Donald started nagging and criticising *her*, but she wouldn't tolerate him or anyone else insulting her husband.

She should have had more sense than to come here.

In Challerton Mrs Pocock was on her own in the shop, for once, and greeted her with the news that a new family had moved into the village. Phoebe had already heard that, but she didn't know anything about them yet.

'No one knows much about them because they don't mix,' Mrs Pocock confided. 'The husband's lost a leg and been invalided out of the army. Hatterson, they're called. He's poor Bill's nephew and inherited the house. *Young Hatterson* suffers from severe headaches, someone told me, but Thad Diggan who lives next door says he's just plain bad-tempered and his poor wife is worn down with running round after him. She's very civil when she comes shopping, though, I have to give her that.'

She hesitated, then added, 'And I think you ought to know, Mrs Latimer, what this Hatterson is saying about the people interned at Greyladies. It's shameful, that's what it is. Those old men and women aren't our enemies, as everyone here knows. Some people don't have the sense of a day-old turnip, whatever airs they give themselves!'

'What exactly is he saying?'

'That we shouldn't allow Huns to stay in our village. That we should chase them out of Challerton, *burn* them out of Greyladies, if necessary.'

Phoebe stared at her in shock. 'If I hadn't seen for myself a mob destroying the Steins' shop, I'd find it hard to believe that an Englishman could make such vile threats.' She shivered at the memory of the mindless anger on the faces that dreadful day. 'Did Hatterson actually say this in public?'

'Not in public, no. He was talking to someone at the rear of his house. Mr Diggan overheard him. He said Hatterson got very vehement and *sounded* as if he actually meant to do it. It's a bit of a worry.'

'Dear heaven, what are we to do about him? I wish Corin were here.'

'If anyone tries to attack you, Mrs Latimer, I'll be running up to Greyladies with my rolling pin, and I won't be the only one to come to your aid.'

'Thank you. I'll have to try to meet this man, see what he's like.'

'Well, all I know is, he might be a Hatterson by name, but he's not like our Bill, who was a decent old soul. This one has never been to Challerton before. And if he hadn't lost a leg in the service of his country, I'd tell him he's not welcome in my shop if he goes on saying such things, I would indeed.'

'We'll be all right, with four soldiers stationed at Greyladies. And a doctor, orderly, nurses and two cooks. Hatterson won't be able to do much against so many.'

'Cowards never act alone. I wouldn't put it past him to find others. Wait till you meet him, you'll see what he's like from the sour expression on his face. A nasty creature, he is, snapping at you for no reason. *I* think he's blaming every German or

Austrian for the loss of his leg, which is just plain stupid.'

Phoebe was surprised at this tirade. Mrs Pocock was usually placid and good-natured, finding something to like in everyone who came into her shop.

'I told him straight: *our* foreign gentlemen and their wives at Greyladies have been in England for long enough to learn civilised ways, I said.'

She was so indignant. 'Mr Hatterson must have been very rude to you. I don't think I've ever seen you so angry,' Phoebe said.

'Yes, he was. He came into my shop once and listened to me talking to someone, then interrupted and told me I was easily fooled. When I told him to mind his manners and said I'd not have talk of violence in my shop, he said people who didn't get rid of Huns were damned traitors.'

'I can't believe he said that.'

'That's what he said, "damned traitors". My husband came out of the back room then and told him to keep a civil tongue in his head or get out of our shop. But did he apologise? No, he did not. He just shrugged and said, "I'll have half a pound of cheese as well, please." I was so shocked, I'd started to serve him before I knew it.'

She shook her head. 'I can't forget the look on his face when he said those things, Mrs Latimer. Mark my words, he meant it about burning the internees out. He seems to blame them for losing his leg. You should tell the commandant to watch the house at night.'

Someone else came into the shop then, so she whisked out her handkerchief, blew her nose and took a deep breath. 'Now, what can I get for you today, my dear Mrs Latimer?'

'Just some jam, please. We're running rather short.' And

she had quite a craving for toast with jam these days. 'We didn't manage to make enough jam last year.'

'We only have plum, I'm afraid. But it's Mrs Olworth's jam that I'm selling for her, because she had a glut of plums last year, and heaven knows, the poor woman needs the money now her husband's gone and died on her. You'll have to give her the jar back, though.'

As she started back, Phoebe slowed down to study the house where the newcomers now lived. There was no sign of life at the front of the building and the garden, which had been Bill's pride and joy, was looking untidy; it hadn't been cleared for the winter. She supposed the occupants were in the kitchen keeping warm.

On that thought she shivered and began to walk more quickly. It felt like rain and the wind had a real bite to it.

Just before she reached the big house, she heard the sound of a bicycle behind her and a voice calling, 'Mrs Latimer! Mrs Latimer! Telegram for you.'

She spun round, her heart thumping in her anxiety. Surely this couldn't be one of *those* telegrams? Corin wasn't fighting at the front.

The lad handed over the envelope. 'Shall I wait for a reply?'

'Yes, please. Give me a minute.' She tore open the telegram, then sighed with relief. 'No reply needed.'

'Is it bad news?'

'Just that my husband might not be able to come home for Christmas.'

'Sorry to hear that, Mrs Latimer.'

She watched the delivery lad tear away on his bicycle. That was the village for you, or it had been until now. Everyone kept an eye on what other people were doing, helped out as needed, which was nice in some ways, annoying in others.

She reread the telegram. Corin's father was ill with pneumonia and his life was feared for. Her husband had been given compassionate leave and was going north to Manchester at once.

It might be a very quiet Christmas, even a sad one.

She wasn't going to tell Corin about the baby in a letter, though, because she wanted to see his face when he found out. Like her, he very much wanted children.

And if they had a son, then *he* could inherit Corin's family home near Manchester one day. That would make her feel so much better about depriving her husband of his birthright.

He said he didn't mind, that what she did at Greyladies was a sacred trust and through it she did a lot of good in the world, but of course it made him sad sometimes to lose his home. She knew him too well for him to be able to hide his feelings from her.

After some thought, Phoebe went into the new part of the house to pass on to Captain Turner what Mrs Pocock had told her.

'Is she sure the fellow was advocating violence?' the commandant said. 'Perhaps the good lady misheard.'

'It was Mr Diggan who heard it and he told Mrs Pocock. She's nobody's fool and says this Hatterson fellow seems to blame all Germans for losing his leg.'

The captain glanced down instinctively at his own missing limb. 'That's foolish. No, no. The man may shout and complain, but I doubt he'll actually do anything. Not in a small place like Challerton. Who would support him? They're a friendly lot in the village, I've always found.'

'Most of them are, but one or two families aren't quite as friendly, and there are other villages and hamlets nearby, not to mention Swindon. If Hatterson's been talking about it to one person in secret, he must already have found others who agree.'

'Don't worry. I'll inform all my staff and we already keep a careful watch on the house and grounds at night.'

But Phoebe still felt uneasy. She didn't feel that the commandant was taking the matter seriously enough. She decided to take a good look at Mr Hatterson on Sunday in church, and try to eavesdrop on what he was saying to people in the churchyard afterwards.

If he continued to urge violence against the internees, she might have to organise something herself, hire some of the village lads, perhaps. No one was going to damage Greyladies if she could help it.

When she returned to the old part of the house, she told her two maids what Mrs Pocock had reported.

Cook hesitated and said, 'I've heard my cousin saying something similar. She hates the Germans since her husband was killed. She wasn't talking about burning down Greyladies, though. What a shocking thing to suggest! I shan't sleep a wink at night now.'

That made Phoebe even more worried. She'd told Captain Turner that there were other disaffected people around, and that had immediately been confirmed by her own servant.

She would speak to him again if she heard so much as a whisper of unrest.

Chapter Three

As she walked past the church in Nether Bassett, Olivia nearly bumped into the vicar's wife who was coming from the opposite direction. 'Oops! I'm sorry, Mrs Simmons. I wasn't looking where I was going.'

'That's all right. Excuse me saying so, but you look rather upset, Mrs Harbury. Are you all right?'

'Not really. Does it show that clearly?'

'That you're angry? I'm afraid it does. Look, why don't you come in and have a cup of tea? It can help to talk to someone and I never betray a confidence.'

Olivia hesitated, then followed the vicar's wife inside. 'This is a lovely house. I always admire it as I walk past.'

'It's far too big for the two of us and I wish there were less of it to heat and clean. It took two years of pleading before the church would even put in a gas cooker and gaslights in the main downstairs rooms. I'd just like to see them cook meals on that monster.' She gestured towards a large, old-fashioned kitchen range. 'It still heats the water and it keeps the kitchen warm, but that's all it's good for.'

She gestured to a chair. 'I hope you don't mind sitting in here? It's much warmer.'

'I don't mind at all.'

Her hostess put the kettle on, then cocked one eyebrow. 'So . . . what's been upsetting you, my dear Mrs Harbury?'

Olivia didn't like to be disloyal and didn't know Mrs Simmons very well, so hesitated.

Her hostess asked quietly, 'Captain Ballam returned this afternoon, didn't he? Is it something to do with him?'

Why try to deny it? 'Yes. My cousin hasn't changed since he was a boy. He's just as annoying. More!'

Mrs Simmons laughed. 'Let me guess. He's been ordering you around.'

'Trying to. How did you know?'

'He kept telling my husband how to run this parish when we first came here. Fortunately, my husband has had many years' experience of smiling blandly, saying very little and doing nothing unless he agrees with it.'

'I wish I could be the same. Donald always tries to order people around, but when he said something about my husband, it was too much to bear, and I walked out. If he doesn't stop carping, I shall have to leave earlier than planned.'

'We're going to miss your cheerful face in the shop when you do go.'

'I wouldn't like to spend my life behind a counter, but it's very interesting to see how things are done and I've enjoyed meeting people.'

They chatted together with the ease of old friends, and Olivia gradually calmed down.

Only when Mr Simmons came in from visiting a parishioner did she realise it had grown completely dark outside. 'I'd better get back or my cousin will be sending out search parties. Thank you so much for the cup of tea . . . and the soothing chat.'

'I'll walk back with you,' Mr Simmons offered.

'It's only three hundred yards and the village is quite peaceful. If I screamed for help, a dozen people would be with me in seconds. There really is no need. You look tired.'

Mrs Simmons stood up. 'I'll see you to the door and watch you down the street.' As they stood at the step, she hesitated then asked, 'I wonder if you care about women's position in society?'

Olivia was surprised by this, so asked cautiously, 'Do you mean votes for women, and – and things like that?'

'Yes. I would never have gone as far as the sorts of things the suffragettes did because I abhor violence, but I very much agree with what they were trying to achieve. I do not consider my mind to be inferior to that of a man, and if a woman does the same sort of work, as they have during the war, and shows she can cope, I feel it's only fair she should be paid the same amount of wages.'

'I couldn't agree more.'

'Good. I meet with a small group of like-minded ladies every week and we discuss what we can do to change things and help other women, both now and after the war. We've helped quite a few people in the area. Would you like to join us?'

'I'd love to, as long as the meetings are after my shop hours.'

'They are. Um, I'm afraid I can't include your sister-in-law in the invitation. Mrs Ballam holds rather different views on women's role in the world.'

Olivia chuckled. 'She doesn't hold any views whatsoever

of her own. It's Donald who doesn't believe in women getting the vote. And whatever he tells her, she believes. I promise not to bring her.'

'We meet here on Wednesdays at four o'clock. Everyone brings a plate of food and we have tea together after our chat. Not too much food and nothing lavish because some of the women don't have much money.'

'I shall look forward to it.'

When Olivia went into the living room Donald greeted her with, 'You shouldn't have been out on your own after dark.'

Cecily nodded vigorously in agreement.

Olivia tried to keep her tone light. 'Why on earth not? You keep telling me how safe Nether Bassett is. And before you ask, I was chatting to the vicar's wife. Now, if you'll excuse me, I'll go and finish eating my meal.'

'One moment, if you please.'

She waited, saying nothing, wondering what else he had found to complain about.

'I wish to apologise to you. If you thought I was . . . um, denigrating your husband and the great sacrifice he made, that was definitely not my intention.'

'Ah. Well. That's all right, then.' She went into the kitchen and closed the door on them. When she took her plate out of the pantry, she also got out her book.

It was bliss to eat a meal alone. She took as long as she decently could over it, sure they wouldn't miss her company.

By the time she returned to the sitting room, Donald was growing tired and had decided to go to bed early 'just this once'.

Olivia made sure Cecily could manage to help him and

sought her own bed, smiling as she put on her nightgown and picked up her book again. Meeting Mrs Simmons and her group of ladies would be something to look forward to.

And if Donald or Cecily asked what the meetings were about, she'd say . . . She thought for a moment and chuckled aloud. She'd say the meetings were for women who'd lost someone close and wanted to pray together.

On Wednesday after work, Olivia got ready to visit the vicar's wife again. She felt happy to be going out but tried to hide that since she was supposed to be praying for her late husband.

Donald swung into the kitchen on his crutches and scowled at the plate she was about to wrap in a tea towel. 'I don't know why you're going to this thing today.'

'Because I want to.'

'And why you need to stay for tea afterwards is beyond me. Don't those women have families to look after? A few private prayers should be more than enough to mourn the departed. This public parading of grief is unnecessary.'

She glared at him. 'Has it occurred to you that women who have lost their husbands can get lonely? They go for the company as much as anything, and there's nothing wrong with that.'

'Some people may need that, but *you* have Cecily to keep you company. When I return to my posting, you'll have to take her with you to the meetings, because she'll be lonely.'

'I don't *have* to do anything at your order, Donald.'

He went red in the face and seemed to puff up a little, like an angry rooster. 'I never thought you'd be so ungrateful for the shelter of my roof.'

'Well, *I* never thought you'd expect me to stay and look after your wife for the duration of the war, and what's more, I won't do it.'

She picked up her plate, saw that someone had pinched a scone, leaving a gap at one side – no need to guess who had done that – so took another scone off the plate of four she'd left for her cousins' tea.

'Hoy! You said those were for our tea.'

'Well, you took a scone from my plate, so you've already had one of yours. And how would it look for me to go there with a half-empty plate? As if we couldn't afford to contribute our share, that's what.'

'Oh, there's no talking to you.'

'No, there isn't. And certainly not in that tone of voice.'

She left via the back door, banging it good and hard behind her.

She'd tried to excuse his grumpiness by telling herself he must be in pain, but really, other people coped with pain without taking it out on the people they were living with. He'd even made poor Cecily cry this morning.

Olivia heard laughter as she knocked on the door of the vicarage and her heart lifted.

Mrs Simmons' elderly maid opened the door. 'Do come in, Mrs Harbury. I'll take your plate into the dining room, shall I?' A whistling sound came from the kitchen and she swung round. 'There goes the kettle! Could you please hang your coat and hat up, and join the other ladies?' She hurried through a door at the back of the hall.

Olivia went into the sitting room, pausing in the doorway to get her bearings. To her relief, and in one case her surprise, several women she knew by sight from the shop were there.

The vicar's wife beckoned her over. 'You all know Mrs Harbury by sight, I think?' She named each of the ladies, giving only first names and adding with a smile, 'We don't stand on ceremony here, Olivia. Pauline was just telling us about her trip to London and the dreadful conditions some poor women are living in now they've lost their husbands. We see the same problem in Swindon.'

'It's not only because they have children to look after, but because women's wages are so low,' a younger woman said. 'And the girls find it hard to obtain as good an education as the boys. I get so angry when my older girls are kept at home regularly on Mondays to help with the family's washing. The only time boys are kept at home is to help with the harvest. Half the school was missing this summer.'

Olivia recognised her then as the local schoolteacher. Cecily had said scornfully that it was a two-room school for the children of common persons, but the children in the senior class clearly had a teacher who cared about their welfare.

The conversation ranged from whether the government would give women the vote after the war, which some people expected to happen and others doubted, to the higher education of girls and women. The schoolteacher had a very intelligent girl in her class she wanted to help. The family was poor and would need their daughter's wage, so they couldn't afford to keep her at school, much as they'd have liked to.

The ladies decided that when this school year ended, they would each contribute some money and offer the parents a small sum per week to allow the girl to stay at school for another year and become an assistant teacher.

It was just the sort of lively conversation Olivia had been missing and she was enjoying it greatly.

There was such a loud knock on the front door, everyone fell silent.

'That has to be Babs,' Mrs Simmons said with a smile. 'Mrs Horner-Jevons from the big house,' she said to Olivia, 'only she prefers to be called Babs. She lost her husband last year and lives in London. But she still comes back to the village from time to time. I don't think you've met her yet. I'll let her in myself. My maid will be having her own tea now.'

Calling, 'I'll get it, Susan,' she hurried out to the front door.

The woman she brought back was tall and plump, wearing trousers and a knee-length tunic, with a rather mannish hat. 'Sorry I'm late. I nearly drove my car into a herd of cows,' she announced cheerfully. 'They were going in for their evening milking and I couldn't see round the corner, could I? Luckily I managed to stop in time, but the man with them shouted at me.'

'What did you do about that?' one woman asked, winking at Olivia.

'Shouted back at him, of course. After my husband died, I decided I had to stand up for myself.' She took the plate Mrs Cummins offered her and piled it high with sandwiches, cakes and scones.

'I hope you don't mind, but I didn't have time to make anything. However, I bought a nice surprise instead. No, I'm not showing you till after we've all eaten.'

When the table had been cleared, she went out into the hall and brought in a rather tarnished silver dish. Whipping the cover off, she displayed its contents, a heap of Cadbury's Dairy Milk chocolates.

There was a chorus of oohs.

'I was in London and I went into a shop which had just got a new tray of chocolates sitting on the counter. Five pounds of them all whispering, "Buy me." So I bought two pounds and if you ladies can't finish them, I will.'

There were more delighted exclamations. Such chocolates were expensive and often bought one at a time for a little treat. They weren't even sold at the village shop, which offered only ordinary Cadbury's chocolate, which arrived in big bars that could be broken into smaller bars for customers wanting a treat.

Babs smiled as she watched each woman choose a chocolate in turn, then go round again. She did her share of consuming the treat, then moved across to sit next to Olivia. 'I don't know you, do I?'

Almost immediately the two of them were chatting like old friends.

Later, as they got ready to leave, Babs stopped Olivia just outside the front door. 'I'm trying to set up a Women's Institute nearby. Do you fancy helping me?'

'I'm not quite sure what you mean by a "Women's Institute".'

'Ah, then we'll have tea together and I'll tell you all about the movement. The idea comes from Canada and they set up the first one in Wales in June at that village with the long, unpronounceable name. I just call it Llanfair PG. A Women's Institute is a local group of women from all social classes who meet every month in sisterhood and equality. The AOS is taking it on board and—'

'Just a minute. I don't know what the AOS is.'

'Agricultural Organisation Society.'

Olivia was still puzzled. 'Why should they be involved?'

'They are there to encourage self-help and mutual cooperation in the farming community. WIs bring people together to share information and skills.'

'Goodness, that sounds wonderful.' Olivia really liked this idea. After all, women couldn't gain the vote or other changes on their own, that was certain. But if they could learn to work together, they might stand more chance.

As Mrs Simmons came across to join them, Babs added pointedly, 'After I've got my present Women's Institute off the ground, I mean to try to set one up here in Nether Bassett.'

'Not yet,' the vicar's wife said. 'We have to move carefully on things like that or we'll upset the local dignitaries. I'm preparing the ground, but it'll be better to work towards it gradually and get the support of certain gentlemen.'

'Hang the local dignitaries!' Babs said.

'Unfortunately my husband can't afford to get on the wrong side of them. I mean it, Babs. We need to go slowly, but I *will* work on it.'

'Oh, very well. As long as you're preparing the ground.' She turned back to Olivia. 'Why don't you come to tea at the hall on Saturday and I'll tell you more about the WI movement? We need women like you to help set groups up.'

'I'd love to.' She would be glad to find a new interest now she was on her own in the world.

'I've got to visit someone on the other side of the village, so I'll pick you up on the way back and drive you to my house. It's a bit far out in the country for comfort, but now isn't the time to try to sell it, let alone move. I'm not staying there after the war without Humfy, though.' She looked sad for a moment as she explained. 'My husband. Lovely man, if a bit bossy. He was killed last year. I believe you lost your husband recently too.'

'Yes.'

'It takes time,' she said in a gentler tone.

When Olivia was more in control of her emotions, Babs went on, 'There are going to be a lot of us widows after the war and we have to stick together. I for one don't intend to sit quietly in a corner waiting to die. Do you?'

'Certainly not.'

It was like meeting a whirlwind, Olivia thought as she walked home. A delightful, friendly whirlwind of a woman who made her feel alive again.

It was like having cold water thrown into her face to be met by Donald's scornful remarks, especially when she mentioned the chocolates.

'I think that's disgusting!' he said. 'You are not to go again. Those women are only pretending to mourn loved ones. They just go there to gossip and indulge themselves in unnecessary luxuries.'

'Don't be silly. And anyway, you can't stop me.'

He goggled at her.

'If you feel it necessary to turn me out of your house, I'm perfectly happy to go home,' she added.

'I shall speak to you again in the morning when you're not so tired.' But he was unused to being defied and in his anger managed the crutches badly and stumbled. He yelled in pain as he hit his leg on the wall, and when Olivia would have helped him right himself, Cecily pushed her aside, shaking her head and gesturing to her to leave them alone.

So Olivia went upstairs and leant on the window sill, staring out at the village, not really ready to go to bed yet. Well, it was only seven o'clock.

She had enjoyed the small gathering, but most of all, she had enjoyed meeting Babs. What a wonderful woman she was, so full of life. She must be quite wealthy if she owned a big country house and a place in London. Why had Cecily never mentioned her?

The Women's Institutes sounded interesting. Perhaps this meeting might lead to a rewarding friendship and something worthwhile to do. It was worth trying, anyway. She really liked Babs.

On the Sunday before Christmas, Phoebe went to church with one of the nurses from Greyladies. As they walked into the old building, heads turned and she saw to her surprise that someone was sitting in her family's pew.

The stranger turned as she stopped at the end of the pew and gave her an insolent smirk.

'This pew is reserved for people from Greyladies,' she said quietly. The Latimers had contributed to the building of the church and this pew had been theirs ever since it had opened. Anyway, she didn't like the looks of this man and didn't want to share her pew with him.

'If you can spend your life with Germans, you can share a pew with a man injured in the service of his country.'

There was a rumble of anger, and two of the farmers who occupied pews near the front on the other side stood up and came to stand by her.

'We have our ways in this village,' one told him. 'And *you* need to fit in with the rest of us if you're going to be living here. Hattersons sit in the fourth pew from the back, on the left as you go out.'

Hatterson glared at them and didn't move until two burly young men moved along the side of the church to stand at the other end of the pew he was occupying.

The verger came hurrying to the front. 'This way, if you please, Mr Hatterson. I'll show you to your own family's pew.'

Why hadn't the verger intervened before? Phoebe wondered. For a moment she thought Hatterson wasn't going to move, then he got up and edged very slowly along the pew, as if it was hard for him to move. As he reached the end, he pretended to stumble and forced her to move quickly back out of the way.

With a smile on his face he continued to limp down the aisle.

'Sorry you were troubled, Mrs Latimer,' one of the farmers said. 'We'll keep an eye on that pew for you on Christmas Day.'

'Thank you for your help. Apart from anything else, I didn't want to share our pew with someone so angry.'

'He's trouble, that one is.'

She agreed. Hatterson had a thin, mean face, with an aggrieved expression on it, as if he hated the world.

She had a feeling he was going to cause more trouble. After she sat down, it took her a moment or two to calm herself. She'd thought Hatterson was going to send her flying when he stumbled. He'd wanted her to think that, had enjoyed frightening her.

She prayed very fervently that he wouldn't cause trouble in Challerton, that he'd not find others with his views about the internees. Wasn't the war causing enough trouble for people without him stirring up more?

What good would it do anyone to hurt the rather elderly people interned at Greyladies?

She wished more than ever that Corin was coming home; she wasn't even sure he'd get back for Christmas now. And of course he had to stay till his father was out of danger, or the worst happened. But still, she would feel better if she could share her worries with her husband.

And share her joy, too. Again her hand went to her stomach.

That next morning Phoebe was on her own, and as it was raining she decided to walk round the ancient part of Greyladies and check that there were no leaks or signs of mice. Most of the old building was empty, except for the furniture and other objects from the new part which were stored there.

She enjoyed the feeling of peace in a world dominated by war and related activities. There was a lot she could be doing today but after yesterday's nasty little scene in church, she craved an hour of peace.

Even when Corin was home, she enjoyed being on her own in the old house occasionally. It was like spending time with a dear friend.

She wondered what her husband was doing at the moment, wished desperately that she could talk to him, hear his voice. She hadn't slept at all well last night.

When a light appeared in the shadows at one end of the

attic, she stopped, not afraid, never afraid in this house. Was it . . . ? Yes, it was . . . Anne Latimer's ghost shimmered into sight, transparent with that wise, kindly expression.

When the figure was completely formed, the Lady looked solemnly across at her descendant, then gave a half-smile, which felt comforting.

'Thank you for visiting me,' Phoebe said softly, though she wasn't at all sure her words got through to the spirit.

Raising one hand, the Lady gestured down the narrow attic stairs, as if to tell Phoebe to go down. As the gesture was repeated, she moved to do that, wondering why she was being directed downstairs. She didn't question that there must be some good reason.

On the gallery landing, she had a feeling that she was meant to continue to the hall, so did that. As she drew near the turn at the bottom of the stairs, the telephone rang, so she ran down the last few treads to answer it.

If she'd been still upstairs she wouldn't have been able to get to the phone in time.

Corin's voice came down the line, tinny with a faint hissing sound in the background. 'Hello, Phoebe darling. I'm so glad I caught you at home. I'm missing you.'

'Have your parents got a telephone now? Give me their number, then we can keep in touch.'

'They don't have one. I've had to use a public telephone to make this call.' He chuckled. 'I'm not used to these kiosk types and I didn't have a penny to put in the door slot to get inside to use the phone. There's a shop nearby, but it had a sign saying "No change given without a purchase". I had to buy some boiled sweets to get the necessary penny, then I had to pay extra for making a long-distance call. I bet that shopkeeper makes a fortune from people using the kiosk.'

His amused tone vanished when he spoke about his father. 'He's a little better than he was, but progress is slow, and my mother's desperately worried about him. He hasn't been well all year. I wish they'd told me. I'd have made an opportunity to visit.'

'I'm sorry he's ill, Corin.'

'The doctor told Mother frankly that Father's health is failing and there's not much anyone can do about it. He may last a year or two, if he's careful, if we're lucky. He's only sixty-two, Phoebe. It doesn't seem fair. Are you still there?'

'Yes. I don't know what to say, darling. Is there anything I can do to help?'

'Not that I can think of. I'm afraid I'll have to stay here for a while longer, just to be sure he recovers, so I'm not sure about Christmas.'

They both sighed at the same time, then Corin said, 'Why don't you cheer me up by talking about what you've been doing. Is everything all right at Greyladies?'

She decided not to tell him about Mr Hatterson and the possible threat against their home, so talked about Mr Stein and his language classes.

But of course Corin realised from her hesitation and tone of voice that something was wrong. 'Darling, you promised you wouldn't keep anything from me.'

So she explained what was going on in the village.

'Damn the fellow! Who does he think he is to incite violence? The British government knows perfectly well how to deal with aliens who are our enemies, and they don't need mobs creating havoc . . . or worse. It would be especially bad if something happened to those internees at Greyladies, because their skills and knowledge are contributing to the British war effort. Have you met this Hatterson? Can't you talk to him, make him understand?'

She had to tell Corin about the scene in church and how Hatterson made her feel nervous.

'In that case, you'd better stay away from him. Sometimes men who've lost limbs can behave unreasonably. When I come back, I'll go and see the fellow and warn him not to cause trouble. We should—'

There were some fizzling sounds and Corin's voice became faint, the sound cutting in an out. 'I think . . . something wrong . . . Take care, my d—'

The line went dead. She looked at the phone, willing it to start working again, but it didn't. After a moment or two, she hung up the earpiece on its stand. It looked, she always thought, like a big metal daffodil. She stayed nearby for a while, just in case. But it didn't ring again, so eventually she went to work on her accounts.

Thank you, Anne Latimer! she thought. *I'd not have reached the phone in time without you.*

It had been a comfort to speak to him. She'd needed that. She felt very alone in the world sometimes, even at Greyladies.

An hour or so later, Ethel Kiddall, their new middle-aged maid, came to find her mistress in the old hall, which had once been the hall of a medieval manor but was now their living, dining and library space all in one.

Phoebe looked up from the trust fund accounts, which she tried hard to keep in order, but which still puzzled her from time to time, because the money came in from so many different sources. She wished sometimes that her predecessor had had longer to show her how things were done.

'Miss Bowers is here, ma'am. Are you at home?'

'Yes, I'm always at home to her. I'll come across and sit with her by the window.'

The former village schoolmistress, who was in her late seventies, was looking as spry and neat as ever.

'Do sit down. How nice to see you.'

Miss Bowers stared at Phoebe. 'Is everything all right, dear? You look a little tense.'

Trust her to notice. 'Oh, well, Corin has just told me that his father's health is failing. And—'

'That's not it. I should think you're worrying about this fool who's come to live in the village. Indeed, Hatterson is the reason I came to see you today, to make sure you were on your guard. We all saw how rude he was to you in church.'

'Have you spoken to him, Miss Bowers? Someone said you live near him.'

'Two doors away. He turns off the street to avoid me if he can. He says he's too busy to gossip. I noticed the other day he was carrying a copy of that dreadful rag that calls itself a newspaper. *John Bull*, indeed! The man who owns it is always calling for a vendetta "against every German in Britain". Shocking stuff. As if every member of a race can be bad.'

She let out a very unladylike snort and went on, 'I don't like the looks of Hatterson, I must admit. He has a sour twist to his mouth. And he limps badly. Surely they can find him a better artificial leg than that?'

'Commander Turner has an artificial leg and he doesn't limp at all.'

'It looks to me as if Hatterson is exaggerating the limp to gain sympathy – and to get out of doing anything around the house. I live two doors away from him and I've never seen him do any gardening, front or back.'

'Some men never do anything in the house. Let's sit down and share a cup of tea.'

'What a good idea!' The old lady patted her hand. 'You'll be all right, Phoebe dear. We only have a few malcontents in the village. People round here are mostly decent. And you have soldiers on guard at Greyladies.'

'Only four of them. There's no real need to guard the people interned here. They don't want to go out and face more violence and they're happy to help the government.'

'The Lady won't let anything happen to this house, I'm certain.'

'I wish I were as sure as you are, Miss Bowers. Can a ghost really stop a mob if it decides to burn the place down?' That was Phoebe's biggest worry. The old part of the house was built using a lot more wood than the new part. A fire could rage through it very quickly.

'Anne Latimer's legacy has lasted nearly four hundred years. *I'm sure Greyladies will last well beyond our time.*'

Phoebe stared at her in surprise. 'Your voice echoed on those last words, Miss Bowers.' Sometimes, when a person spoke of the future in the house, there was an echo behind the words and what they'd said then always came true.

'Yes, I heard the echo, too. That's a good sign, my dear girl.'

'I'm sure you're right.' She pulled herself together. 'No, you *must* be right. The Lady will continue to watch over us.'

'Have you seen her lately?'

'Yes.'

'That's good.'

But was a ghost omniscient? Phoebe wondered later as she got ready for bed. Dare she trust in Anne Latimer's very occasional appearances and warnings?

In this modern world, people trusted in machinery, not prophecies and guardian spirits. Perhaps that sapped the ghosts' power.

Oh, she was being silly. She was down in the dumps because Corin wasn't likely to be home for Christmas. She missed him dreadfully and had been so looking forward to seeing him again. She must pull herself together and get on with things.

Chapter Four

Alexander Seaton got off the London train in Swindon. He hadn't been back here since the war started, but his cousin Mildred had written to say his mother was dying, so he felt it his duty to make one last attempt to reconcile the differences between them.

He remembered that last quarrel all too clearly. He'd gone home for the first time in years for his father's funeral and afterwards, his mother had insisted he come back to Swindon to look after her and run the family business.

'You are, after all, my only living son. It's your duty.'

'I know nothing about carting goods, Mother. It's better that you sell the business and invest the money wisely. I can advise you about that and—'

'*You* advise me? *You* who sell second-hand furniture, who shamed the family by running a market stall! What do you know about handling large sums of money? I shall take advice from those who know.'

It was no use protesting that he sold fine antiques, and had only run a market stall when first starting up his business. She burst into tears and refused to listen.

'I shall leave everything to the church. I have no one else to leave it to. I have nourished a viper in my bosom.'

This reference to Aesop's fable made him want to smile, in spite of the seriousness of the situation. But the urge to smile soon faded as she continued to rant at him. He didn't expect her to leave him anything. He didn't want or need his father's dirty money, earned by ill-treating his workmen.

She continued at the top of her voice, 'If your poor brother had lived, he'd not have deserted me. Ernest was a good boy, obedient. *He* would have taken over the family business and made it even more successful.'

Alex doubted that. Ernest had been three years older than him, a bad child not a good one. He'd stolen his little brother's pocket money, filched coins from his mother's purse and, as he got older, regularly came home drunk, boasting about the women he'd had.

In the end Alex had left home at twenty – or rather, been thrown out – because he'd refused to continue working in the family business. He knew the men despised him for his puny body and his frequent illnesses. Worst of all, he was overcome by severe fits of sneezing if he got too close to the horses, fits so bad that sometimes he could hardly breathe.

The way his father treated the men working for him had also upset Alex. His body might be weak, but he hoped he was an honest man who wouldn't dock employees' pay for no reason when they already had trouble making ends meet on the low wages paid.

In fact, *Seaton and Sons, Carters* disgusted him and he wanted nothing more to do with it.

Luckily he'd inherited a little money of his own from his grandmother, only two hundred pounds but he'd saved another hundred from his wages. He moved away from Swindon and started up a market stall in London, selling any second-hand object or piece of furniture he could see a profit in. Not second-hand clothes, though. The smell of them turned his stomach.

He'd been lucky, made friends with an elderly man who could no longer lift heavy pieces, but who knew and loved old furniture. Horry had taught Alex all he knew, including how to chat to people passing by and entice them to look at the goods.

When Horry died three years later, Alex mourned him greatly. It was as if he'd lost a beloved grandfather. To his surprise, Horry had left him everything. Not a fortune, but enough money to make a difference.

Alex had already proved to be able to spot something valuable beneath an item's grime. He now made a name for himself clearing out the houses of middle-class people who'd died. He paid higher rates than usual for the valuable items he unearthed, too, because he didn't want to cheat people.

Gradually he moved on to sell better quality second-hand furniture in a shop. His first shop was small, but in it he learnt how to display his goods to the best advantage. Once he could afford more spacious premises in a better area, he opened *Seaton Antiques*.

He also proved that you didn't have to treat those who worked for you harshly. He found Tom Pascoe and trained him. Tom became his second in command, and by the time war broke out, he knew his antiques nearly as well as Alex did. Unfortunately he'd been called up and Alex worried about him, but Tom's wife had taken over his job and was proving almost as good as her husband, lacking only experience to equal him.

Oops! Alex realised he'd been standing outside the railway station, lost in thought while the other passengers took all the cabs. After a few minutes a horse-drawn cab turned up and took him to his mother's house.

He paid the driver, picked up his small suitcase and stood by the gate staring at *Cumberland Villa*. It hadn't changed much, was still a solidly built house three storeys high, standing in the middle of a street of similar dwellings.

But unlike the others, his family house was now in great need of repairs and maintenance, which would never have happened while his father was alive.

Why was he standing here like a timid fool? Because he was dreading this meeting, absolutely dreading it. Indeed, his mother might have him shown straight out again, as she had done after his father's death. But people usually said their goodbyes to the dying, so here he was. He had to live with his own conscience, after all.

Picking up his suitcase, he walked up the footpath. Before he could use the knocker, the door opened and his cousin Mildred stood there. She hadn't changed, was still plump with a kindly expression. He hadn't seen her for a year, because she hadn't been able to get up to London. Today she looked exhausted. Had she been coping with his damned mother on her own? Surely not?

Mildred was a year younger than him. Her mother had kept an eye on him in his childhood, and he and his cousin had been more like brother and sister. The two of them had shown him the only love and kindness he'd ever known from his family.

She didn't move for a moment, then held the door open. 'Come in, do. I'm glad you came, Alex, but I'm afraid you're too late. Your mother passed away just after midnight.'

He was ashamed of the relief that surged through him and hoped it hadn't shown on his face.

'The undertakers have finished laying her out and have just brought her body back. Do you want to see her?'

'Not really.'

'You ought to, dear. It won't look good if you don't.'

'Who's to know?'

'These things get out. Her maid will know, for a start, and she's heard nothing good of you, so will think the worst of you. And the undertakers are still here. And since I shall still be living in Swindon, I'd rather not have people gossiping about our family.'

He shrugged and put down his suitcase. He'd do almost anything for his cousin. Besides, a corpse couldn't say spiteful things to you. 'Well, if *you* think I should . . .'

'I do.'

Mildred took his hand, as she had when he was a child, and led him into the dining room. A highly polished brass and mahogany coffin with a cloth over one end sat on two trestles covered in black velvet. She lifted the cloth and there his mother lay, dressed in her usual black silk, with an old-fashioned lace cap on her white hair.

Well, at least this time she wasn't glaring at him. In fact, she looked so peaceful he'd hardly have recognised her. He didn't want to linger, so stepped back, averting his eyes. 'Cover her up.' His voice was harsh. He couldn't help that.

'We'll wait in here for a minute or two before going into the sitting room,' Mildred said.

'You always were good at keeping up appearances.'

'I prefer not to upset people and you should too.'

'Why? I doubt I'll ever be coming back to this house again, perhaps not even to Swindon. My mother always said she was going to leave everything to the church. She *should* have left it to you for taking care of her. You ought to have a halo to wear as well.'

'I did my family duty, that's all.'

'I hope she was grateful.'

Her tone was brisk and matter-of-fact. 'Of course she wasn't.'

'No, of course not. So . . . where are you going to live now if the church takes the house?'

'I'm going to get married and live with my husband.'

Alex stared at her in shock. 'You've been courting? You never said a thing about that.'

'It was better to keep it secret. Your mother would have thrown a fit of hysterics if she'd had the slightest suspicion.'

'What's his name? How did you meet him?'

'It's Edwin Morton, your mother's lawyer. She was always calling him in to change her will, so he came to the house quite often. She grew a little forgetful and would sometimes get up and leave us to walk round the garden, so he and I would chat as we waited for her to remember he was here. He's a widower, a couple of years older than me.'

She blushed. 'We're not going to wait to get married, because I've waited long enough. Edwin is getting a special licence and it'll just be a quiet wedding.'

Alex gave her a big hug. 'I'm really happy for you, Mildred, and I wish you well. If anyone ever deserved to be happy, it's you. You've had years of caring for bad-tempered old women: first your mother, then mine.'

'My mother was only bad-tempered when the pain was bad, and even your mother didn't give me too much trouble because I knew how to manage her. But that life is all in the past now. Alex dear, can you stay for a few days?'

'I wasn't going to but I can if you wish. Why?'

'Two reasons. The main one is that Edwin and I want you to be one of our witnesses at the wedding. And secondly, there's the reading of the will.'

'I told you, Mildred, my mother won't have left anything to me.'

'She did mellow somewhat towards the end, and I'd guess she's left you some keepsake or other.'

He frowned at her. 'Do you know something about her will?'

'No. Edwin would never betray a client's trust. All he would say was that you had an interest and should stay for the reading of the will. I've had a bedroom prepared for you here.'

He looked round and shivered. 'This house has such unhappy memories.'

'Then let's see if we can make some better ones tonight. We haven't had a good chat for ages.'

'I'll stay if they take the coffin away. The thought of her lying down here . . . No, I couldn't face that, wouldn't be able to sleep. Do you think I'm being foolish?'

'No. I was feeling the same but wasn't brave enough to admit it. I'll tell the undertakers to take her away again till the funeral, and blame it on myself.' She reached up to lay one hand gently on his cheek. 'I'm so very glad you came, Alex.'

He leant forward to plant a cousinly kiss on her forehead. 'I am too. I'm always glad to see you, my dear.'

'Why don't you wait for me in the front parlour while I speak to the undertaker?'

He was tired, glad to sit down in front of a cheerful fire.

There was the sound of hushed voices from the hall, then Mildred came back to join him, sitting next to him on the sofa. 'I've sent for a tea tray. While we wait, tell me how you're keeping.'

'I'm well enough. My health is much better than it was when I was a child.'

'Your father should never have sent you out with the drays. You got soaked to the skin so many times and we nearly lost you to pneumonia twice.'

'He had very fixed ideas about my working my way through the family business. Ah well, he's long gone now and my health continues to improve. I didn't even have a cold last winter. I feel like a fraud for failing the army medical.'

'Your heart has a slight murmur and your lungs were weakened. It seemed obvious to me even before you volunteered that you couldn't have coped with the training, let alone the dreadful conditions out there in France. Why did you volunteer, my dear?'

'I just . . . thought it was my duty, wanted to do my bit. But I must say I was dreading it.' He hated to be such a weakling. Other men of thirty-eight passed their medicals and went to serve their country.

Twice recently, women had stopped him in the street to hand him white feathers, which he thought a cruel thing to do to anyone. He had told them outright that he'd failed the medical and they should make sure who they were dealing with before doing something as unkind as accusing strangers of cowardice.

One woman had said he should be wearing a Silver War Badge to show he was ineligible, so he told her this was still a free country and men should be left to follow their own consciences, even pacifists. That had upset her.

He realised he'd been silent for longer than was polite. One of his cousin's gifts was that she would give you time to think. 'Sorry. I was remembering something. Tell me what you've been doing besides looking after my mother.' He leant back and enjoyed the sight of her rosy face as they chatted.

She told him briefly about her war activities, rolling bandages and packing boxes of comforts for the troops. 'Now, that's quite enough about me. There's nothing interesting about rolling bandages, however necessary they may be. Tell me how your shop is going. It looked so beautiful last time I visited London. You should have been an artist.'

'Business is good. Because new furniture is in short supply, good quality second-hand furniture is even more in demand.'

'Second-hand furniture indeed! You deal in valuable and rare antiques.'

'I deal in many other things these days. If people are selling furniture and bric-a-brac because they're in distress financially due to the war, I try to help them out, even if they aren't offering something I would normally buy. I originally opened a second shop to sell these cheaper and yet still good items, not expecting to make much money from it. But it's proved an excellent business venture.'

'I'm sure you've helped a lot of people whose goods didn't bring you a profit.'

'But they do bring a profit. Oh, not as much as my more valuable pieces, but a profit nonetheless.' He sighed. 'Lucas Marsh manages the other shop for me, and although he's in his late forties, he's in good health and very capable. His assistant volunteered, so he's another whose wife has started helping out. She's doing very well, but . . . Oh, never mind that.'

'No, tell me. But what?'

'They're going to introduce a Military Service Bill into Parliament next month. They say it'll be only for single men, but there have been massive casualties and I can't see how they can avoid conscripting married men sooner or later. I hope they don't call Lucas up. Surely he's too old. Only they have to replace the men they've lost.'

'It's dreadful how many men have been killed,' Mildred agreed. 'My Edwin has such poor eyesight, I doubt he'd pass a medical. It's very selfish of me to think like that, but I pray they won't take him away from me when I've only just found him.'

When Alex went to use the lavatory, he stared at his thin face in the mirror, wishing he wasn't staying in this house of unhappy memories. Then he cheered up at the thought of attending Mildred's wedding. He was looking forward to meeting her husband-to-be. Why, there might even be time for her to have a child. She deserved that.

He wished he'd had a child, but had never met a woman whom he could imagine marrying.

Two days later the funeral was held, with less pomp and ceremony than he'd expected.

'Didn't my mother specify the details of today?' Alex asked Mildred over breakfast. 'I'd expected more . . . fuss.'

'Yes, she did. However, *I* didn't see the point in wasting so much money on her obsequies. You'd think she was Queen Victoria from the list she gave me. As if the funeral attendants wear weepers on their hats these days!'

'They do look rather silly trailing strands of crepe down their backs.'

'What gave me the courage to defy her wishes was that there are women and children going hungry, men dying in agony because of the war and others injured and struggling to make a living. I couldn't bear to waste money on your mother's follies when it could be put to better use. You don't mind, do you?'

'I agree with you absolutely.'

'She'd already bought a plot in the churchyard and chosen her coffin. Let that suffice. A few of our neighbours and some people from her church will be attending, out of courtesy. She had no friends left alive.'

'I don't think she ever had any real friends.'

'No. She wasn't like my dear mother.' Mildred was silent for a moment or two, then said, 'Those attending are coming back here afterwards for light refreshments, but I hope to get rid of them within the hour, then we'll have the reading of the will.'

'You're more decisive than you used to be.'

'When I came to look after your mother, I had to learn to stand up for myself.'

'Well, I'm grateful that you did it and glad it led to you meeting Edwin.'

The funeral went smoothly and Alex hoped he played his part properly, but the service, graveside ceremony and slow drive back to the house seemed to go on for ever. And then he had to speak to those who'd attended and listen to their condolences as they made free of the generous refreshments, not easy to provide in a time of food shortages.

He didn't even know half of them, probably would never meet them again.

At long last the funeral gathering drew to a close. Alex saw the last guest out and lingered for a few moments on the doorstep, breathing in the cool, fresh air.

But there were still things to do, so he closed the front door and went back to join Mildred, her fiancé and his partner, Mr Telsom.

'We can have the reading of the will now, if you wish, Mr Seaton,' Edwin Morton said in his quiet, rather musical voice.

'Yes. Let's get it over with. Then if I need to leave the house to the new owner, I can go to a hotel.'

'I doubt it'll come to that.' Edwin gave a faint smile.

'We'll go into the dining room, shall we?' Mildred led the way without waiting for an answer.

Alex noted that she smiled briefly at her fiancé as she sat down and that Edwin returned the smile with a warm, loving look. It was good to see that.

There were some papers waiting on the table and it was Edwin's partner who went to sit in front of them.

Once the other three people were seated, Mr Telsom cleared his throat. 'I drew up the most recent will, Mr Seaton, because it would have been a clash of interests for my partner to do it by then.' His glance in Mildred's direction said why. 'The will isn't complicated, so with your permission, I'll summarise its main points.'

Alex hoped that meant his mother had left something substantial to his cousin.

'Very well. Agnes Rosina Seaton left everything she possessed in equal parts to her son Alexander James Seaton and her niece Mildred Rosemary Seaton.'

The words were out before Alex could stop them. 'I don't believe it!'

Mildred reached out to take his hand. 'It's what you deserve, dear.'

The two lawyers waited to continue, their expressions polite and non-committal. He supposed a lot of strange things were said and done when wills were read. It took him a minute or two to calm down, and his first impulse was to refuse the bequest.

But that would have been stupid and he had never thought himself lacking in common sense.

'I'm sorry. I was rather surprised.' He turned to Mildred. 'I'm glad she remembered you. If anyone deserves that money, you do.'

'It wasn't always easy to look after her, I will admit.' She smiled across the table. 'But doing it led me to my dear Edwin, which is far more important than the money.'

'What does the estate consist of these days?' Alex asked. 'My mother was never very good with money.'

'This house and its contents, a few hundred pounds in the bank and very little else,' Mr Telsom said. 'My partner and his wife-to-be have no desire to live here, so they wish to sell everything. How do you feel about that, Mr Seaton?'

'I'm of the same mind. However, since I'm in the trade, perhaps it'd be best if *I* sell the furniture and other items. I have a lady and gentleman who work for me and who clear out houses of deceased persons. I'm sure with their help, I can get far more money for the contents than my cousin could. There are one or two items I should like to keep, and of course I'll pay a proper price for them.'

'What a good idea!' Mildred said. 'I wasn't looking forward to going through my aunt's things, I must admit, because I don't think she ever threw anything away. Is that everything, Mr Telsom?'

'Yes. I'll leave each of you a copy of the will and take my leave.'

'What about her maid?'

'She refused even to consider leaving the poor woman anything.'

'Then I think we should give her something, Alex. If she hadn't been so old, I doubt she'd have stayed with my aunt.'

'Give her what you think right. And a medal with it, for putting up with my mother for so long.'

She smiled but wagged her finger at him in mock reproof.

Edwin showed his partner out and came back to join them. Mildred was standing near the fire staring into it and he went across to put one arm round her shoulders. 'Are you all right, my love? You were looking rather sad just then.'

'I'm fine, but I do find it sad that no one will miss her.'

She looked across at Alex. 'Well, that's done now. On a happier note, I'll remind you that Edwin and I have booked our wedding for tomorrow morning at eleven.'

'I shall look forward to it.'

'And after the wedding, I'll move straight into Edwin's house. I shall be glad to leave this place. It's never been a happy house, has it?'

'No, never. I'll get up early tomorrow and sort out the things I wish to keep, then I can catch an afternoon train to London immediately after the wedding. I shall be glad to leave the house, too.'

'We'll leave the maid to look after things till your employees arrive. Or if she gets another job, which she hinted she might have a chance of, we'll simply lock the place up. They can stay here, if they like.'

'I'm sure they'd appreciate that.'

It was just the three of them for dinner and afterwards they sat by the fire chatting. The more time he spent with Edwin, the more Alex liked him.

'Can I ask what made my mother change her mind about leaving anything to me?'

'I did,' Mildred said. 'I didn't tell anyone but she talked once or twice of leaving everything to me. I told her that if she didn't leave a good part of the money to you, *people would talk*. She was always terrified of being gossiped about – I don't know why, because she never did anything scandalous. I'm not sure I feel comfortable about taking half the money, even.'

Alex let out a harsh laugh. 'That's the main thing that makes *me* feel it's right to accept the bequest, that you get your share. I'm not short of money, Mildred. My business is very successful, even now.'

He wasn't sure whether to say it, but took the risk. 'I hope it's not too late for you two to have children, because then I'll have someone in the family to leave my money to.'

'I share that hope for children,' Mildred said. 'But I'll remind you that it's not too late for *you* to marry and have children, either.'

'Who would want to marry an old crock like me, whose hair is rather thin on top and who is definitely on the scrawny side?'

'Many women, because you have a kind heart and a decent nature.'

Alex could feel himself flushing. Personal compliments had been rare in his life and he never knew what to say or do when they were offered.

He went up to bed and left the others chatting, but Edwin didn't stay late and Alex heard the front door open and close about ten minutes later.

He hoped he'd never have to come back to this house again.

He smiled in the darkness. He was very much looking forward to the wedding. That would end his visit on a happier note.

When Mildred came downstairs to go to her wedding, Alex almost didn't recognise her. Happiness had even lent her the illusion of prettiness – or perhaps it wasn't an illusion. Perhaps this was the real Mildred and the other rather plain woman had been the illusion.

The ceremony at the registry office was brief, with himself and Mr Telsom acting as witnesses, and Mrs Telsom attending as a guest. Afterwards, they went to a local hotel where Edwin had ordered an excellent luncheon, together with a bottle of French champagne.

Alex snatched a moment with Mildred before he left. 'If you need anything, ever, you know I'll help you.'

'Don't worry about me, dear. I trust Edwin absolutely. And remember, if you have to come to Swindon, you must stay with us from now on.'

She chewed the corner of her lip, something she'd done from childhood when she was uncertain about what she wanted to say.

'What is it?' he prompted.

'It's you. Alex, please try to find yourself a wife.'

'I'm far too busy to go courting.'

'No need to *go courting*,' she said firmly. 'Just keep your eyes open, and if necessary, take a risk. You can be too careful about these things, you know.' She grasped his hand and gave it a little shake. 'Promise me that if the opportunity occurs, if you meet a woman you really like, you'll make the effort to get to know her.'

'Mildred, dear—'

'Promise me!' She laughed suddenly. 'It's the wedding present I want most.'

'Oh, very well. I promise.' He couldn't imagine it happening, though.

She patted his cheek. 'I know you won't break your word. Ah, Edwin! Come and say goodbye to my cousin.'

Donald watched sourly as Olivia put on her outdoor things. 'I don't like you associating with that Horner-Jevons woman. I don't know what poor old Humphrey was thinking of to marry someone as unconventional as her. Cecily tells me she goes out in public wearing *trousers*. Has she no shame?'

'So do you. They're very practical garments. I'm thinking of getting a pair made for myself.'

'I'll burn them if you do.'

'While I'm wearing them or after I take them off?'

'Don't be ridiculous.'

She studied him. Her feelings for him were undergoing a change. She'd always been a little afraid of upsetting him, he was so big and strong, but after spending more time than usual with him, she now considered him a stuffed shirt with a narrow view of the world, who backed down when challenged.

And he was rather stupid too. From the way he talked about what he would do after Britain won the war, it was clear that he expected life to go back to how it had been before.

She too believed they'd win the war, whatever it took. But she was equally sure most people wouldn't go back to their old ways of living and thinking. Young men who had never gone more than ten miles away from their villages had now seen big cities and travelled to foreign countries. They'd met all sorts of people, and though they'd seen some harrowing sights, they must have learnt a great deal too.

She was sure they would have been changed by their experiences.

And so many men had lost their lives, like her husband. The women they left behind would have to make new and different lives for themselves. It stood to reason that with so many young men being killed, there would be a lot of young women unable to find husbands at all.

She opened the front door to see if there was any sign of Babs's car, shivering as a cold wind sucked the warmth from her body.

'Shut that door!' yelled Donald.

'Yes, your majesty,' she muttered and chose to wait for her friend outside, where the air might be cold, but no one yelled orders at her.

Babs turned up a few minutes later to pick Olivia up. 'Can you get into the car without help?'

'Of course I can.' She opened the door and climbed nimbly in.

'Did you sell a lot of groceries today?' Babs asked in a teasing voice.

'Yes, of course. With Christmas coming next week people are trying to buy little treats, especially those whose sons and husbands will be home on leave. Are you staying down here in the country for the holiday?'

'No. I'm going up to the London flat and will be having friends round and going to a few parties. You could come with me, if you liked. It's a big flat and I have plenty of room for guests. I doubt you'll have much fun with dear Donald.'

'Don't tempt me. My cousin is driving me mad.'

Babs laughed. 'I met him a couple of times when Humfy was alive. He's an absolute blockhead. He wouldn't have been made a captain if the casualty rates among officers weren't so great.'

She scrubbed her eyes with the back of her forearm and sniffed. 'Sorry. That reminded me that the son of a close friend was killed two days ago. Pilot. Shot down over the Channel. Only twenty-three. Such a charming young man.'

'I'm sorry.'

Babs thumped the steering wheel with one clenched fist, causing the car to swerve slightly. 'How many lives are going to be lost before these stupid men learn to get on with one another? If we women ruled the world, we wouldn't go to war like this.'

'Wouldn't we? Who knows? I've met some quarrelsome and bigoted women in my time.'

Babs glanced quickly sideways. 'You sound and look a bit downhearted.'

'I am. It's living with Donald that does it. I can cope with him for a day or two, but weeks of him . . . I shall flee for my life once Christmas is over.'

'Change your mind about Christmas and join me in London.'

'I can't, Babs. Not this year. Cecily is hopeless without good help in the house and we can't seem to find her a full-time maid.'

'Offer more money.'

'Donald refuses to pay any maid more than he did before the war.'

'You'll soon be able to go back to your own home.'

'The trouble is, my house is full of Belgians. I'm not sure it'll be much better there, because at least here I have my job in the shop, where I meet a lot of people.'

'You need another job, then. Which is where the Women's Institutes come in. Leave it with me. Ah, here we are.' She slowed down and swung left into a drive.

Her house was large, four windows wide at the front. But it was just a square lump of a building without any charm. Whoever had designed it had done a poor job.

'Dull-looking place, isn't it?' Babs stopped the car in front of the house. 'I'll leave the car here and drive you back later. Yes, I will! It's going to rain and I'm not having you walking two miles and getting soaked.'

'I did bring an umbrella, but thank you.'

'Come on in. We'll have a glass of wine and a few chocolates.'

'Wine?'

'The only thing that's good about this house is the wine cellar. When I sell it, I'm also going to sell the flat in London and buy a house there. I'll take all the wine with me. Then I'm going to drink it, bottle by luscious bottle.'

She gestured to a portrait on the wall of a gentleman with ruddy cheeks and a rather full figure. 'Humfy's father. Only interested in hunting and fishing, but he did enjoy a drink, so I have him to thank for the wine. Humfy followed his example and drank more than he should sometimes. I'm glad of that now. At least he enjoyed what life he did have before the bullet found him.'

A maid stuck her head into the room without knocking. 'Oh, there you are, Mrs J. Do you want some tea bringing in?'

'Yes, please, Annie. Just a few sandwiches and some cake. But we'll drink wine with it, so no pot of tea. This is my friend Mrs Harbury, by the way.'

'Nice to meet you, Mrs Harbury.' She left the room.

'She's a treasure,' Babs said. 'I'd be lost without her.'

'I wish she had a sister to work for Cecily and Donald.'

'I'll ask her if she knows someone looking for work. But your cousins will have to pay higher than pre-war wages.'

'I'll see if I can convince Donald. Perhaps when he accepts the fact that I really am leaving, he'll reconsider it.'

After they were settled with a platter of food in front of them, Babs said briskly, 'Right. Let's talk about the Women's Institute movement.'

'I'm looking forward to hearing more about it. It must be something new.'

'Very new, just starting up and hasn't really got off the ground in England. It's thriving in Canada, though, and it's getting started in Ireland. You know how long it can take to accept something new in England. And one problem is, everyone knows their place in society. You'd think we'd asked them to commit murder by suggesting they form an association where all the women in each village are on equal terms at meetings.'

Olivia smiled. 'That *is* outrageous. I can't imagine Donald allowing his wife to join such a group. Why, she might have to sit next to her own maid! A lot of other people would be very much against such egalitarianism, though, women as well as men. And where would each group meet?'

'There! I knew you were a practical sort. How should I know where they'd meet? Each village is different. Church hall, maybe.'

'Only if the clergyman agreed. They're not all like our Mr Cummins, who has a very modern attitude towards the world.'

'He and his wife are dears. You'll find this hard to believe, but I heard that the vicar of one village instituted a curfew for women when they tried to set up a Women's Institute and forbade them to go out after dark.'

'*What*? You're joking.'

'No. It's the absolute truth. If I'd lived there I'd have gone out every night and danced on the vicar's doorstep. But he's not the only one to try to stop us: some husbands don't like their wives going out in the evening, especially if that means leaving them to look after the children. Whose children are they, I ask? It takes two people to make a child.'

She let out a defiant snort. 'Hah! We'll find a way to get the institutes started. You'll see. We need to give women somewhere to speak out, train them to speak out for their own future. One woman's voice isn't enough. We need a big, loud chorus.'

'A lot of women won't dare speak out, even so. They've been brought up to keep quiet and let men do the talking about the wider world.'

'That's the beauty of it. They'll learn to speak out by running their own group.' Babs drained her glass of wine and poured herself another one. 'Can't you say something nice about the idea?'

'Sorry. I love the idea of Women's Institutes. I just think it'll be hard to get them going. The best way might be to get an important person in each village on our side.'

'But that would go against what we're trying to do. We want ordinary women to speak to such people as equals!'

'They'll learn to do that gradually.'

Babs leant back, scowling. 'Gradually isn't good enough. I never was very patient when a thing needed doing.'

'Sometimes you have to be patient.' Olivia took a deep breath and said it. 'But if I can help in any way, then I will, because I really do like the idea. I can start after I go back to live in my old home in Swindon and— Hey! What are you doing?'

For Babs had pulled her up and was waltzing her round the room. 'I knew you'd help. I just knew it! You have that independent look to you.'

So Olivia danced with her friend and at that moment something tight and painful inside her loosened just a little.

Chapter Five

On Thursday 23rd December, Phoebe sat down to a solitary dinner in the great hall at Greyladies. When her husband was away, she used the smaller table near the window and in the daytime had a lovely view over the gardens. She sometimes wished she could eat in the kitchen with Ethel and Cook, for company. But that would make them feel uncomfortable.

The meal was excellent, as usual, but Phoebe didn't feel hungry. She pushed her food round her plate then piled it to one side, hoping it looked as if she'd eaten more than she had.

She paused, fork in the air. Was that the sound of footsteps outside the back of the house? If so, they were too slow and faint to be caused by one of the soldiers who made regular patrols round the building. Anyway, tonight's guard had clumped round the house and passed her window only a few minutes ago.

The footsteps were coming closer. Surely it couldn't be a trespasser trying to spy on what was going on inside the house? Her heart began to thud and a sudden urge to hide from view made her slip from her seat and move out of sight of whoever might be outside the window.

As she flattened her back against a bookcase, she wondered if she was being foolish. Was there really someone prowling outside, or was she just imagining it?

She was debating whether to return to her meal when she heard more faint sounds, closer this time. Someone was walking across the gravel outside and trying to keep quiet. The sounds were regular, definitely footsteps, definitely not a product of her imagination.

She remained perfectly still, listening intently, feeling rather ridiculous to be hiding like this in her own house. She would draw the curtains at night from now on. She didn't usually bother doing that, as the moonlit gardens could look so pretty and there was no one who overlooked these private gardens.

This was all Hatterson's fault for making her feel nervous. How dare he urge people to burn down Greyladies? What had she ever done to him that he wished her ill? In church, it had felt as though he was threatening her. He wouldn't have dared try to occupy their pew if Corin had been with her.

She'd have to face Hatterson again in two days' time, because it was unthinkable that she should miss the Christmas Day service. Perhaps the men who'd come to her aid last week would keep an eye on her pew and stop any trouble before it began.

And perhaps she was worrying about nothing.

She jumped in shock as a harsh man's voice suddenly yelled, 'Kill the Huns!' and the glass in one of the nearby windows smashed as something was hurled through it. She let out an involuntary cry as the missile landed close to where she had been sitting.

She stared at a chunk of rock with a pointed end, lying on the floor, surrounded by shards of broken glass. There were pieces of glass glinting on the tablecloth too in the light of the oil lamp.

The rock might have injured her if she hadn't had the sudden urge to move.

Wind whistled in through the hole and outside someone laughed and yelled, 'Kill the Huns and all the traitors who give them shelter!'

Then other voices cried out, the door to the kitchen was flung open and someone else hammered on the big door that connected the great hall in the old house to the new house.

For a moment Phoebe sagged against the bookcase. Before she could pull herself together, Ethel was there with an arm round her.

'Are you all right, Mrs Latimer?'

'Yes. Thank you.'

'Don't move to where they can see you,' the maid said. 'They might still be out there. We locked the kitchen door as soon as we heard the window smash and Cook's got her meat mallet handy in case she needs to defend herself.'

The connecting door opened and Captain Turner came striding across the hall towards her. 'What happened? I heard the sound of breaking glass. Are you all right?'

'Yes. Someone threw a big stone through the window. Luckily, I'd heard footsteps and moved out of sight.'

He walked across to examine the smashed window. 'This could as easily have been a bullet, you know.'

'Yes.' She shuddered. No use telling a down-to-earth man like him about the sense of warning she'd felt. He wouldn't believe in ghosts. She hadn't been certain about their existence herself till she'd come to live here.

'From now on, you must never sit with the curtains open after dark, and it might be a good idea to move your table to another part of the room. It's too close to the window.'

'Shall I draw the curtains now, sir?' Ethel asked.

'Not yet. My men are going round the outside of the house, searching for signs of the intruder. The light from inside will help them and *I* want to make sure it's them walking past, not an intruder.'

He turned back to Phoebe. 'Have you any idea who it might be?'

'The person who threw it yelled, "Kill the Huns",' Phoebe said. 'He laughed, such a nasty laugh.'

'It was a man?'

'Yes.'

'If what he's after is the Germans, why didn't he throw the stone through one of *our* windows at the front? There are no German internees in this part of the house.'

'He did it because I own Greyladies, I suppose. He yelled, "Kill the Huns and all the traitors who give them shelter." Though why he should think I can control what the War Office and army do about requisitioning my house, I can't imagine.'

After a couple of steadying breaths, she added, 'It must be that newcomer to the village, Hatterson. The one I told you about.'

'I shall go and check up on him as soon as my men have made sure there's no one lurking outside. I'll leave two soldiers on patrol instead of one tonight.'

There was a knock on the connecting door and Turner yelled, 'Come in!'

Sergeant Baxter joined them, saluting smartly. 'All clear outside, sir.'

'Then you and I will go into the village and seek out this Hatterson fellow.'

'I heard he was causing trouble, sir.'

'Yes. If he can't prove where he was tonight, I'll have him arrested for damaging army premises.'

He turned back to Phoebe and Ethel. 'Please draw the curtains now. Every single curtain on the ground floor.'

Ethel moved forward. 'It'll be safer if I draw them, ma'am.'

'What if you get hurt?' Phoebe protested.

'My men have checked the grounds,' Captain Turner said. 'And the missile was aimed at you, not at those in the kitchen.'

'Will you come back and tell me what you find out about Hatterson, Captain?'

'Yes, of course.'

The two men left and Ethel went round drawing all the curtains in the great hall, then in the rooms leading off it. She seemed more animated than usual. She was one of the women Corin's aunt Beaty had rescued from a life of poverty after her husband had been killed. She had barely said a word to Phoebe until tonight.

When she'd finished drawing the curtains she stood with hands on hips. 'I hope when they catch him, they give him a good thumping, Mrs Latimer, I do indeed. Men like my Stan have given their lives in the fight against the Germans and this man is causing trouble here at home. Has he no loyalty to our king and soldiers? No respect for the dead?'

'I suppose he thinks he's being loyal by attacking Germans.'

'Well, he's not. Early on in the war a German doctor saved my son's life. The man was a prisoner of war, but he was working in a military hospital in England because they were short of doctors who knew how to operate on the worst wounds. I didn't like the thought of him touching my Danny, but the other doctors told me they trusted him absolutely, because he cared more about saving lives than taking them.'

She gulped and for a moment couldn't continue, then more words poured out. 'After my Stan was killed, I couldn't manage. I was short of money – they don't give widows much, you see, and there's the full rent still to find before you even buy your food. But also, I couldn't seem to think straight, let alone hold down a job. When your country's at war, you think you're prepared to lose someone you love, but it still hurts. It hurts so much. My Stan was just an ordinary fellow, going bald and skinny, but we were happy together. He volunteered. I do wish he hadn't.'

She took another deep breath and continued. 'If Lady Potherington hadn't found me and sent me to work here, I don't know what would have become of me, I really don't. I'm very grateful to you for taking me in, don't think I'm not.'

'You're a good worker, Ethel.'

'I always do my best. But what surprised me, Mrs Latimer, is that I found some other Germans here who are kind people and polite. Cook told me they're working for our side like that doctor was. So this Hatterson doesn't know what he's talking about. The Germans aren't all bad, are they?'

'No, they're not. I didn't know you had a son serving in the army, Ethel.'

'Yes. My Danny recovered from his wound, but they sent him back to the trenches. I pray every night he'll come through safely. Every single night. Down on my knees I go, to do it proper. I never miss.'

'I'll pray for your son too from now on.'

Ethel sniffed away incipient tears. 'Thank you, ma'am. I'd appreciate that. I hope I haven't spoken out of turn tonight, but that stone upset me. Throwing it was *wrong*. Now, I'll go back to the kitchen and get Cook to serve you some more food. This plate will have bits of glass on it. Shame, that is. You'd hardly begun your meal. And I'll bring a clean tablecloth, too. You can't be too careful with broken glass.'

She was back soon, fussing over her mistress, and Cook herself brought a new plate of food. Phoebe was touched by their concern and forced most of it down so as not to offend them.

The thought of Ethel's confidences stayed with her as she sat writing some overdue letters. People could be wonderful. There were all sorts of heroism. Just carrying on was brave when you were worried sick about your son.

An hour later Captain Turner came back to report on what he'd found.

'Hatterson insists he was at home all evening, never left the house, and his wife bears that out.'

'She would.'

'Yes, that's what we thought, so we asked the neighbours, and one of them said she'd seen Hatterson sitting reading near the window.'

'*Seen* him?'

'Just the top of his head. Inside the house he wears a little hat, don't know what you'd call it, sort of a soft, knitted fez. It's to cover his baldness and keep his head warm. It pokes up over the back of the chair when he sits in there, they said.'

'Who said?'

'Someone we all trust . . . Miss Bowers.'

'Oh.'

He spread his arms in a gesture of helplessness. 'She wouldn't lie.'

'No. But her eyesight isn't good. She could be tricked.'

'That's what she said. But apparently Hatterson sits reading in that armchair most nights, with his back to the window, like tonight.'

'Then who threw the rock?'

The captain shook his head. 'I don't know. But Hatterson had a triumphant look to him, as if he'd got the better of us. The sergeant and I both agreed about that. Miss Bowers emphasised that she didn't actually see his face, or notice him getting up and down, just saw the hat. Though, of course, she wasn't watching him every minute. Only, her house is just along the street from his and he sits in the bay window with the light on, so she's well placed to notice what's going on.'

'I don't know what to say, except that even if he didn't throw the stone, I feel he was involved.'

'I agree with you absolutely, Mrs Latimer. We'll be watching him carefully from now on, I promise you.'

When he went back to the front part of the house, Phoebe was so upset, she paced up and down for quite a while.

There was something about Hatterson that made her shiver, something unclean . . . evil. What would he do next?

In Nether Bassett that same day, there was the sound of a car engine and Babs came breezing into the village shop. 'Afternoon, Mrs Cummins. I wonder if I can have a private word?'

'Certainly, Mrs Horner-Jevons. Please come through to the back.'

'After you finish here, I'll take you home,' Babs called to Olivia, speaking as loudly as if she was fifty yards away. 'I've got something to tell you before I go up to London.'

When Mrs Cummins returned, she was smiling and put something into a box near the till. No mistaking that large piece of thin white paper with black writing on it for anything but a five-pound note, though they didn't often see those in the shop. Their customers mostly dealt in coins or occasionally one of the new ten-shilling notes, which had only been issued last year. Some of the older customers were still rather suspicious of the red and white banknotes, and preferred to stick to coins.

'Don't forget: I'll be back for you in half an hour, Olivia,' Babs called as she left.

Mrs Cummins was still smiling. 'She's a real lady, that one. And I don't care if she does wear trousers, which someone as plump as her shouldn't, because it isn't flattering. But there you are, people can't see their own behinds, can they? She looks better in a skirt, like she's wearing today. But Mrs J could go around wearing tiger skins and I'd still think well of her.'

Olivia hid a smile. 'Praise, indeed. Why do you say that?'

'Because she comes in every Christmas, like she did today, and gives me five pounds to buy extra food for people who're a bit short. It's a godsend to some of them, I can tell you. And she trusts me to know who needs help, doesn't even ask for an account of how the money was spent. Well, she knows I'll not cheat her.'

She turned away as the door opened and a customer came in.

Olivia felt a warm glow at the thought of Babs's generosity. If she ever had a lot of money to spare, she'd help poorer women more than she was able to at the moment. Men earned wages their families could live off, even if it was a struggle for the lower paid, but employers expected to hire women for half those wages, even widows with families to support. How were the women supposed to manage? Life could be so unfair.

Today she was glad when her time at the shop ended, because she was looking forward to seeing Babs, wondering what this was about.

The motor car was standing outside but Babs wasn't in it. She was haranguing a man about drinking too much and leaving his wife without money for food. The man stood with head bowed, listening to her in silence, even though he towered over her.

'I'm going to call in at the pub and tell them not to serve you more than one pint a night,' Babs finished up. 'And I'll set someone to watch that you don't have any more than that.'

'Two pints,' he pleaded. 'A man gets thirsty, working hard all day.'

'One. And if your wife grows any thinner, I'll have you banned from the pub completely.'

She strode back to the car and swung up into it. 'I'm an interfering old woman, aren't I? But I can't bear to see men wasting so much money on drink when their families are going hungry.'

'You seem to care about a lot of things,' Olivia remarked.

Babs shrugged, her smile fading. 'It helps to pass the time. And Humfy would have told me to do it now that he can't. He knew everyone in the village, played with some of the men when they were all lads.'

She started the car, an easy job even for a woman because the large Wolseley had one of the new starter motors on it and didn't need hand cranking. She raised her voice above the sound of the motor as she drove. 'I've got some very good news for you. You won't have to feel guilty about leaving, because I've found your cousin's wife a maid.'

'My goodness, how did you manage that?'

'I put the word out through my servants that I knew a lady in the country who needed a general maid. The woman who came to see me about the job has been living in London. When a Zeppelin came over and dropped bombs nearby, destroying her neighbour's house and killing the whole family, she grew terrified, and is desperate to live in the country till the war is over and her husband comes home. If you'll kindly introduce me to your cousins, I'll tell them about her.'

She glanced down at herself with one of her jolly chuckles. 'I hope you appreciate that I've dressed in a skirt today so that I won't shock the captain too much.'

This was going to be an interesting meeting, Olivia thought. Even the way Babs talked to people would upset Donald, who liked meek, quiet-voiced women. But if you wanted to get something done, you couldn't be meek. She was learning so much from watching her new friend, who seemed absolutely fearless when dealing with people.

As Olivia got out of the car she said, 'Give me a couple of minutes to warn them that they've got a visitor, then follow me in.'

She went into the house, calling, 'I've brought a visitor.'

Cecily came out of the sitting room, saying in a low voice, 'I was watching out of the window and saw who it was. I don't know if we have anything suitable to serve Mrs Horner-Jevons for refreshments. And I'm only wearing an old dress.'

'Never mind that. She's not here to take tea and she won't give two hoots what you're wearing. She wants to speak to you and Donald.' She glanced into the sitting room and saw her cousin sitting on the sofa with his foot up. 'Don't try to get up when she arrives, Donald. Babs knows you've been wounded.'

There was a knock on the front door and a voice called, 'All right to come in?'

Cecily rushed across to open the door wider. 'Yes, of course, Mrs Horner-Jevons.'

'This is my cousin's wife, Mrs Ballam,' Olivia said 'And her husband, Captain Ballam.'

'We met a while ago. Pleased to see you again.' Babs followed her hostess into the sitting room.

'Won't you sit down?' Cecily indicated a chair. 'Would you like a cup of tea?'

'No, thank you. I'm here on business. You may not know it, but I help women who're struggling because they've lost husbands, or lost their homes in the bombing. I heard you were looking for a maid.'

Cecily gave her husband a worried glance.

'We *were* looking for a maid,' he said. 'But as we can't find one, my cousin will have to help out instead.'

'I've already told you, I'll be leaving after Christmas,' Olivia said firmly. 'I won't change my mind, whatever you say, so you definitely need a maid.'

As Donald opened his mouth to argue, Babs spoke again, slightly more loudly, drowning out his first words so that he stopped speaking. 'I know a woman who's terrified of staying in London because of the bombing. Her husband is serving in France, so she'd need to be able to see him when he comes home on leave, but apart from that she has excellent references; she used to work for a titled lady.'

Cecily gave her husband a pleading look.

He hrrumphed, caught Olivia's eyes and said, 'I'll think about it. I prefer to do the hiring of servants, because I'm used to dealing with people. Besides, I like to know the person to whom I'm paying out my money.'

'Fine. But if you won't take my word that she's suitable and you need to interview her before you employ her, you'll have to pay her train fare to and from London, because she can't afford it.'

He stiffened visibly. '*What*?'

'And her wages would be . . .' She turned to Olivia and winked. 'What would you say, Olivia? How about a pound a week and all found.'

'Yes, that sounds reasonable.'

'*A pound*! We've never paid more than ten shillings a week,' Donald said immediately. 'I don't think—'

'You're out of touch, then. Prices have risen and so have servants' wages. I thought your need was urgent, what with Olivia going home to Swindon after Christmas, so I came to you first. But if you're not interested in hiring the woman, other people will snap her up.'

He turned to Olivia. 'It really would be better if you stayed here till the end of the war – better for both you *and* Cecily.'

'No, Donald. My mind is quite made up.'

He glared at her, then turned to Babs. 'My cousin and I will have to discuss this and get back to you, Mrs Horner-Jevons. After all, she and my wife have been managing perfectly well without a full-time maid. And I'm sure when she has time to think, she won't want to leave us in the lurch.'

Olivia leant forward and said loudly and clearly, 'I am leaving – after – Christmas, Donald. Cecily *will not* be able to manage without a maid.'

'But—'

For once, his wife interrupted him, her voice fluting with nervousness. 'Tell us about this woman, Mrs Horner-Jevons. It's hard to make a decision without having met her.'

'Pansy is forty-five and a hard worker. She used to be head housemaid for a friend of mine until she married. After running her own home for a few years, she has discovered that she also likes cooking, so she'd be ideal for you. If you don't wish to employ her, I can find her a job like that.' She snapped her fingers in the air.

'Donald, dear, I do think we should reconsider.' Cecily blushed and added, 'Especially now, with a baby on the way.'

'Ah. Oh. Yes. I suppose . . . given the circumstances. If Olivia *will* be so selfish. I might find the extra money for a while. Just until the war ends.'

'Good. I'll send Pansy a telegram and she'll be here within the week, but you'll have to give her the train fare.' Babs turned to Olivia. 'And you're still coming to spend New Year's Eve with me in London as we agreed, aren't you?'

Olivia had agreed to no such thing, but her new, livelier self gave in to another of Babs's winks, not to mention the thought of some more stimulating company. 'Yes, I'm looking forward to it.'

'Good. I'll send someone with the car to pick you and

your luggage up on the 30th, because you'll have to go home to your Swindon house first to get your glad rags. Bring something really pretty to wear on New Year's Eve. Humfy and I always threw a big party, and he'd want me to carry on doing it. I dare say we'll be dancing until dawn. When those officers come home on leave, they like to enjoy themselves.' Her face took on a fleeting look of sadness and she murmured, 'And who can blame them?'

Not waiting for an answer, she stood up and nodded to her hosts. 'I'll take my leave now. I'll call in next time I'm down in the country to see how Pansy is liking it here, Mrs Ballam. Though, of course, she'd get in touch with me if things weren't going well, because she knows I can always find her another job.'

Donald's face turned red with annoyance at this not-so-subtle threat, but he didn't say anything else.

'I'll see you out, shall I?' Olivia walked with Babs to the car and leant against it on the side away from the house, shoulders shaking with laughter. 'You have the devil in you sometimes, Babs. Oh!' She clutched her stomach. 'Did you see the shock on his face?'

'I can be a bit of a devil, can't I? But I got what I wanted and what Cecily clearly needed, as well. And poor Pansy really is terrified of staying in London. She'll have him eating out of her hand in no time. She's much cleverer than he is.'

'You got what you wanted in more ways than one. You also nudged me into staying with you for New Year's Eve.'

'Well, you need to start living again, my dear. We widows can't wallow in our sorrow for ever. Nothing will bring our men back, will it?'

'No. You're right. Life has to go on.'

There was another moment's silence, then Babs got into the car. 'I'll send someone to fetch you!'

Olivia went back inside to find Donald very stiff and on his dignity, so she went into the kitchen on the excuse that she was parched and needed a cup of tea.

Cecily came in and beamed at her. 'Thank you so much for helping me get a maid. I've been trying to persuade Donald to pay higher wages for a while now. He simply doesn't understand what it's like running a house.'

'That's all right. Congratulations on the baby.'

Cecily went pink, a soft expression on her face. 'I'm so looking forward to having children. I love babies.'

'Good. What do you want? A girl or a boy?'

'I don't mind. I shall love it, whichever it is.'

'I'm sure you will.'

Olivia turned to fiddle with the teacups. Once again she couldn't help feeling jealous of another woman who'd got the thing she had wanted so desperately for years: a baby.

She hoped she hadn't let her sadness show. She didn't want to spoil Cecily's pleasure.

Alex found life in London rather dull. He couldn't forget how radiantly happy Mildred had looked at her wedding. He couldn't ever remember feeling as happy as that, not even when he found a particularly fine piece of old furniture or a painting by a well-known artist.

He might have made a lot of money, but something had always been missing from his personal life.

So when an acquaintance invited him to tea that afternoon to meet a lady friend of the family, who had returned to London from the country, for once he accepted, instead of pleading the need to work. It was probably another go at matchmaking. People would introduce him to single women every now and then. But none of the women had attracted him and few seemed able to hold an intelligent conversation.

He felt sorry for the poor women who were paraded before him, but he couldn't live with a woman who bored him to tears.

He had no expectation that this tea party would offer anything different, but he felt like getting out of the shop and talking to people.

The phone rang just then, so he picked up the earpiece and leant forward to speak into the 'mouth' of the candlestick telephone. 'Seaton's Antiques.'

'I'm so glad I caught you.'

'Mildred! How's married life?'

'Wonderful, but never mind that. Alex, some things have been unearthed at your mother's and I think you should see them, decide what to do about them.'

'Well, can't you post them on to me?'

'I'd rather not. They're . . . um, rather delicate. Besides, if you agree with me, and I think you will, you'll need to come down to Swindon anyway.'

'That sounds ominous.'

'It could be.'

'Can't you tell me anything about it?'

'No, dear. You never know who's listening.'

She was right, really. Some telephone operators did eavesdrop on conversations, everyone knew that. 'Very well. I'll come down. But it'll have to be after Christmas. I have one or two projects that are at a crucial stage. One is for a war charity for whom I'm running an auction that should raise rather a lot of money.'

'After Christmas will be fine. It's just that we both need to decide what to do about this.'

He frowned as he put down the phone. Mildred wouldn't ask him to go to Swindon for no reason, or exaggerate the seriousness of something. Why on earth couldn't she give him a hint about the reason, though?

He looked at his watch. Nearly time to set off for the tea party. He'd lost all interest in it now and wished he hadn't accepted the invitation.

When Alex saw that the woman attending the tea party was Babs Horner-Jevons, his spirits lifted immediately. He hadn't seen her for a good while, not since before her husband died, in fact.

She wouldn't be looking for a husband, and even if she was, she'd no more want to marry him than he'd want to marry her. However, she always had something interesting to say and he enjoyed her company.

'I didn't realise you two knew one another,' his hostess said.

'I've been a friend of Humfy and Babs for years.'

As the two of them chatted, he saw his hostess smiling smugly, so he leant closer to Babs and whispered, 'She's got us married off already.'

She let out one of her delightfully infectious gurgles of laughter. 'Oh, dear. Shall we tell her now that we're just friends or shall we let her hope?'

'If you know the lady of the house, you can tell her. I've only met her once or twice and never had a real conversation with her, so I wouldn't presume to speak to her about such a delicate subject.'

'We'll let her hope, then.' Her expression grew sad. 'I still miss poor Humfy.'

He gave her a moment to blink away the tears in her eyes, then asked, 'What are you doing with yourself now, Babs? You don't seem to have been around lately. Have you retired to your country home?'

'I've been spending a lot of time there, yes, but not because I'm spending my days weeping. Humfy would come back to haunt me if I did. It's a convenient place to stay for something else I'm involved in.'

She began telling him about the embryonic Women's Institutes she was helping set up and he listened with interest because he hadn't heard about this new organisation.

'I've found someone to help the cause, a new friend, but she's going to be a good friend, I'm sure. The trouble is, she's stuck in deepest Wiltshire. I was going to give her a lift up to town, stopping on the way to leave some of her luggage at her house in Swindon and let her pick up some party clothes. But my car's broken down and I can't get it repaired until after the new year, because they haven't got the right part.'

'Can't your friend come to London by train?'

'I suppose she could, but it'd be very awkward. There isn't a branch line to the tiny village where she's staying. And the thing is, I'm worried about her bossy cousin. I wouldn't put it past him to try to stop her coming if I'm not there to support her. Ballam's a dull brute and he's nursing a war wound, enjoying playing the hero and making everyone run round after him.'

Alex had met a lot of men like that. Backbone of the army

in one sense but he doubted they'd be pleasant to live with.

'Ballam wants Olivia to look after his wife when he goes back to his regiment. Mrs B is a limp sort of female who can't manage on her own. Oh dear, why do cars always break down when you need them? I really need to rescue Olivia.'

'Another lame duck you're taking under your wing?'

'Olivia? Well, she needs help at the moment but I would never call her a lame duck. She says she hasn't been herself since her husband's death, but I could tell she's getting over her loss now. The two of them were like me and Humfy, very happy together.'

She sighed and fell silent again for a moment or two. 'I've just about forced Olivia to come to my New Year's Eve party and afterwards I'm going to nudge her into a wider social life. I'll also get her involved in the Women's Institute movement as an organiser. That'll take her out and about.'

'You don't do things by halves, do you?'

Babs gave him a very direct look. 'If I see something that needs doing, I try to do it. I don't always succeed, but I always try.'

'I admire that. Look, as it happens, I can help out. I have to nip down to Swindon after Christmas, because something's come up. I could easily go and pick your friend up at the same time, if you like.'

'Alex, would you?'

'For you, Babs, only for you. But you'll have to promise she won't bore me to tears.'

She chuckled. 'She definitely won't. You'll like Olivia, I'm sure. One can't have too many friends as one dwindles into old age.'

'You will never dwindle into anything, my dear. You'll be nagging the undertakers to help one of the mourners as they screw down your coffin lid.'

She gave a shout of laughter, then laughed even more loudly as she saw their hostess nudge her husband again.

Alex hadn't enjoyed himself so much for a long time.

It was strange, though. He had never been attracted to Babs as a woman, much as he enjoyed her company and friendship.

Who knew why you were attracted enough to some people to marry them and not at all attracted to others in that way, even though they'd be perfectly suitable spouses?

Perhaps he was so fussy he was destined to remain a bachelor.

But a small flicker of hope refused to die, which was why he'd come to tea today. He had promised Mildred to keep his options open, and he would keep that promise.

Chapter Six

Christmas seemed even quieter than usual that year. Alex had heard about another friend losing a son in France and that reminded him of how little he was able to personally contribute to the war. He seemed to have spent his whole life trying to keep up with other, stronger men.

The highlight of his day was when Mildred rang to wish him a merry Christmas. She sounded extremely happy and that cheered him up.

He had insisted his cook–housekeeper and maid spend the afternoon and evening with their families, but when they'd gone the house was too quiet. He even missed the faint sound of the maid humming as she went about her work or the clatter of pots from the kitchen.

Worst of all, the silence emphasised how alone he was.

Snap out of it, you fool! he told himself. *Self-pity will get you nowhere.*

He took out a recently published novel given to him by a friend, who'd assured him he'd enjoy reading something a bit different. He looked at it and shook his head. *Tarzan of the Apes* wasn't his sort of book, he was sure, but he didn't feel like reading about eighteenth-century jewellery, which was his only other unread book, so he'd give the story a go, at least.

Once he started reading, he couldn't stop, had to follow the ridiculous tale to see how it ended. It couldn't really happen that a human child would be raised by apes and then turn out to be a lord, he was sure. But the imagination was a wonderful thing and it was sometimes intriguing to play the 'What if?' game.

The day passed quickly and he didn't go to bed till he'd finished the whole book. He blessed his friend mentally.

When he got up the following morning, he decided that he'd drive down to Swindon tomorrow, a day earlier than originally planned. He enjoyed driving and the weather looked fairly settled. Mildred and Edwin had offered him a bed and wouldn't mind him turning up unannounced, he was sure.

As they sat round the breakfast table, Olivia watched Cecily become paler by the minute. The poor thing hardly ate any breakfast these days, because she felt sick in the mornings, but she seemed to feel she should still get up with her husband.

Olivia had been obliged to cook Donald's breakfast for the past three days and then watch him stuff his face with food. No wonder he was getting rather stout if he always ate so much.

Suddenly Cecily gulped, pressed her handkerchief to her mouth and rushed out, sending her chair tumbling backwards.

'It's a poor lookout her doing this to me every morning,' Donald grumbled.

Olivia wasn't letting him get away with such selfishness.

'What do you mean by "poor lookout"? And what exactly is she doing to *you*?'

'Well, it puts a man off his food to know his wife's about to be sick. If she has to do it, she should control herself till the meal is over.'

'It doesn't seem to have put *you* off your food. You never leave a crumb. You should be kinder to her. She can't help feeling sick in the mornings and she *can't* control it. Many women are like that.'

'She might be able to wait if she bends her mind to other things.'

'Donald, it's impossible to think of something else when you're about to be sick. Do be reasonable. She's carrying your child, possibly a son. You don't want to upset her with your complaints.' She saw the stubborn look settle on his face and added slyly, 'Cecily might lose the baby if she gets too upset. Your job is to keep her calm, not scold her.'

He stared at her, mouth slightly open as if she'd told him something outrageous, then let out an aggrieved sigh. But for the rest of the day she noticed him studying his wife surreptitiously and he did stop nagging Cecily to snap out of it, at least in Olivia's hearing.

The long, tedious day ended at last and she filled hot-water bottles for them all, then took hers up to bed before Donald could find her any more little jobs to do for him. Cecily helped Donald get ready for his makeshift bed, taking him in a glass of water and the chamber pot before coming upstairs.

Olivia let out a low groan of relief as she pulled the covers up to her chin, enjoying the luxury of silence.

Babs had phoned that evening to tell her that a Mr

Seaton would be coming in two days' time to drive her up to London.

Not long now, she thought as she felt sleep taking over. I shall definitely not miss running round after Donald.

What a poor husband he was. Selfish to the core. She had been so lucky in Charles.

The stone-throwing attack on Greyladies went unsolved and left Phoebe feeling as if her assailant had won that trick in the game.

It had to be Hatterson, or someone connected to him, but he didn't seem to associate with anyone in the village, so who could be helping him?

The soldiers had asked around, but no one had seen any strangers in the neighbourhood. Or at least, no one admitted seeing any strangers. She knew there were still people who resented the internees living in luxury at Greyladies, so who knew whether they might be giving shelter to strangers.

She went to church on Christmas morning, but Captain Turner insisted on escorting her. It felt strange going out to worship on a Saturday.

He had told the internees they would be safer staying at Greyladies for the moment and most of them had agreed, because they'd already faced hostility and even violence before being brought here. They decided to say prayers together in honour of the day and one man would play hymns on the piano, which had remained in the front part of the house. Phoebe allowed them to use it because one or two of them were very musical.

As she and Captain Turner walked to church, she enjoyed

the crisp morning and the sunlight on her face. Of course, it wasn't warm, but still, the brightness cheered you up. However, when they reached the church, she noticed some members of the congregation standing by the door, making no attempt to go inside. They were looking worried and murmuring to one another.

Something was definitely wrong. She let go of the captain's arm and hurried forward to find out.

'They're fighting in there,' a woman whispered to her. 'Don't go inside till it's over, Mrs Latimer. It's that Hatterson creature again.'

'Oh, no!' Could she not even have a peaceful Christmas Day?

Captain Turner pushed through the group and said, quite unnecessarily, 'Stay there, please, everyone.'

But Phoebe followed him into the porch and watched from the doorway as he strode down the aisle.

At the front of the church the verger and one of the farmers were trying to drag Hatterson and a complete stranger from the Latimer pew but were hampered by the pew's narrowness and high back.

Hatterson's wife was cowering in one of the rear pews, looking distressed.

The two intruders were putting up a spirited fight, jabbing at those trying to remove them from the pew with walking stick handles.

'Will you get out of that pew!' the verger shouted. 'This is a church and you're causing a disturbance.'

Hatterson yelled, 'No, I won't get out. Us Englishmen have a right to worship where we choose and—'

He fell silent as the captain came to a halt next to the pew. 'Kindly stop causing a disturbance and take your place with the rest of the congregation! This is the Latimer pew and you have no right to use it.'

'*She* lets those Huns sit in it!' Hatterson yelled, stabbing his finger in Phoebe's direction. 'Look at her! Standing there as if she owns the place. If Huns can sit here, so can us Englishmen.'

'Don't be ridiculous!' the captain roared. 'Get out of this pew and don't try to sit here again or I'll arrest you.'

'The magistrate would just let us go again. There's no law against sitting in a pew in church.'

'There is a law against causing an affray.'

After standing staring at him defiantly for a few seconds, Hatterson shrugged and when his friend nudged him to move out of the pew, he did so, but very slowly indeed.

Phoebe stepped to one side as they walked back down the aisle but Hatterson paused when he was level with her. 'It isn't finished yet,' he whispered. He didn't even look at his wife, sitting there with her head bowed.

She watched the two men leave the church and wondered where they'd gone, what mischief they were plotting now, then she took her place at the front with the captain by her side.

'What did that fellow say to you?'

She repeated it.

'Don't worry. We'll keep you safe.'

But could they? It seemed to her that Hatterson was winning something with each incident, if it was only the planting of worries in her mind.

She had trouble concentrating on the service and not a word of the sermon sank in. It was a relief when it ended.

As they stood up to leave Captain Turner hesitated, then turned to the farmer now standing across the aisle with his wife behind him, waiting to follow them out of the church. 'Could you please escort Mrs Latimer home for me when she's greeted her friends, Ruddle? I think I'd better hurry back to Greyladies immediately, in case those two try to cause any more trouble there.'

At the farmer's nod, he left at once.

'You don't need to come home with me, Mr Ruddle,' Phoebe told him as they walked out into the churchyard. 'I'll be quite safe walking through Challerton.'

'You let him go with you,' Mrs Ruddle said. 'It doesn't pay to take chances and I've got family to keep me safe.'

Her husband nodded agreement. 'I'd rather see you back, if you don't mind, Mrs Latimer. The captain's right to be concerned about your safety. That Hatterson fellow seems to have it in for you and I'd not put anything past him. His poor old uncle would be turning in his grave if he knew what was going on. What a pity Bill's other nephew was killed.'

'Well, thank you. That's very kind. I won't stop to chat today, so that you can get back to your family.' Phoebe took the arm he offered and they set off at a rapid pace.

Everything seemed peaceful enough until they reached the side gate to Greyladies and found signs of a struggle. The bare flower bed had been trampled, with earth scattered over the gravel path. Nearer the house one or two small rocks were lying on the path and the remains of a wooden sign on a pole were lying on the ground in two pieces. You could still tell that it had said, 'Kill all Huns!'

From the rear of the house came shouts and grunts.

'I'd better go in the front way,' she said in a low voice.

Captain Turner opened the door before they even got there and called, 'Come inside quickly, Mrs Latimer. Good thing I saw you coming. We're keeping the front door locked.'

'Is everything all right?'

'There were several men here yelling and shouting when I got back, all strangers except Hatterson, and some of them are still causing a nuisance round the back.'

Her heart sank as she turned to thank her protector.

'I'll just stay a while in case you or the good captain need help,' Mr Ruddle said.

'We can't ask you to do that.'

'You didn't ask. Besides, it's my village too and I don't like people causing trouble here.'

The captain shot the bolts on the front door. 'I'd better get back to my men. Mrs Latimer, please stay out of sight of the windows. This way, Mr Ruddle.'

The burly farmer followed him out of the big entrance hall towards the servants' quarters, which had an exit at the side.

Phoebe went straight through the new house to the old part, and made her way to the kitchen, from where you could see more of the rear gardens. Since no one was in sight outside, she risked opening the back door just for a moment to see if she could hear anything.

Yes! There were people yelling over near the crypt, their voices echoing in the frosty air. Well, they'd not be able to get inside the crypt from the garden, if that had been their intention. There was a locked iron grille across its entrance, protecting the last remaining room of the original abbey where the grey nuns had once worshipped. The only other way into it was through the cellars of the old house, and even then you had to know the trick to opening the entrance to the secret passage.

As the sounds grew fainter, someone cleared their throat

to one side of her. She jumped in shock to find Ethel standing there. 'Didn't you go to church?'

'Yes, but when I saw you leaving I came back quickly, in case you needed me.'

'You came back on your own? I thought you and Cook were together.'

'I ran all the way. I've always been a good runner. I checked it was safe before I went round the back. Cook's following me with a friend to keep her safe. She's too old to run, she says.'

'It's very kind of you to think of me, but please don't take such a risk in future.'

Ethel gestured towards the churned up gravel outside the kitchen, where a tin of white paint had been upended, leaving a sticky mess. 'Lucky they didn't get to use that. I've seen people painting words on buildings in Swindon and it's a devil to get off. Eh, what is the world coming to when this sort of thing happens in England?'

Phoebe couldn't say anything because of a lump in her throat. She felt deeply upset at being helpless to stop this trouble, and horrified at the violence that was breaking out across the country, a lot of it aimed at people with German ancestry, some of whom had been born in England and had never even visited Germany.

'We shall have to be on our guard, Mrs Latimer. We could do with some big dogs to give us warning.'

'We'll take care and we do have the soldiers helping guard Greyladies.'

'Four of them, and they have to sleep and eat sometimes. They can't always be patrolling the gardens. And this is a big house, with all sorts of nooks and crannies to hide in.'

'I know. What worries me is Hatterson. If he can find others like him and bring them here, next time he may come back with a whole crowd of troublemakers. I saw a mob attack the Steins's shop in Swindon once. It's terrifying how mindless people seem to become when they go on the rampage like that.'

The two women waited a few moments, but nothing else happened, so Ethel said, 'We both need a nice strong cup of tea.' She moved back inside the kitchen and put the kettle on the hot part of the stove. 'Did you lock the outside door of the kitchen again, ma'am?'

'No, I—'

The door began to open and for a moment they froze, then Phoebe threw herself against it and locked it. Someone cursed outside and they saw a man running away.

'Who is he?' Ethel whispered.

'I don't recognise him. I don't think he's from the village.'

There was a sound behind them and they both swung round. But it was only Cook.

'I hope you don't mind me using the front entrance, Mrs Latimer. One of the soldiers was there and told me not to come round the back way because they'd had intruders. On Christmas Day, too. I don't know what the world is coming to.'

She looked towards the window. 'There doesn't seem to be anyone around now, though.'

'There was a minute ago,' Ethel said. 'Bold as brass he was, about to walk in and help himself to our good food, I should think.'

Phoebe didn't correct her, but she thought it was more likely the intruder had intended to do as much damage as he could.

'They've gone off towards the crypt now,' Ethel said.

'Well, you keep that back door locked. I need to get on with my cooking and I don't want any hooligans interrupting me. I've planned a lovely meal for you, Mrs Latimer. You've not been eating much lately and you need to keep up your strength.'

She sounded as if she was encouraging a child to cheer up, Phoebe thought. She had a sudden idea. 'Can't you two share the meal with me for once? It won't feel like a celebration if I'm on my own.'

'That wouldn't be right, ma'am.' But Ethel sounded uncertain.

'I think it'd be a good thing to do on Christmas Day,' Phoebe insisted. 'And I'd feel much safer eating in the kitchen, I must admit.'

'Yes, of course. I never thought of that. Cook and me will set the table properly, though. I like my tables to look nice. You could go and sit by the fire in the great hall till we're ready for you, ma'am. Don't go near those windows, though. I'll come for you when it's time.'

Phoebe did as her maid ordered, smiling at their reversal of roles. It was good to see Ethel coming out of her shell. She poked the fire to get it burning more brightly, though the big room was always on the chilly side in winter.

She sat in an armchair placed temptingly near the fireplace and picked up a book, but couldn't settle to reading. She didn't feel like embroidering, either. Her mind kept going round in circles, as she worried how to protect herself and her house.

When the door opened, she didn't turn round for a moment, expecting to hear Ethel's voice. No one spoke and her heart skittered. Had one of the troublemakers managed to sneak inside?

She snatched up the poker and whirled round, brandishing it.

But the man staring across at her from the doorway was her husband. She closed her eyes for a moment in utter relief.

'What the hell has been happening here?' Corin demanded. 'And put that poker down before you hurt yourself.'

She let it drop in the hearth with a clatter.

His eyes were raking her from head to toe. 'You're quite sure you're all right, my darling?'

'I am now.' As she ran towards him, she burst into tears of sheer relief. 'Oh, Corin, Corin!'

They met in the middle of the room, his arms going round her. He pulled her close, murmuring her name, raining kisses on her face.

Her feeling of apprehension vanished and the world seemed to shift into a happier state, a feeling that all was right now. It always did when they were together.

In the far corner of the room a light glowed and as they pulled apart, they both noticed it.

'Merry Christmas, Anne Latimer,' Phoebe said softly.

The light glowed more brightly for a moment, then faded.

'You've got me believing in ghosts now,' he muttered. 'These lights can't come and go from nowhere, but they do.'

'She likes to show us she's still here, keeping an eye on Greyladies.'

There was a knock on the door and Ethel came in. 'I'll just set the table in here, shall I, Mrs Latimer? Welcome back, Major. You're just in time for the Christmas meal. Cook's done us all proud.'

Phoebe would have moved away from her husband when the maid was there, but his arm tightened around her waist, so she stayed where she was, feeling his love fold round her.

She saw Ethel's eyes go to that embrace and her maid smiled briefly, then blinked her eyes furiously. Phoebe suddenly realised it would be the maid's first Christmas without her husband and she must feel his death even more at such a time.

'Thank you, Ethel,' she said. 'For everything you've done in the past day or two. I don't know how I'd have coped without you.'

The maid straightened up and the sadness was replaced by pride. 'I always try my best, ma'am. Cook says the meal will only be a few minutes.'

As she left the hall, Corin turned to Phoebe. 'What has she been doing?'

'Keeping my spirits up. And her own. She lost her husband earlier this year, but she's coming through it. I think she's going to make a wonderful maid and it's good that she feels needed here.'

By the time Ethel served the food, Corin knew about the happenings at Greyladies and in the village.

'I'll put a stop to that,' he said.

'How?'

'I'll find a way, believe me. I'm not having troublemakers upsetting you.'

Alex had a pleasant drive to Swindon after the various Christmas festivities were over. He went straight to Mildred's house, but there was no one at home and the curtains were drawn. Damn! He should have telephoned.

He decided to try Edwin's office to find out where they were but it was closed, with a neat notice in the window saying '*Closed until 1st January*'.

Where had Mildred and her husband gone? She hadn't said anything about them going away when she phoned.

Alex went back to her house and there was still no one around, so he asked the neighbours if they knew where Mr and Mrs Morton were.

The neighbour on the right shook her head. The one on the left side said, 'I think they went to stay with Mr Morton's cousin in the country. It was very sudden and my maid says they gave the maid extra time off to visit her family. Mr Morton told her they'd be home again tomorrow. He never stays away for more than a day or two.'

'Thank you. I'll come back tomorrow, then.'

Alex went to sit in his car, thumping the steering wheel with one clenched fist. Why hadn't he phoned to tell her he was coming a day early?

Because he'd been a bit unsettled, that's why, had wanted to get away from his solitary existence. He'd simply assumed Mildred would continue to live a quiet life. But why should she do that now she was married?

He was tired and it wasn't worth going back to London, only to drive down here again tomorrow. He didn't feel like the false Christmas bonhomie of a hotel, so decided to spend the night in his old home. Not a cheerful prospect, but simple enough to do since he had a key.

But even if he had a bed for the night, what was he going to do with himself for the rest of the day? It was chilly and threatening rain.

Suddenly he remembered Babs's friend, Mrs Harbury. She had a house in Swindon. If he visited her today at the village where she was staying and explained his dilemma, perhaps she wouldn't mind leaving her cousins early and spending the night in her own home. That'd save him some time tomorrow. He didn't want to linger in a place he still thought of as his mother's house.

Mrs Harbury might even be glad to leave early. Babs said she wasn't enjoying her cousins' company. And she had to sort out some party garments for the visit to London. He smiled. Well, you couldn't go to one of Babs's splendid parties dressed drably.

He wondered what the lady was like? Would she mind these rather ad hoc arrangements? If she was a friend of Babs, she probably wouldn't be the sort to stand on her dignity. He smiled involuntarily at the thought of Babs and dignity. The two simply didn't mix.

He checked Mrs Harbury's address. Yes, she was staying in the village near Babs's country residence and he knew the way. He got out of the car to crank-start it. He was hoping to purchase a car with an electric starter motor, though he'd probably have to order one and wait.

He'd sort out this problem with his inheritance as soon as Mildred and her husband got back. He couldn't understand why they were being so mysterious about it. They probably needed his signature on something.

He doubted there were any skeletons in his mother's cupboard. The mere idea made him smile. She must have been one of the most rigidly correct people in England.

Chapter Seven

Nether Bassett was just as Alex remembered it from driving through a couple of times on the way to visit Babs and her husband: a pleasant if rather nondescript village, with only enough inhabitants to support one general store and one pub.

He stopped at the store to ask directions to Captain Ballam's residence, because he had only the house name *The Laurels* on the address he'd been given.

As he was about to leave the shop, he noticed that dandelion and burdock was available to buy by the glass. It made him realise how thirsty he was and he couldn't resist asking for one. He had a weakness for the dark-brown herbal drink, preferring it to beer or wine.

A few minutes later, feeling refreshed, he got back in the car and drove in the direction the shopkeeper had indicated.

The house was at the better end of the village, one of a group of relatively modern dwellings. They'd probably been built around the turn of the century from the looks of them, and weren't nearly as picturesque as the older cottages. They were probably a lot more convenient to live in, though.

He wondered why Mrs Harbury's cousin had chosen to

live in such an isolated place. Perhaps it was cheaper than somewhere in a town. Or perhaps Captain Ballam enjoyed country pursuits such as hunting and fishing.

When Alex knocked on the door, it was opened by a woman with the most glorious hair he'd ever seen. It was bright red verging on auburn, with golden glints where the afternoon sun touched it, and although it was drawn severely back into a low bun, little curls had escaped along her forehead and at the nape of her neck.

It'd have been a shame to have hair as pretty as that bobbed in one of the new shorter styles. He still wasn't sure about those, but all the ladies he knew who'd taken the step of having their long hair cut off were thrilled with how easy it was to manage.

There were a few threads of silver at this woman's temples, and that only added to her attraction in his eyes. He was too old to find young women attractive. The lady's eyes were green – not a wishy-washy greenish hazel but almost an emerald green, and they were sparkling with life. She looked intelligent and full of suppressed energy, rather like Babs.

'I'm Alex Seaton, Babs's friend.'

'Pleased to meet you. I'm Olivia Harbury.'

'I guessed you must be. Babs asked me to give you a lift back to Swindon and then on to London.'

'Yes, but have I got it wrong? I thought you were coming tomorrow.'

'No, you weren't wrong. However, my circumstances have changed, so I wondered if I could take you to your house in Swindon today, and pick you up from there tomorrow afternoon to go to London.'

Someone called sharply, 'Olivia! Why are you leaving the door open and letting all the warm air out?'

She glanced impatiently back over her shoulder. 'We have a visitor, Donald. A gentleman has come to—'

'Well, find out who he is and what he wants quickly. He'll probably have come to see me.'

She rolled her eyes and murmured, 'My cousin thinks the world revolves round him. To answer your question, I shall be delighted to leave today. Give me a few minutes to finish packing, then I'll bring my final suitcase down and we can be off.'

She gestured to a large suitcase in the hall. 'I packed that one today. We'd better carry it out to the car together. It's full of books that Donald was going to throw away, so it's rather heavy, I'm afraid. I had to slide it down the stairs one step at a time.'

'I have a trolley in my car for moving heavier items. We can use that.'

'Oh, good.'

She was the same height as he was, tall for a woman and healthy-looking, and he liked that. In fact, he liked everything about her.

The voice from the sitting room was louder this time. 'Olivia, what *are* you doing?'

'Coming.' She stood with her eyes closed for a moment as if praying for patience, then whispered, 'I can't get away without introducing you to my cousin, but please don't take any notice of what he says. He doesn't want me to leave, but I'll go mad with frustration if I have to stay here any longer.'

'It's all right. Babs warned me about – um, your situation.'

She grinned at that euphemism and led the way into the

sitting room, introducing him to her cousin then hurrying out without allowing herself to be drawn into a conversation, or possible argument.

Ballam stared at him. 'Please sit down, Mr Seaton. I don't think we've met before. Do you live nearby?'

Alex leant back and studied his host as if he were a customer in the shop before answering. Ballam didn't look intelligent. No sense of humour, either, he'd guess. And he bit his fingernails so badly there wasn't much nail left. He must be a worrier underneath all that bluster. It stood out a mile that he was an autocrat in his small kingdom here, expecting to have his own way in everything. No wonder the man didn't get on with Babs.

'I live in London, Mr Ballam, and my business is there.'

'And that business is . . . ?'

How rude to ask that so bluntly. 'I deal in antiques.'

'Oh, second-hand stuff. I shouldn't think there's much money in that. Look, I'll be frank with you, Mr Seaton. I don't like the idea of my cousin going off with a complete stranger. I think it'd be better if she waited and took the train to London in a few days' time. She's too recently widowed to attend parties anyway.'

'That's her decision, surely?'

'I'm her cousin, the head of the family now. I keep an eye on her and advise her.'

There was the sound of footsteps running lightly down the stairs and Olivia called, 'I've just got a few more bits and pieces to fetch down, Mr Seaton.'

'Olivia, would you please come here?' Ballam bellowed at the top of his voice.

She stuck her head round the door. 'What's wrong now?'

'I'm not happy about you going off with a stranger.'

'Oh, that. We've discussed it already and I haven't changed my mind about leaving. Anyway, if he's a friend of Babs, he's not exactly a stranger. Don't listen to him, Mr Seaton.'

She went out again and Alex could hear her running up the stairs.

'*Olivia! Come back!*'

Ballam had a fine pair of lungs, Alex thought. He obviously hadn't been gassed in the fighting. He must be very difficult to live with.

Olivia was down again in a couple of minutes, acting as if Ballam hadn't just tried to stop her leaving. 'Everything's down now, Mr Seaton. Would you help me carry them out, please? I'm sorry I can't introduce you to my cousin Cecily, but she's not feeling at all well today and is lying down.'

'All the more reason for you to stay a little longer, Olivia,' Ballam said. 'I don't know how you can desert her at a time like this.'

'Ah, but your wife has *you* to look after her, so I know she's in safe hands, and anyway, Pansy will be arriving soon.' She turned and led the way into the hall, so Alex followed her.

'Is Ballam always like this?' he whispered.

'Oh yes. Always. Donald likes to rule the roost and he's a bit hampered with his leg injury, so he's taken to yelling for attention at the top of his voice. Let's take these out, then use your trolley for the big suitcase, shall we?'

She was strong for a woman, her movements sure, and she had beautiful hands. He always looked at people's hands. In fact, she reminded him of a figure in a painting by Dante Gabriel Rossetti, an artist whose work he greatly admired.

Within five minutes they had loaded the car, said goodbye to a furious cousin, and driven off.

As they left the village, Mrs Harbury let out such a huge sigh of relief that Alex chuckled. 'It's all right. We've escaped from the lion's den.'

'You must think me foolish to let Donald upset me like this, but I've been here for over six weeks. I didn't expect him to be home except for an occasional visit or I'd not have agreed to stay for more than a couple of nights. Even Cecily is hard to live with. She's not interested in anything except for her husband and home.'

'Many women are like that.'

'Well, I'm not. Luckily I found a temporary job at the village store, which got me out of the house. But when Donald was injured and sent home to convalesce, Cecily was fluttering around like a trapped butterfly, no use to anyone, poor thing. So I had to stay on long enough to get him settled and find them a maid.'

She stared at the road ahead for a while, then added quietly, 'It took me a few weeks to make up my mind to be ruthless about leaving, because Donald means well, I grant him that, at least. And anyway, I'm a bit lost still without Charles.'

'Your husband?'

'Yes. And he was my best friend, too.'

Charles had been a lucky man, Alex thought.

They chatted intermittently for the rest of the drive into Swindon, not needing to force conversation because the silences were comfortable, too.

'Could you direct me to your house now, please?' he asked as they reached the outskirts of the town.

'Yes, of course. Sorry. I wasn't thinking. It's just outside Old Town. Turn left at the next crossroads.'

The house was a commodious villa. When the car stopped outside, a woman peered out of the bay window, then vanished and opened the door.

'That's one of my lodgers. They're Belgian refugees.' Olivia was out of the car before he could help her. She kissed the air above each of the other woman's cheeks in the continental manner, then launched into speech. '*Bonjour, madame. Tout va bien?*'

'*Très bien, merci. Vous revenez?*'

'*Pour une nuit seulement. Je vais à Londres demain, chez une amie.*'

Her French was quite good, Alex thought. And as Olivia had told him during the drive to Swindon, the Belgian lady looked capable, not at all put out that her hostess had come back unexpectedly.

Having explained about this brief one-night visit and her stay in London, Olivia introduced Alex and they started to unload her possessions from his car.

Two men came out to help with the luggage and were introduced in their turn.

'You have a house full,' Alex commented.

'Yes. The poor things fled when the Germans invaded Belgium and Madame found refuge with an old lady nearby. When the old lady died suddenly, her relatives wished to sell the house and asked Madame to leave. I'd met her at the shops, so I volunteered to take her in and then the others turned up one by one. By that time there was a second wave of Belgians fleeing to Britain and accommodation was very scarce. But since people were needed to work in factories to produce war materials, they were welcomed.'

She paused. 'I'm probably telling you something you already knew. Sorry.'

'I knew vaguely but didn't think about the impact of the refugees, the difficulties of finding them accommodation and so on.'

Her voice sounded sad as she added, 'I found it comforting to do something for the war effort.'

She paused, shaking her head as if to banish unhappy memories. 'After I lost my husband, I felt as if the house needed other people in it. It's far too big for one person and I shall sell it eventually.'

'Yes. I know what you mean. My house is the same.'

'You've lost someone? I'm sorry. Babs didn't say.'

'No, no. It's not that. Sadly, I've never married. I bought a house that was close to my shop, but it's proved to be far too big for one person. Sometimes I feel like a billiard ball, ricocheting around it. Only I didn't want to live in a flat. I like to walk round my garden in the evenings, and in the summer I like to pick a flower in the morning for a buttonhole.'

After another comfortable silence, he said, 'I'll come for you sometime tomorrow afternoon, possibly even late morning, if that's all right, and drive you up to London. I'm sorry I can't be more precise about the time – and if my business takes longer than I expect, we may have to finish our drive after dark.'

'It doesn't matter what time you come. I'll be ready. Babs never goes to bed before midnight, anyway. Oh! Just a minute. What are you doing about a meal tonight? You said your house had been closed up.'

'I'll buy some bread and ham, probably.'

Her eyes were twinkling as she said, 'I can't let you do that after you've been so kind as to rescue me from my cousin. I can't give you the medal you deserve for that but I can offer you a meal. Madame Vermeulen is an excellent cook. Let me just check that she can fit another person in.'

'I don't expect you to—' But he was talking to himself.

She came out almost immediately. 'You are cordially invited to dine here tonight.'

'Are you sure?'

'Yes. Madame loves cooking for people. She misses her family greatly.'

'Are they still in Belgium?'

'Some are. Others are scattered across the country. I think she said one brother and his family are in Glasgow. It seems there are quite a few refugees there. Anyway, come back at half past six and we'll feed you.'

'I shall look forward to it.'

Olivia watched him go, thinking what a neat figure he made, and how well he dressed, stylish but not in any exaggerated way. It was as if his trim body reflected a soul that was also in good order, knowing itself and its place in the world. He had a charming manner and smile.

Oh, how wonderful it was to be free of Donald and his carping ways! She went into the house and looked round with a smile. Everything was immaculate – well, she hadn't expected anything else. She encouraged Madame Vermeulen to tell her the latest local gossip over a cup of tea.

Afterwards she went upstairs to the two rooms she'd kept

for herself, a small bedroom which had once been a child's room, and a larger bedroom, now her sitting room.

She lit the gasolier, looking up at it and thinking that if she stayed, she might consider getting electric lights installed. Babs had them and they were wonderfully convenient, with no need to clean them so often, and the light they threw was much brighter and clearer than anything else.

She unpacked her things, putting them away neatly, then started sorting out clothes suitable for the visit to London. She had a suspicion Babs and her friends would dress up for the New Year's Eve party, so hunted out some pretty garments she hadn't worn since she'd lost Charles, removing their dust covers and holding first one then another against herself.

The last one, a dark-green dress with a lace overlay that looked like a jacket, was so new she had never worn it. To do so now seemed to be signalling to the world that this was the new independent Olivia, coming out of mourning.

The dress was a bit old-fashioned, because skirts were shorter these days and much fuller. Fashions had changed quickly once the war started, becoming more practical than hobble skirts and draped skirts, which were narrower at the ankle. She studied the hem of her dress and nodded. If she got up early she could shorten it, and as the skirt became fuller a few inches above her feet, though not as full as many of today's skirts, that would seem slightly more fashionable.

It was a long time since she'd cared about how she looked socially. She felt pleased to have found such a pretty dress, but it made her sigh, too, and murmur, 'Oh, Charles! I do miss you, my darling.'

She might never have worn mourning for him, but her heart still felt wounded and she was still learning to live without her husband.

Alex felt like an intruder as he let himself into his mother's house. That was ridiculous when he and Mildred owned it now, but there you were, he couldn't help how he felt. It was icy cold inside and since no one else was now living here, he could do what he wanted about where he slept.

He took off his hat, but kept his overcoat and scarf on as he walked round the lower floor, noting with approval the signs of packing and clearing out by the couple he employed. The Townleys were very good at their job and there didn't seem to be much left to do downstairs now.

This couple, in their late fifties, had fallen on hard times financially till he met them when they came into the shop to sell a piece of silver. They knew exactly what it was worth, which was unusual. He'd got chatting and realised he might be able to use their skills.

They were, as always, meticulous about staying in touch, sending him a note each evening to be delivered by first post the following morning. In them they'd explained what they had done that day and before they went home for Christmas, and they'd apologised that the house was taking longer to clear than expected. The old lady had been a hoarder, but among the clutter were quite a few objects of value so they didn't want to rush things.

The rooms looked like a warehouse now, with furniture pushed into groups of like items, boxes neatly labelled and stacked according to their contents. The mantelpieces and windowsills were bare of his mother's motley collection of ornaments and someone had taken the trouble to dust them.

On the first floor, he found a bedroom that was being used by the Townleys, but like the other rooms, it had been stripped of everything except the bare necessities they needed.

The house felt even colder upstairs, and some rooms had not yet been touched. But he didn't fancy sleeping among the dusty clutter. He decided to use the kitchen, where he could light a fire in the big stove to boil a kettle on and keep warm.

If he remembered rightly from his childhood, there was a small room off it where Cook had slept. He went down and yes, he'd remembered correctly. It too had been cleared out, but the bed still had a mattress and seemed quite comfortable, so he decided to sleep there.

After lighting a fire in the kitchen range, he went upstairs to hunt for bedding. It felt eerie, walking through the shadowy spaces. He had to use his electric torch because it was now nearly dark. And while the rooms at the front of the house were partly lit by the street lamps, the ones at the rear were dark, looking out only on to the large garden.

There wasn't even gas lighting upstairs. His mother had preferred oil lamps in the bedrooms, not caring that they gave the servants a lot more work or that other people found them inconvenient and old-fashioned.

Mildred deserved a medal for living here with the old termagant.

'Ah!' He found some blankets, a pillow and a sheet, and took them downstairs, spreading them on an old wooden clothes horse in front of the stove to take the damp chill off. They would be well aired by the time he got back. He would only be here for one night, after all.

As he warmed his hands in front of the stove, he glanced automatically at the kitchen clock. It was still there on the wall, but below it on a side table was a collection of clocks from all over the house. Of course they had all stopped and needed rewinding.

Not one of the clocks in the house was particularly valuable, though he would be able to sell the clock from the sitting room and the grandfather clock from the hall in his antique shop. The others would bring a pound or two each in his second-hand shop.

He didn't want to be late, so took out his pocket watch to check. He was fond of this gold hunter because it was one of the first luxuries he had bought when he started earning decent money. He could afford a much better watch now, but he wouldn't bother to change this one, which kept excellent time and reminded him of how far he'd risen in the world.

He flipped the lid of his watch open with one finger. Yes. He must set off soon.

He was looking forward to spending more time with Olivia. He ought to stop thinking of her as Olivia, had no right to use her first name. But it was a pretty name and she was a strikingly attractive woman. Not pretty exactly. Elegant, lively or charming were better words to describe her.

He laughed at himself for mentally quibbling over such unimportant details and for thinking about her in that way. She was still in mourning for her husband, he could tell.

But he did like her.

Probably, after the festive season was over, he'd not see her again, whatever Babs said about them all becoming good friends. It wasn't as easy as she seemed to think to make good friends, especially when you were rather shy in company.

He wished he had even a tenth of Babs's confidence when dealing with people socially. He wished a lot of things about himself were different, which just showed what a fool he was. You couldn't change the body you'd been born with.

The Belgians lodging in Olivia's house didn't stand on their dignity at meals. They spoke in a mixture of languages: English, French and Flemish. They gesticulated wildly and interrupted one another as they talked about their day, and no one seemed to notice that Alex was rather shy.

The Belgians' main aim tonight seemed to be to bring their hostess up to date with what had been happening in Swindon during her absence.

One of the four men had independent means and didn't need to seek paid work. Two others worked in the Great Western Railway workshops, helping to turn out carriages for the military. One of them had found a weekend job as well, tutoring a lad of twelve who was often ill and had missed a lot of schooling. He had grown fond of the child that reminded him of a nephew who had gone on to America after the family fled from Belgium. One day he'd join them, perhaps, but not with empty pockets.

They all paid Madame Vermeulen a weekly sum for acting as housekeeper and for their food. She managed her own expenses out of that, but wanted to set up a lodging house after the war was over. And she very much wanted to stay in England, if that was allowed.

'I would like the sea to remain between myself and the Germans for ever,' she said. 'It feels so much safer here. You English are lucky to live on an island.'

She was delighted when Alex enjoyed his meal and

complimented her on her cooking. Nothing she'd served was expensive; everything was exquisitely cooked.

The other man, who had come over to Britain early in the war, wasn't strong enough to work in a factory. He had intermittent work in a bookshop and was finding it hard to manage on his earnings.

During a lull in the conversation, he asked Alex quietly whether he bought antique jewellery.

'Yes, I do.'

'Perhaps I show you some pieces later and you give me an idea of their price?'

'My pleasure.'

'*Merci bien.*'

But Alex could see the sadness on the man's face and guessed he didn't really want to sell the items, which were probably all he had left after fleeing from Belgium. He'd seen this dilemma before, particularly agonising when the only thing left to sell was a woman's wedding ring.

Because he didn't enjoy taking away an object a seller loved, he'd evolved a way of dealing with it that satisfied his conscience and he would offer the same choice tonight.

As everyone left the table to go into the sitting room, Claude tugged at his arm. 'M'sieur? It will not take long, I think. I do not have much to show.'

He hated to see that anxiety and embarrassment on his companion's face. 'I'm happy to do it now.'

'*Un moment, s'il vous plaît.*' He ran up the stairs.

Olivia came to the door of the sitting room. 'Ah. I wondered where you were, Mr Seaton.'

He explained quickly what he was doing.

She nodded. 'That's kind of you. Join us for a while

when you've finished speaking to Claude.'

The man returned carrying a leather drawstring pouch. He waited till she'd left to tip several pieces of jewellery out of it, each wrapped in a small piece of silk. Moving the last pieces of crockery aside, he set out the pieces in a row, only five of them.

Alex studied the jewellery carefully. They were fairly ordinary pieces, but one was of much better quality than the others. It was easy enough to name a price for each. He offered fair prices, which he knew would be slightly higher than other dealers might pay. This was not to get the custom at all costs, but because he had been short of money in his younger days. He knew only too well how hard it could be to manage, so was content with a small profit from such people.

The man looked puzzled. 'I show them to another gentleman and he tell me much less.'

Alex bit his lip, trying to formulate a tactful version of the truth. 'I am perhaps more generous than he can afford to be, because I am not short of money. What is more, if you wish me to, I'll keep any piece you sell to me until one year after the war ends. If you can raise enough money by then, I'll sell it back to you at the same price.'

The man stared at him, his face twisted as he tried in vain to stem his tears. Alex got up. 'You may need a few moments to consider it.' He pretended to examine the contents of a small bookcase near the window to give Claude some semblance of privacy.

When the muffled sobs had stopped, Alex risked a quick glance round.

'I am sorry to be so . . . weak,' his companion said. 'But you give me hope. These are all I have left from my family.'

'I'm glad to give you hope.'

'Can I sell you this and keep the others?' He held out the most expensive piece.

'Yes, of course.' Alex took out his wallet and counted out the money on the spot, then found one of his business cards and put it on top of the small pile of five-pound notes. 'You can find me at this address if fortune favours you.'

The man took Alex's hand in both his and said in his heavily accented English, 'I shall pray for you, m'sieur. You have a deep sadness in you. I can see these things. But you are a kind man and I think fate will deal more generously with you from now on.'

Then he put the money carefully in his wallet, wrapped the other pieces and slipped them back into the leather pouch, and left the room.

Alex stood for a moment, surprised at what the man had said. He didn't believe in foretelling the future, but Claude had been right about his feelings. He did feel sad sometimes, mostly to be so alone. He'd have loved to marry and have children.

Fate hadn't dealt generously with him in this respect and why that should change now, as Claude had said, he couldn't imagine. It was, he had found, better not to hope for too much for himself.

He heard a sound and turned to see Olivia standing in the doorway.

'I have to confess that I eavesdropped,' she said. 'I was worried about poor Claude. People have tried to cheat him before with low prices. But I needn't have worried. You were very generous in your payment.'

He could feel a betraying heat in his cheeks. 'We should all help one another when we can. And I would still make a small profit if I sold that brooch. They're very fine diamonds and the workmanship is exquisite.'

She too came and clasped his hands. 'Thank you for being so kind to my friend.'

Alex could feel the softness and warmth of her hands on his even after she let go. 'If you don't mind, I shall take my leave of Madame and your other lodgers now and go home. It'll be a busy day for me tomorrow. I'll come for you as soon as I can.'

He walked home through the dark streets, feeling happier than he had for a good while. Perhaps Babs was right. Perhaps she, Olivia and he would all become friends. Such a friendship would definitely brighten his life.

But Olivia was a lovely woman, and if fate had made him a better specimen of manhood, he'd try to be more than friends.

He'd never met a woman who attracted him as much as she did.

After an excellent night's sleep, Alex nipped out to the local bakery and bought himself a buttered roll, still warm from the oven. He took it home and ate it with a cup of tea without milk.

He waited until ten o'clock, pacing round the house, staring out at his car, impatient to get this puzzling matter over and done with.

At half past ten he muttered, 'Hang it! I can't bear to wait any longer.' He carried his single piece of luggage out to his car, glad to be leaving the dark and oppressive house.

It seemed to take longer than usual for the engine of the car to catch as he cranked it and he was beginning to worry that something had gone wrong. It would spoil everything if he had to find a mechanic, or worse still if his car needed repairs. He was looking forward to seeing Mrs Harbury again.

Suddenly the motor started up. 'Well, thank goodness for that!' he muttered, adding, 'And I've got to stop talking to myself.'

He drove to Edwin and Mildred's house, telling himself it was far too early for them to have returned, and he'd probably have to find a tea shop to wait in. But that would be better than the chilly, echoing rooms. To his huge relief, however, the curtains at Mildred's were drawn back, so they must have returned.

He knocked on the door, eager to get this over and done with so that he could pick up Olivia and enjoy her company during the drive to London. Perhaps if he could get away before noon, they could stop to enjoy a luncheon together on the way. He'd enjoy chatting to her again.

Mildred opened the door herself, greeting him with: 'Goodness, you must have set off from London at the crack of dawn to get here so soon. We've only just got back ourselves. We spent Christmas with Edwin's cousins in the country.'

He couldn't lie to her and confessed that he'd come to Swindon the day before on a whim.

She linked her arm in his and took him into a small sitting room at the rear of the house. 'You should have rung and told us. We could have taken you with us to the country, if I'd thought. Where did you stay?'

'In Mother's house. What a gloomy place it is! How did you bear it for three years? It feels far worse than when I used to live there.'

'I stood it because it was my duty. But I will admit that after your father died, your mother became even grumpier and after she fell ill – and she really was ill, Alex – she grew positively cantankerous. It was as if her misery had embedded itself in the very walls. Sometimes I just had to get out of the house, however much she scolded me when I got back for deserting her.'

'She was an expert at scolding!' he said with feeling.

'Yes, but fortunately I had my own money from my mother, and I wasn't dependent on her charity. She had nothing to threaten me with and didn't dare go too far in what she said, in case I left.'

'Where did you go for relief from the misery?'

'Anywhere I could be with normal people, like the library or shops. I met friends in a tea shop every Tuesday and Friday afternoon, too. In summer, if it was fine, I'd go to the nearest park. I love to watch children playing. They're so free and joyful.'

She smiled. 'I'm so much happier with my Edwin, I can't tell you how much! But what a shame you didn't know we were away. I hate to think of you on your own.'

'It doesn't matter. I'd have been on my own at home as well.'

Tears welled in her eyes and she leant across to take hold of his hand. 'My dear Alex, I do worry about you. I pray you too will meet someone to love.' She touched his lips lightly with one fingertip to stop him speaking. 'You've given up hope of it, I know, as I had when I met my dearest Edwin. But I shall keep reminding you that miracles do occur. I'm the living proof that older people can find a person to love.'

'I'm not much of a prize, Mildred.'

'You're belittling yourself again. Stop it. I've been hoping that our mutual friend Babs would introduce you to someone suitable.'

He was moved by her concern. 'Well, as it turns out, she did. I had dinner with a friend of hers yesterday evening in Swindon, and with the lady's lodgers as well. She's a widow called Olivia Harbury.'

Mildred's face brightened. 'That's wonderful. How did that come about?'

'I'd agreed to drive Mrs Harbury to London today, so I picked her up in the village where she was staying with an obnoxious fellow, who's her cousin, and I left her at her own house for the night. In return she invited me to dine there.'

'I won't tease you, but am I right in thinking that you like her?'

'I do. But she's still grieving for her husband. Anyway, it's early days yet. She's a very new acquaintance. Now, let's change the subject. I must say, it makes me happy to see that you're starting to enjoy a more normal social life, Mildred.'

'It was the best Christmas I've ever had. We were determined to ignore the war for once, so we played charades and told riddles. When we tired of that, we talked of the theatre and books we'd read, *not* about who'd been killed or how the latest offensive was going. Edwin's cousins are delightful people.'

There was the sound of a door opening and closing. She cocked her head on one side and glanced at the clock on the mantelpiece. 'That's probably Edwin coming back. He nipped into the office to get some documents from his safe. We didn't like to leave them lying around here while we were away.'

She opened her mouth as if to say something, half-closed it and (Alex was quite sure) substituted the more mundane question, 'Did you have any breakfast?'

'Yes, Mama Mildred,' he mocked. 'Even a mere man can recognise a bakery when he needs food.'

'Of course you can. So we'll have our normal morning tea and then . . .'

'Then you'll tell me what all this fuss is about.'

Her smile vanished. 'Yes. Something must be done about it, that's for sure.'

The way she was acting was making him feel anxious. It wasn't like Mildred to keep something from him.

Chapter Eight

Phoebe didn't tell her husband her special news on the evening of his return. She could see he was exhausted and deeply worried about his father. She didn't want this joyful news linked to such sadness.

And then on Boxing Day, just as she was about to tell him, they had visitors from the village, and later some of the internees they knew, like the Steins, came to wish them well. So there never seemed to be a suitable time.

In the evening the internees put on a concert, and though the elderly voices might have sounded rather thin at times, the musicians playing instruments put on virtuoso performances. The two best pianists provided 'Fûr Elise' by Beethoven and 'The Moonlight Sonata' by Chopin. A violinist played 'Love's Old Sweet Song' very sweetly.

After that they had a sing-song, with old favourites such as 'My Grandfather's Clock' and 'The Last Rose of Summer', which all the foreigners seemed to know, since a lot of them were musical.

But someone started them on 'Home! Sweet Home!' and that reduced several people to tears, so they went on to some of the war favourites like the recently written and very popular 'Pack Up Your Troubles in Your Old Kit-Bag', which cheered them up again.

Phoebe decided the news couldn't wait any longer and planned to tell Corin when they went to bed. At least no one could disturb them there. But he was delayed by Captain Turner asking him if he could spare a moment, and she fell asleep before he joined her.

When she woke, Corin was beside her, smiling, and she decided she wasn't letting him leave the bedroom till he knew he was going to become a father. She rang for Ethel to bring them a tea tray.

'We'll have breakfast half an hour later than usual,' she told the maid and could see Ethel smile fondly at them both, as if she understood what was going on.

Corin lay back against the pillows, his eyes gleaming. 'Any particular reason for that instruction?'

'My reason isn't what you're hoping for – at least, not yet.'

He tried to pull her to him for a kiss, but she held him off. 'Not yet, darling. I have something very important to tell you first.' She took a deep breath. 'I— I mean, *we* are expecting a baby.'

He stared for a moment open-mouthed, then beamed and pulled her closer. 'Why didn't you tell me as soon as I got back?'

'You were so sad, and then there didn't seem to be a quiet moment. I wanted us to have time to rejoice together about our coming child. I meant to tell you last night, but I fell asleep. I seem to need more sleep these days.'

'You haven't been sick in the mornings. I thought women were sick a lot.'

'Some are, some aren't. I must be one of the lucky ones.'

She snuggled against him as his arm went round her, resting her head in the crook of his shoulder. If only they could be together like this every morning! They'd got married during a war that seemed to have been going on forever so they'd never had a normal life.

'Have you seen the doctor about your condition?'

'No. It's early days and I've spoken to Mrs Archer in the village. She was a trained nurse before she married Peter Archer. She's a very experienced registered midwife, with a certificate from the Royal College of Physicians of Ireland, no less. I've spoken to her and I liked her manner. Indeed, she's well thought of by everyone in the district, including Miss Bowers.'

'That's good but I want you to have a doctor's care as well. You're far too important to me to take any risks.'

'Oh, pish! What risks? I'm feeling fine. Having children isn't an illness. It's a perfectly natural thing.'

'We must tell the maids, so that they don't let you lift anything heavy.'

She chuckled. 'They've not said anything but it's clear they've guessed. We live too closely together for them not to notice certain signs.'

'Nonetheless, I shall ask them to take particular care of you. Oh, my darling, isn't it wonderful?'

They lay closely entwined in blissful silence, then he stirred. 'Do you know when it's due?'

'Early June. We'll have plenty of time to think about names and discuss them on your next leave.'

'If it's a boy, my family usually alternates Corin and Angus for the firstborn sons.'

She wrinkled her nose, not pleased by this suggestion.

'You're the only Corin I want, and I'm not fond of Angus for a name, though I suppose we could use it as a second name if you feel strongly about it. I like the name Robert, actually.'

'Hmm. Not bad. We'll see. What about girls' names?'

'I can't seem to think of those. Perhaps that means it's going to be a boy. I'm certainly hoping so. If I give you a son, your home can stay in the family, because a male can't inherit Greyladies. It isn't even certain a daughter would, because something mysterious always leads to the next chatelaine, and the only thing certain is that she will be a Latimer.

When Phoebe had first come to the house, she'd not known anything about the legend of the grey ladies, or the wonderful trust fund that provided money to help less fortunate women.

After a few more quiet moments, he nuzzled her neck. 'Are you still able to pleasure your poor deprived husband? I won't press you, if you don't feel like it.'

'Always ready for you.' She lifted her face for his kiss.

They were even later going down to breakfast than she'd intended and she blushed as she met Ethel's knowing gaze.

After they'd eaten, Corin went down to the village on his own, claiming he needed a brisk walk but in reality intending to speak sharply to this Hatterson fellow, and also to size him up.

A little dab of a woman opened the door to him and said her husband was away, then tried to close the door as he was saying something.

Corin put out one hand to stop her. 'Wait a moment, please. Where is Mr Hatterson? I need to see him urgently.'

She shook her head. 'Sidney wouldn't like me discussing

his business with anyone else, and anyway, I don't know where he is.'

'Well, when is he coming back?'

'He wasn't certain.'

'Does he often go away like this?'

She hesitated, then said, 'Please understand . . . since Sidney's lost his leg he's changed. He's always angry, even though we inherited his old uncle's house and aren't short of money. You can't really blame him for being upset about the leg, though. He was a very active man. If he's upset you, I'm sorry.'

In spite of himself he felt for her. 'It must be hard for you, as well.'

She shrugged. 'I'm not the only woman whose husband has been changed by the war.'

'Well, it's important that I see him in person, so I'll call again tomorrow.'

She gave a small nod of farewell and closed the door quietly.

He heard the bolt slide and wondered why she felt the need to lock up.

He didn't take her word about her husband's absence, but called on Miss Bowers, who confirmed that Mr Hatterson had gone away in a motor car with another two men in the early hours of the morning, waking her and the other neighbours up.

'The men were strangers, not people from hereabouts and the car wasn't one I'd ever seen before.'

He knocked at the house across the road, but the woman there couldn't tell one car from another. 'All I know is I don't want to see it again. Woke the baby, it did, and it was two hours before I could get him to sleep again.'

Old Mr Diggan was passing in the street and, as he lived next to the Hattersons, Corin asked him if he knew anything.

'Well, I know they woke me. I looked out of the window to see what was going on, but he was just getting into a car. I think the same men have called for him before. They may be friends of his, if he has any friends. What did his wife say?'

'Not much.'

'Never does. *He* does enough talking for them both. I hear his voice sometimes if the window's open. On and on he goes, talking *at* her, not chatting, if you know what I mean. And he thumps her. She tries to hide it, but I've heard her scream, heard the furniture knocked over and seen the bruises. I never thought I'd have a neighbour like that in Challerton! No, I did not.'

'Well, thank you for your help.' Corin walked slowly back to the big house, wondering now whether Hatterson had left Challerton to avoid him. Surely not? The man wouldn't have known he was expected back. What was going on here, then? Why leave in the middle of the night?

Whatever it was, he hoped Hatterson wouldn't continue to rant on about Huns. People could turn very nasty about the presence of Germans, and had already in some parts of England, smashing businesses and looting them, injuring the poor foreigners, who had nothing to do with the war.

And why these people would attack his wife and the rear house, which didn't contain any Germans, was beyond his understanding. All he knew was that he felt helpless to protect his wife. Unfortunately, the army and the war waited for no man, so he would have to leave in two days' time.

Perhaps Captain Turner would be able to use the attack

as an excuse for getting more men posted to Greyladies?

He answered that thought himself as soon as it popped into his mind. *That wasn't likely.*

General Sir Douglas Haig had taken over command of the British Expeditionary Force in Europe, and rumour among the officers was that he believed in all-out offensives. That would take more men away from Britain. And it'd kill more men in that hell across the Channel. Corin didn't think most of the civilian population understood how bad things were in the trenches, at least he hoped they didn't.

He didn't intend to leave Challerton without doing *something* to protect his wife and home. He had made it his business to get to know people in the neighbourhood earlier in the war, while he was commandant at Greyladies. He intended to ask for help and advice from one or two older men who were considered leaders in the local community.

And perhaps Miss Bowers might be able to think of something. The former headmistress of the village school was in her late seventies now, but still spry with a sharp brain. Her love for Greyladies was matched only by her love for the village and the people she'd taught in its school over the years.

He wondered sometimes about Greyladies. Sometimes chatelaines like Phoebe stayed only for a few years, as Harriet, the previous lady, had done; sometimes they stayed there for the rest of their lives.

He couldn't help wondering into which category his Phoebe would fit, and whether he would ever live in his own home in the north again. He had more or less given up his own family inheritance when he married her, and if – *when* his father died, he would put in a manager and find a smaller house for his mother to live in. He'd already discussed that with her. He wasn't selling his home.

He'd even changed his name to Latimer to marry Phoebe, and hoped he'd hidden how much that had upset him.

He hadn't expected to love someone so deeply after his first wife and unborn baby had been killed because of her reckless driving. But then he'd met Phoebe, who wasn't reckless and who was . . . simply the most wonderful woman in the world.

She would be careful now she was carrying his child, he knew, but she was also very protective about the house and that might inadvertently lead her into danger. He'd lost one wife and child, couldn't bear even the thought of losing Phoebe.

Dammit! Why did this have to happen while he couldn't help being away for most of the time? He wanted to be here protecting the woman he loved.

And yet his country needed his services desperately too. The battle to defeat Germany was going to be hard fought.

Edwin came into the hall bringing a swirl of cold air from outside. He hung up his outer clothes then joined Mildred and Alex in the sitting room. Putting his briefcase down on the table, he looked solemnly at his wife. 'I have a client coming to see me in an hour's time, so let's get started straight away.'

She nodded and turned to Alex. 'This is to do with your older brother.'

He was puzzled. 'Ernest died in 1905. How is he connected with anything that happens now?'

'We've found out he was secretly married and had two children.'

Alex couldn't speak for a few seconds, he was so shocked. '*Ernest had children?*'

'Yes.'

'Did my mother know?'

'We're not sure, but your father definitely knew. We found the relevant information among his papers. As to your mother knowing . . . well, the documents didn't seem to have been touched for a long time, they were so dusty.'

'Father wouldn't have told her,' Alex said. 'He was a firm believer in shielding ladies from unpleasant facts. And my mother wouldn't even have looked at business papers.' He frowned. 'When did Ernest marry? He died so suddenly. How did he have time to produce two children?'

'They were only nine months apart, a boy and a girl, and he'd been married for years.'

Alex let out a low whistle. 'Did he make provision for them?'

'No. Not at all.'

'Typical of him. Do we know where they are now?'

'We think they're still alive but we don't even know their names. Your father didn't have a copy of the marriage or birth certificates among his papers.'

'He was planning to keep the children's existence secret, then. You know what he was like, Mildred.'

'Yes. Edwin didn't believe me when I told him about my uncle's slyness.'

Her husband patted her hand. 'I'm beginning to,' he said grimly. 'The last address we have was in Swindon, but I sent my clerk to check the house and Ernest's widow and children were no longer living there. Actually, though your father didn't make regular provision for them, he didn't completely ignore them either. He occasionally responded to requests for specific help with things like clothing or schooling.'

'He'd have made the mother beg for it,' Alex commented and Mildred nodded agreement.

Edwin tapped the papers with one finger. 'Reading between the lines, Ernest's widow must have been a capable woman, and hard-working, because you know how difficult it is for single or widowed women to earn a decent living wage. Though Mrs Seaton may have found it easier since the war because women working in men's jobs are getting similar pay to the men, if not quite as much.'

They all fell silent, then Alex said, 'I wonder what his wife's first name is. I have trouble thinking of her as "Mrs Seaton" because that brings my mother to mind.'

'I've applied for a copy of the marriage certificate,' Edwin told them. 'That should tell us. And the birth certificates, of course. We do know the father's full name, at least, so it should be relatively easy to find. We might even have the copies by tomorrow. We'll know all their names then.'

'Good. And Mildred . . . I think the children have a right to inherit something from the estate,' Alex said. 'Don't you?'

She looked triumphantly at Edwin. 'I told you he'd say that. Yes, of course I do, Alex.'

Edwin cleared his throat to get their attention. 'If they wanted, the children or their guardian could make a legal fuss and try to claim a sizeable share of your mother's estate. I wouldn't object to Mildred giving up part of her inheritance to them – the money wouldn't matter at all to me – but a scandal could affect me adversely and I'd object to anything that caused one. I'm about to open my own practice, you see.'

'Then we'll give them a decent share before they even ask,' Alex said at once. 'An amount they can't quibble about.'

'First we have to find them.'

'It shouldn't be too hard. Someone will know where they've moved to. May I read the relevant papers?' Alex took the various documents from Edwin and started to go through them. There weren't many.

The other two chatted quietly till he'd finished.

'Any questions?' Edwin asked.

'Only how best to set about it. My father's notes show that he'd checked out the marriage and births, and was satisfied that they were Ernest's children. Why didn't he do more to help them? They should have been brought up as members of our family.'

Then he let out a scornful laugh. 'No. He wouldn't have wanted it known that my brother had married beneath him. He believed in people marrying their own sort, in breeding their children as you would horses, from good sires and dams. He once said a runt like me should never have children.'

Edwin stared at him in shock. 'He didn't! Oh, that's despicable.'

Alex shrugged.

'It looks as though he did nothing whatsoever to get to know the children, even after you left home.'

'After I was thrown out,' Alex corrected. 'Well, why should he? Father was stubborn to the core, wouldn't expect to die for many years, probably had a plan to get me back after the war and make me toe the family line. I don't think he realised how successful I'd become financially. There was nothing he could threaten me with that would have made me go back to working with him.'

There was another of those silences before Edwin spoke. 'Are we agreed, then? I shall employ someone to find where the children are as soon as we have their full names.' As the others both nodded, he frowned and added, 'The trouble is, the man I used previously for such delicate investigations is fighting in France. I'll have to find someone else.'

'Shall I take that upon myself?' Alex asked. 'I'm used to investigating paintings or other *objets d'art* and I have some good connections.'

'Thank you. That would be very helpful. It's always best to use people you trust in such cases.' He began to gather the papers together. 'I'll lock these away again. There's no other useful information in them about the children, not even their or their mother's names.'

Mildred looked at her cousin. 'Well, now that's over, do you want to stay for luncheon? We could eat early.'

'No, thank you. I need to get back to London and I have to pick up Mrs Harbury first.'

'I'll get my clerk to send copies of what papers there are to you in London,' Edwin said. 'And now I really must go.'

'So must I.' Alex looked at his watch, pleased that it was only quarter past eleven. So much had happened that it ought to be later, he felt.

He was still trying to take it all in. From being a man with no close family except Mildred, he had now become an uncle. And he might find himself becoming some sort of guardian to the two children if their family was in difficult circumstances. He wouldn't mind that.

How old would they be now? Going on for twelve, he'd guess. He hoped their mother was looking after them properly . . . and loving them. All children deserved love.

He hoped they were getting a decent schooling, too. In this modern world, education was far more important than at the end of the last century.

He walked out to his car, wondering whether this was fate being kind to him by giving him a family. Or was it being unkind by giving him more problems to sort out?

Who could tell? It was no use starting anything today, though. He had promised to take Olivia to London and once there, to attend Babs's party. He was looking forward to it for he wanted very much to spend more time with Olivia.

But would she want to spend more time with him after today's journey? Would she too see him as a runt, who wasn't fit to serve his country?

When the telephone rang, Corin hesitated to pick it up, dreading a summons to return to duty at once.

But he couldn't refuse to answer the phone or a summons. He unhooked the earpiece with one hand and leant forward to speak crisply into the mouthpiece, holding it steady with the other. 'Latimer here.'

'Good morning, Major. I hope you found your wife well,' his commanding officer said.

'Good morning, General. Yes, my wife is very well.'

With one hand Corin gestured to his wife to move away and give him some privacy.

She nodded and blew him a kiss, vanishing in the direction of the kitchen.

'And your father?'

'Not well, sir. The doctors don't give him long to live, a few months perhaps.'

'I'm sorry for that. Particularly sorry that I'll have to take you out of circulation for a while at such a crucial time. We have a special project to plan and need your excellent attention to detail. I'm afraid you'll not be getting much leave while you're working on it.'

'Oh dear.'

'Something wrong?'

'There's a man causing trouble in the village because of the German internees. He's been threatening my wife and has brought others in. They've already damaged the house, broken windows . . . and they're threatening to do more.'

'Don't you have soldiers based there?'

'Yes. But they're . . . not the lively sort and there are only four of them. It's a big house, and frankly, I'm worried about the safety not only of my wife, but of the internees.'

There was a moment of silence. 'I'll make a note of the problems at Greyladies and get my adjutant to see what we can do to help. Now, let me tell you about this project . . .'

Corin knew that half-promise of help was the best he could expect from such a busy man. He listened intently, holding back a sigh. The project sounded interesting, but what a time to be pulled out of circulation!

When he put the phone down, he stood for a few moments getting his thoughts in order, then went to find his wife.

She took one look at his face and said, 'I can see from your face that it isn't good news.'

'No. I don't have to go back early at least, but when I do, I'm being seconded to a special project which is at the planning stage. I shan't be able to get away much while working there, I'm afraid. I shall worry about your safety.'

'I'll be all right. I'm not alone here, after all.'

'I've still got time to do something about it. I don't know

what yet, but I shall find a way. Well, for a start, I'm going to make sure you have a gun loaded and ready, so that you can defend yourself. And you must promise to keep it handy. I know you don't like guns, but sometimes, with some enemies, using one is the only way to stay alive.'

'Very well, darling.' She laid one hand on her belly. 'There is more than my safety to think about now. I won't allow anything to happen to my unborn child.'

Chapter Nine

By the time Alex turned up in his motor car, Olivia had altered the hem of one of her day dresses and was wearing it. Not her neatest sewing, but who would know? She'd started on the evening gown, simply to avoid wasting time, but that wasn't as important because she wouldn't need it till New Year's Eve.

She felt she looked more like a modern woman now, and knew that was foolish and vain, but didn't try to work out why it mattered so much.

After she opened the door to him, she couldn't think what to say and stood staring like a fool. He stared back at her, not rushing into speech. His smile was warm and he didn't seem impatient to move into the house.

'Bring him in,' Madame said from behind her. 'You can stare at one another just as easily inside the house and we can all stay warm as you do it.'

Olivia felt herself flushing and saw his face grow rosier too. They both launched into speech at the same time.

'How are you?'

'Are you ready to leave?'

'Have you—?'

Both stopped again and Madame looked from one to the other, shaking her head. 'Come into the sitting room, m'sieur. Do you want something to eat before you leave? Or I can make sandwiches to take with you.'

Alex glanced from her to Olivia. 'I know a pub about an hour's drive away. We can get a decent luncheon there and warm up a little. I've got a nice thick travel blanket, so you shouldn't get too cold in the car. If you don't mind eating in a public house, that is.'

'I don't mind at all. Charles and I used to drive into the country sometimes and stop at pubs for luncheon. It can be very pleasant.' Olivia pulled her scattered wits together. 'I'll get my things. I've got two suitcases, but this time they don't weigh a ton.'

'I'll help you with them.'

'Thank you.'

When they set off, Olivia leant her head back against the car seat and sighed. 'So. You managed to sort out your problem quickly?' She saw his expression change. 'You look as though it was rather serious.'

'Yes. Very serious, in fact.' He hesitated.

'I won't pester you, but if you want to talk about it, I'm a very good listener and I can keep a confidence.'

There was such a long silence she thought she'd overstepped some invisible mark in their budding friendship. 'I would value your opinion, actually,' he then said.

He told her what they'd discovered from his father's papers.

'You had no idea your brother had got married?'

'None whatsoever. I can understand why he would keep it secret, though. Our father would have hated such a marriage and might even have tried to get it declared void.'

'Even if your brother and this woman loved one another?'

'Father believed in selecting a spouse primarily for business reasons. I don't think he believed in romantic love at all. His only love was money. He'd have been furious if he'd known how foolish my mother would be with his hard-earned wealth after she inherited it.'

Alex sighed. 'He predicted that I'd be back in Swindon begging his help before a year was up. He'd be very upset to think I succeeded in doing something other than carting. Or "delivering goods", as he preferred to call it in the last few years, because he thought it sounded more modern and genteel.'

Olivia could hear the bitterness and pain in Alex's voice. 'You'd think he'd have been proud of your achievements. You and your brother can't have had a happy family life, from the sounds of it.'

'No. It was a very unhappy household. If Mildred's mother hadn't visited her in-laws regularly I'd have no happy memories. She was as kind to me as was allowed, taking me out to tea or inviting me round to play with Mildred occasionally.'

'Not your brother?'

'He was older, already out at work in my father's business.'

She waited but Alex did not continue. 'What are you going to do about these children, then?' she prompted.

'I intend to find them and make sure they want for nothing from now on. I'll see that they receive a share of the inheritance and remedy any lack of education, if it's not too late to do that. I don't even know how old they are. But those things are only fair, don't you think?'

'Yes I do. But not many men would voluntarily give up their money.'

'I've earned enough by my own efforts to be comfortable. I don't need the inheritance nor do I wish to grab every halfpenny I can.'

'You're a very kind man, Alex Seaton. You were kind to Claude last night, too.'

She watched him flush and guessed he wasn't used to compliments. She felt so comfortable with him, she hoped they would stay friends from now on. Charles would have liked him too, she was sure.

She found Alex's shyness rather touching. She had no experience of a shy man. Charles had been a big man, confident and sunny-natured. He'd been so sure he'd survive the war.

Alex was very different, about the same height as she was, thin but dressed with quiet elegance.

She was sure Alex's father had gone straight to hell for treating both his sons so badly! She must enlist Babs's help in making Alex realise his own worth.

They stopped for an excellent luncheon, chatting like old friends about the changes the war had brought. It was late afternoon when they arrived in London, just starting to go dark.

Babs's house was a four-storey building in an elegant Georgian terrace.

'What a lovely street!' Olivia exclaimed.

'I always think so too. My house is rather different, a detached villa with a walled garden. Perhaps you and Babs could come to tea with me the day after the party, if you're not too tired?'

'I'd love to do that. I'll have to check with Babs first, of course.'

'I hope she'll be free. It'd be better if you came to tea at the shop, because I'd like to show it to you. I have a small room upstairs where I entertain clients.'

'I'd love to see your shop.'

'And . . . I know you're staying a few days, but I'd be happy to drive you home again. I shall have to return to Swindon anyway.'

She looked at him and was going to refuse, because she didn't want to take advantage of his kindness. She had steadfastly refused invitations from other men in the past few months and though she liked Alex, she didn't want to give him false hopes about his relationship with her.

But then she noticed that he was looking nervous and she guessed how much courage it had taken for him to ask her.

'I'd like that,' she said and saw him sag in relief.

By this time the front door was open. Babs hadn't waited for them to knock and was standing beckoning to them impatiently.

Olivia let Alex open the car door for her and tried to walk sedately into the house.

But Babs spoilt this polite behaviour by giving her a big hug and then hugging Alex for good measure. He looked a bit startled by this and patted her back awkwardly.

'Come in, come in! It's all in terrible chaos because they've started getting ready for the party on New Year's Eve – you are coming, aren't you, Alex?'

'Yes, of course I am. I've been looking forward to it. You always throw such splendid parties.'

'Good. We'll have so much fun and we'll dance in the

new year.' She flapped one hand at a hallstand. 'Take off your coat and hat, Olivia. Alex, would you like a cup of tea before you leave?'

'No, I can see you two want to be alone to chat, and I have a business to run. I'll look forward to seeing you at the party.'

'Eight o'clock sharp,' Babs said. 'We're having cocktails. I've got some delicious recipes from an American friend.'

He gave a wry smile. 'I'm not very good with alcohol, as you know. I don't think I'd dare drink a cocktail.'

'Ah, but I have recipes for one or two without alcohol in them. I did remember that about you, Alex, and I have another friend who can't drink. Anyway, who can go on drinking all evening and still stand upright?'

After he'd taken his leave, Olivia said, 'I don't know much about cocktails and I don't have a good head for wine, so I think I'll drink the ones without alcohol as well. Charles liked a glass of beer, or a whisky, and laughed at me for preferring ginger beer.'

'Well, at my party we're all going to pretend the war doesn't exist and we're going to have fun. Dancing and laughter are obligatory, cocktails are optional.'

'That's good.'

'I've got such plans for you and me, and—'

Olivia interrupted. 'Alex has invited us to take tea with him on the first of January at his shop. I said we'd go if you were free. Is that all right? I'd rather you came too, because I don't want to give him ideas about . . . about . . .' She broke off, flushing.

'He's rather taken with you,' Babs said softly.

'Do I sound conceited if I say yes, I suppose he is? Only

it's too soon. Charles has only been dead for a few months and I still feel married to him.'

Babs patted her hand. 'But you might like Alex later?'

'I don't know him well. I . . . might like to get to know him better, though.'

'Then I'll come with you and play chaperone. You won't know it, but very few people are invited to take tea at Alexander Seaton's beautiful shop and they boast about the visit. It's the most elegantly furnished place you ever saw.'

'Oh, well, good. I'll phone him to say we'd love to go to tea. Most people think he's stand-offish, but in fact he's rather shy.'

'Very shy. I've known him a while and noticed that, but he's all right with me now.' She let out a gurgle of laughter. 'Unless I say something outrageous, of course, then he doesn't know what to say or do.'

'You love teasing people.'

'They don't mind. I'm never nasty. So . . . what are you going to wear for the party, Olivia? If you have nothing suitable, we can go shopping in the morning.'

'I have a suitable evening frock that I haven't worn yet and it's not too old-fashioned, or it won't be once I've altered the hem.'

'You must show it to me. Let's go and unpack your things now. I want to talk to you about the Women's Institute and I'll get interrupted if we stay within sight of my housekeeper and people moving furniture about.'

She led the way up the stairs, moving with the bouncing energy of a young woman.

Olivia followed more slowly, feeling welcome, feeling as if Babs was an old and dear friend.

Why had she stayed at Donald's house for so long? She should have pulled herself together sooner.

Only it took time to recover from losing a beloved husband. She smiled as it occurred to her that it was Donald's irritating ways which had pulled her out of the 'slough of despond' and jolted her forward into a new life.

Where this path would lead, she didn't know. It had to be somewhere different. You couldn't recreate a life that had gone for ever and you shouldn't even try.

She wondered how many people understood that. She'd seen some women virtually stop living after they were widowed. Charles wouldn't want her to be like that. He'd say, 'Go out and have fun, old girl, and think of me fondly sometimes.'

She blinked her eyes furiously. She could almost hear him saying it.

Babs was waiting for her patiently at the top of the stairs. 'You were lost in thought.'

'Sorry. I just . . . remembered something.' She followed her hostess through a doorway. 'Oh, what a lovely room!'

The bedroom was luxurious and spacious, like the house, but far more colourful than any bedroom Olivia had seen before. The counterpane was patchwork, in beautiful jewel colours and the curtains matched the main kingfisher blue. Olivia hesitated to put her suitcase on such a beautiful bedcover, but her hostess slung the other suitcase carelessly on the end of the bed. 'Put your suitcase here and unpack quickly, then we'll have a chat,' she said. 'I've got a proposition for you.'

Olivia unpacked, amused that her hostess made no

attempt to look away or give her any sort of privacy.

'You need some more modern clothes,' Babs said abruptly. '*And* underclothes. Yours are all far too sensible. You can alter some of your frocks, but you need new ones with much fuller skirts, really, and far shorter even than the one you're wearing today.'

She stood up and swept a curtsey to show how wide her own skirt was. It must have been four or five yards round the hem. Then she beamed down at it. 'Fashionable skirts are *so* much easier to move about in than those dratted hobble skirts. I didn't wear the things after one try. I'm too plump and too clumsy.'

Her frankness about her own faults took away the last of Olivia's shyness. They seemed to be getting to know one another more quickly than she'd have thought possible. She had a suspicion Babs did most things quickly, even making friends. 'I agree. But I mean to study what women are actually wearing and see if I can alter some of my clothes as well as buying new ones. I hate waste.'

'Um . . . did your husband leave you all right for money?'

'Yes. Not lavishly provided for, but comfortable if I'm reasonably careful.' She held up the green gown. 'I thought I'd wear this for the party. What do you think? I still have to finish shortening it.'

'I like it. That dark green looks good with your hair. You can start altering it while we chat, if you like. Do you have some sewing things with you?'

'Does any woman not take a needle and thread with her when she stays away from home?'

'Most people wouldn't take their sewing materials with them on a trip to London. And these days some women don't dress-make at all. I don't, actually. I'm not at all good at it and there are such excellent ready-made clothes these days. It's not like it was in our mothers' day.'

'No, thank goodness. But I knew I'd have to alter this, so I brought everything I'd need.'

'Well, you get started and we'll talk about the Women's Institute movement while you sew. I'm determined to involve you.' She put one foot up on the bed, knee bent, and clasped her arms round it. 'If you remember, I told you about the group of women who set one up in Wales in June. There are others looking into it, too.'

She pulled a wry face. 'Would you believe it, though, the first national organising committee is composed of six men, with a lady secretary. Isn't that ridiculous for dealing with a women-only organisation? That'll have to change.'

'Will it?'

'Oh yes. Because women like you and me are going to help our poorer sisters to get things going and oh, you know, play a bigger part in public life.'

'I've never heard you sound so serious, Babs.'

'I'm very serious about this. But you catch more flies with honey, so it doesn't do to appear too earnest and annoy the local lady of the manor or the vicar's wife. Or the important men from each area, come to that. Softly, softly, catchee monkey.'

'I've never heard that expression before.'

'Haven't you? It's one of Baden-Powell's. I like to imagine him chasing a monkey round the room, wearing that strange Boy Scouts costume of his.' She chuckled. 'But let's get back to our plotting about getting the men on side for our Women's Institutes.'

Men like Alex, Olivia thought, then felt her cheeks go warm.

'Now, why did you blush suddenly?' Babs asked.

'Just thinking of something. Go on. Tell me how I can help.'

'Well, I thought you and I could go and talk to the organisers of the first English WIs and get some hints from them. They're in West Sussex and Dorset, so we'll go to West Sussex first and we can go on to see a friend of mine in Wiltshire after we've been to Dorset.'

'How will we get around? The train services sometimes get disrupted by troop movements, but isn't it a bit far for you to drive?'

'Not at all. I love driving. And I'll teach you to drive while we're at it. You'll need to be able to if you're going to go round giving talks.'

Olivia blinked in shock. 'Me? Go round giving talks? Why would I do that?'

'I told you: to help people get started.'

'I've never given a public talk in my life. I'd be terrified.'

'Then it will be good for you to work with me at first. It'll build your confidence. What about driving? Does that frighten you too?'

'Not as much. I have Charles's car sitting doing nothing, though I thought I'd change it for one with a self-starter motor. Even my husband found it hard to get the car started manually sometimes.'

'Good idea. I know a chap who can help you with that.' Babs became very earnest again as she continued, 'We can't wait for the war to end before we do anything, you know. I've heard men talking. They expect to push women back into the kitchen again afterwards. In fact, to hear some of them talk, we can hardly find our way up a flight of stairs.'

'Donald has that attitude.'

'I could tell. Well, I intend to think ahead about how to prepare women for new times. It's their world too, so why shouldn't they have a say in how it's run?'

Olivia thought about Cecily, always in the shadow of her dominating husband. So many women were subservient like that, whatever their social class. Charles had never expected her to echo his opinions and run round after him like a substitute mother. 'I agree with you.'

'I knew you would the moment I started talking to you. I'll introduce you to a woman called Madge Watt. She's a bit eccentric and dresses peculiarly, but she's been involved in a similar organisation in Canada and she knows a lot about running women's groups. And there's a man called John Nugent Harris you have to meet, too. The poor chap's lost the use of his legs, but he isn't letting that stop him, drives round in a pony trap. He has an excellent brain. He's trying to get people to found WIs too.'

'Do the women themselves want it?'

Babs grinned. 'Some do. The others will once they see the benefits. I've spoken to John about it a few times. He understands more about women than most men I've met, I can tell you.' She chuckled. 'He says the people we'll be dealing with will be suspicious of us at first, and I think he's right there. You can't pull together a group of uneducated women who've been managing their egg money for years and growing their own food, and expect them to be good at running meetings or to have well-thought-out ideas about the future of womankind. They're used to markets and selling their produce but ask them about their daughter's future life and all they can think of is a husband who's a "good provider".'

She was flushed with enthusiasm, continuing without waiting for Olivia to comment. 'I've discussed it with energetic women of all classes. Women have already been getting together to do war work, or to help hungry children, or to learn new crafts and ways of preserving food. They can go on doing similar sorts of things as an official group. And they'll enjoy the social side of the meetings, too.'

She looked ruefully at Olivia. 'I feel guilty sometimes at throwing expensive parties, when poor children are starving, but I know the officers on leave from the front will be heartened by a party . . . just as I know half of them will be dead by this time next year. So cheering them up is one of my personal contributions to the war. But once we've won it – as I have no doubt we will – I can work to help women.'

She waited a minute or two for it to sink in. 'Sorry to beat your ears when you've only just arrived.'

'I found it interesting. I'm amazed at your energy and the scope of your ideas.'

Babs shrugged. 'There are a lot of hours to fill without my Humfy.'

They were both silent for a moment or two, remembering their dead husbands.

'Anyway, are you in, Olivia? Will you join me in this important work?'

'Yes, I will.' She hadn't realised that beneath Babs's frivolous exterior was a woman who cared so deeply for others. 'Like you, I'll be glad to have something useful to do with my life. But Charles would tell me to have fun too.'

Babs clasped her hand for a moment. 'So would Humfy. So we'll enjoy our party. Who said war work ought to be solemn and worthy?'

They both laughed, then Olivia bent over her sewing again, while Babs chatted about the people who'd be coming to the party.

Chapter Ten

Phoebe stood at the rear door of the old house, waving goodbye to Corin. She kept a bright smile on her face, difficult as that was, but as soon as he was out of sight she felt the smile slip. She would miss him dreadfully, worry about him . . . and also worry about herself and that horrible man in the village.

On that thought she went to put away the small handgun she and Corin had been practising with this morning in the old stables, the one her husband usually carried. He said he could buy another gun in London and would feel better if she had a way to protect herself.

She knew how to load and use the weapon now, but hoped she'd never have to fire it at anyone. Corin had assured her that simply having a gun to aim at them would deter most of the people who might try to attack her or her home.

Although she'd concentrated hard while practising, she hadn't hit the target as often as she'd hoped. But she had hit it a few times and Corin said that her score was as good as the average new recruit, so she didn't feel completely useless.

When she'd worried about the noise of gunfire, her

husband had laughed. 'The people from the village will think it's the soldiers practising. I asked our servants not to tell anyone it's you who's learning and Captain Turner will ask the soldiers to say nothing, either. If I had time, I'd teach the servants how to fire a gun, too.'

When it was time to leave, he'd taken Phoebe in his arms and said quietly, 'Always remember that your life and the baby's life are worth far more than this house. And if it's between your baby's life and a villain's life, you must shoot him.'

As she went inside, she felt a warmth enfold her and knew it was Anne Latimer trying to offer comfort. She wondered sometimes how much a ghost could understand about the modern world and the bitter fighting that was taking place far away from Greyladies.

The warmth faded slowly and she looked across the room to see Ethel staring at her in shock.

'Did you just see our family ghost? You don't have to worry. Anne Latimer is very friendly, especially towards women.'

Ethel let out a deep shuddering breath. 'I saw a light all round you. Would that be her?'

'Yes. Please don't be afraid of her.' She gave Ethel a quick summary of how the first chatelaine of Greyladies had created this house and set up a trust for helping women in trouble.

The maid listened, fascinated. 'No one ever told me history like that, ma'am, as if the people were real. At school we just had to learn things like dates and a list of the kings and queens of England.'

'Well, history was made by real people of all sorts, not just kings and queens. If you're going to continue working here, you might like to learn more about Tudor history, because that's when the old part of the house was built. And you may be interested in what I do to help other women. Would you like me to tell you more about the history of Greyladies and the legacy that has been left?'

Ethel nodded vigorously.

'Good. We'll start tonight after tea.'

'I wonder . . .' Ethel broke off. 'No, that's cheeky.'

'Tell me.'

'Well, there's a group of women in the village who're trying to improve themselves. Some have never had the chance to learn to read and write properly, even, because when they were girls they had to stay home from school to help their mothers with the housework and children.'

She flushed. 'I've been helping them a bit, especially with their reading and writing. I was always good at reading, well, at all the three Rs. The teacher wanted me to stay on and become a teacher, but my family needed my wages.'

'How kind of you to help others now! If you'd like to borrow any of our books to read in your spare time, you're welcome. Just write down what book you've taken in that little notebook in the top drawer of that desk. Miss Bowers does that when she borrows them, too.'

'Really? I can really borrow your books?'

'Didn't I just say so?'

'I . . . was surprised. Thanks ever so much, Mrs Latimer. I'd love something to read.'

'And if you need any time off to help the village women, just ask. I'm glad some of them are trying to improve themselves.'

'They didn't have much choice about the schooling, but

they want better for their daughters these days. I understand how they feel because I was one of the missing scholars till I was nine. Then my dad died and my mum married again. My stepdad insisted on us children going to school every single day. He earned a bit more than my dad had, so we could afford to. They made a big difference to our family, those few extra shillings a week he brought home, and he wasn't a boozer, either, like Dad. Eh, he wasn't a bad old stick, my stepdad. I still miss him. Sorry, ma'am. I didn't mean to go on about it.'

'I found it interesting. You were lucky to have him.' Phoebe hesitated. 'There's one other thing you might like to learn. You know my husband has given me a handgun?'

'Yes, ma'am. Me and Cook couldn't help hearing the shooting.'

'I'd like to show you how to use it too. Just in case someone attacks the house and I'm not here. I'll put the gun somewhere safe, but if I'm out I want you to be able to protect yourselves in any way necessary. Mobs on the rampage seem to lose any sense of reason or decency.'

Ethel gaped at her. 'I've never heard of a mistress like you.' She clapped one hand to her mouth. 'Ooh, sorry.'

'Don't be. We're both women and I think the gap between mistress and maid has narrowed a lot during the war.'

'Well, I thank you for thinking of our safety too. I do indeed.' She drew a deep breath. 'But this won't get the cleaning done, will it?'

Phoebe laughed. 'No. We'll have that lesson tonight about the history of Greyladies and I'll ask Cook when it would be convenient for you two to learn to use the gun.'

'She won't do it. She hates guns. But I'd like to learn how

to fire it. You never know what will come in useful these days. If those Huns invade England, I could shoot them with it.'

The next day, Phoebe heard that Sidney Hatterson had returned to the village and her heart sank.

He stared at her with such a hostile expression as she walked past him near the village shop that she was sure he still meant to do her harm.

The next night, which was New Year's Eve, someone threw another big stone at the old house. Fortunately this one missed the window.

Even more fortunately, the soldier on guard had stopped to smoke a cigarette, so was nearby and didn't have to be summoned to the rear of the big house.

He came running out of the bushes, yelling at the top of his voice to whoever it was to halt or he'd fire.

The intruder fled and the soldier fired his gun after him. A yelp suggested he'd hit the man, but he still managed to escape.

By that time the commandant had come to the front entrance in his dressing gown, standing pressed against the wall just inside the slightly open door, his revolver at the ready.

When the soldier came running round the corner of the house, Captain Turner yelled, 'What the hell is going on, Baker?'

'Intruder, sir. He threw a stone at the back of the house.'

'Well, get after him.'

But by that time it was too late to catch him.

Captain Turner went to check that Phoebe was all right and found her in the kitchen with her own gun at the ready.

'He got away.' The captain gestured to her weapon. 'You'd better keep that handy at all times. I'm beginning to fear it's you they're after, as well as my charges.'

Which worried her so much she got little sleep that night.

Why? What had she ever done to Hatterson?

A lad from the village who'd been paid by Corin to spend the nights keeping watch on the village and old house was in the stables eating the sandwiches his mum had packed for him when the incident happened. When he heard a noise, he dropped the food and stood up in time to see the intruder throw his stone and the soldier come after him shouting.

Since it was a cloudy night, Joe was able to slip out of the building without being seen and follow the intruder. He grinned at how useless the soldier clumping along was at tracking anyone. A proper townie, that chap, and soon left behind by the stone thrower.

He kept to his strict instructions to watch for intruders and check where they went. He was to keep out of sight and make no attempt to stop anyone.

It wasn't Sidney Hatterson, because this man didn't have a limp, but the fellow went into the Hattersons' house without knocking, so Sidney must be involved.

Joe had been unable to distinguish any details of the intruder's appearance because the moon was still behind the clouds. The fellow had a dark cap pulled down over his hair and a scarf wound round his lower face, so all the lad could tell was that he wasn't all that tall and was thin.

He found a nearby garden to hide in and keep watch on the house, delighted to have something to report, but regretting that he'd dropped his sandwich.

No lights came on in the house to greet the visitor, but Joe had excellent hearing and heard doors open and close inside. He thought the sounds must come from the room at the front or he'd not be hearing them, so risked creeping into Hatterson's front garden and getting close to the window.

He gave a pleased nod as he heard two men talking in low voices. His mum teased him about his big ears and how he could hear a pin drop, but it was very useful tonight to have good hearing.

'. . . how you could miss hitting one of those big windows, I really can't understand.'

That was Hatterson. He had such a whining voice, you couldn't mistake it.

'It isn't as easy as it sounds, throwing stones in the dark.'

The other man was a stranger and spoke very differently from local folk.

'I hit a window when *I* threw my stone,' Hatterson said. 'Smashed it good and proper, broken pieces of glass everywhere. *You* missed a ruddy great window completely.'

Outside Joe rubbed his arms briskly to warm himself up. Hatterson had a strange way of rolling his Rs. The lad mouthed the words 'rrreally' and 'brroken' to try it out, then went back to listening.

His mum was right: Hatterson was a real bad 'un.

'It's cold tonight. How about lighting the fire?' the stranger asked.

'Do you want to tell all my neighbours that someone's awake here? Do you think they wouldn't notice the smoke and the firelight? Anyway it doesn't seem cold to me. You should have been in the trenches. Now, that really was cold. You were lucky getting turned down on medical reasons.'

'I'm doing my bit in other ways, aren't I?'

'Not yet, you're not. We have to do something to get

rid of the Huns in that house, not just play at smashing windows. What I'd really like to do is burn the whole damned place down.'

'No! It's been there for hundreds of years.'

'So what? I'd burn all the Huns up with it, too.'

'I don't understand why you're going after that woman in the back, then. The Huns live in the front part of the house'

'I want to get rid of *her* as well. She's given them shelter, hasn't she? She deserves to be got rid of, the snooty bitch.'

'You don't mean you'd—'

'Never you mind what I mean. You and your pals keep in touch and we'll work our way up to a big offensive.' Hatterson sniggered. 'That's what they call attacks in the army – offensives. The offensive thing here is the stink of Huns and Hun-lovers. Did you know they all had a sing-song together at Christmas? Very cosy, they were. My friend up at the big house said it made him feel sick to see them acting like old friends. Well, we'll make sure them sods aren't here next Christmas, whatever it takes.'

'I'm not prepared to kill anyone.'

'Not even a Hun?'

'Not even a Hun. But I would thump one if I got the chance. I'd enjoy doing that.'

The lad outside was shocked by what Hatterson had said.

'You'll do your bit if you have to,' Hatterson snapped. 'And *I* will tell you what to do. I'm the trained soldier here.'

Silence, then he went on, 'You'd better get off home now while it's dark. Be sure you wheel your bicycle on the grass as you go through the village. We don't want anyone hearing you.'

'I was going to grab an hour's shut-eye on your sofa first.'

'They get up early in the country. Someone would see

you going back. You get off to Swindon now, while it's dark. Here. Have a nip of this first. It'll warm you up.'

There was the sound of glasses clinking.

Joe decided he'd better hide again. As he was leaving, he saw something poking out from behind the house and tiptoed along to check it. It was the stranger's bicycle. He was tempted to use his penknife to puncture one of the tyres, but realised that would give away the fact that someone had been watching them. Regretfully he moved across the road and hid in the other garden once again.

He waited to be sure the stranger really had left, then walked slowly back to check on the big house and see if his sandwich was still in the stable. He could brush the dirt off it as long as nothing had been nibbling it.

He was enjoying this little job. It was a nice way to earn some extra money during the slow season on his dad's farm and he was getting practice at doing military stuff.

He had a think about what he'd overhead and decided Hatterson was wrong. Them lot at the big house weren't enemies. They were nice old men and women, who were polite as anything when they went into the shop. He was sure they didn't want to fight anyone.

Major Latimer would be pleased with what he'd found out tonight.

He'd write his daily letter to the major about it first thing in the morning, as instructed. Who'd have thought those boring lessons with Miss Bowers, writing his alphabet and then the same words over and over on his slate, would come in useful? Even his mum said he wrote a clear hand. You wouldn't dare be sloppy with Miss Bowers.

The schoolmistress had always said you had to learn to *think* clearly too, because your brain was the main thing you had to deal with the world. He hadn't cared about that at school, but now he was nearly a man, he could see that she was right.

By next year, if the war was still on, he'd be in the army, then he'd really be dealing with the world. Just try to keep him out! He'd be fighting the bad Huns then, not little old men who wouldn't hurt a fly.

Unlike Hatterson. Nasty sod, that one was.

Babs's New Year's Eve party started just before eight o'clock in the evening, when four young officers strolled down the street and knocked on the door.

The maid let them in and took their khaki greatcoats and caps away.

Babs was talking to the three-man band – well, two men and a woman because of the war – so Olivia was left to entertain the young men. She felt a little nervous but realised they were nervous too and began to relax a little, concentrating on getting them to chat by asking them about themselves.

By the time the sitting room was full of people, young and old, men and women, she had no need to intervene because people had had a drink or two to oil the social wheels and were all chatting away.

The younger men had taken their leave of her very politely after sipping one cocktail, and after acquiring another drink had gravitated towards two younger women. She had no doubt they considered her in the same light as their mothers . . . old. She didn't feel old, though.

All the men here tonight were immaculately turned out, she noticed, with their hair slicked sideways or backwards with brilliantine, and with perfect partings. The younger women had bright-red lips and skirts a few inches above their ankles, something that would have been considered shocking when she was their age. Their beads and jewellery sparkled and their eyes sparkled too.

She began to feel a little weary of struggling through the same sort of conversation with one stranger after another, however polite they were. She wished she had Babs's skill at drawing someone out or making them laugh.

When she saw Alex hesitating in the doorway, looking distinctly nervous, she excused herself and went across to join him. 'I'm so glad you've come. I'm too old to chat to these youngsters. I haven't a clue what they're talking about half the time.'

His face brightened and he gave her such a beautiful, kind smile, it made her feel instantly more relaxed.

'Then chat to me instead, Olivia, because I'm no good at small talk to strangers, either. But you and I aren't strangers now, are we?'

She caught Babs's eye across the room and her friend winked, so she looked away hastily. 'Come and get a cocktail, Alex.'

'I really can't take alcohol. I'd better not risk it.'

'I'm having a drink the barman swears contains no alcohol.' She held her glass of bright-red liquid out to him. 'Try a sip.'

'Are you sure you don't mind?'

'I wouldn't have offered if I did.'

He took a sip, holding the liquid in his mouth for a moment before swallowing it. 'He's telling the truth. There is no alcohol in it. I can always tell. Let's get a glass for me and a refill for you, and find somewhere quieter to chat.'

'The bar is in the breakfast parlour and I think they're going to start dancing in the entrance hall soon. That's why Babs had all the furniture moved out of it.'

'I enjoy dancing. Will you dance with me? I'm far better at that than talking to strangers.'

'I'd love to. I've missed dancing.' The memory of dancing with Charles brought tears to her eyes, but she didn't let them fall.

Alex gave her an understanding pat on the arm and allowed her a moment to recover before speaking again.

When the dancing began, he took her to the back of the hall, where the older couples were moving about more sedately.

'You're a good dancer,' she said after a moment of two.

'One of my few physical skills. I miss the ball more often than I hit it in tennis, I'm usually bowled out with the first ball in cricket and I detest hunting. It sickens me when good horses have to be put down because they've been set to a hedge or wall that's too high for them.'

She moved closer and whispered, 'Don't tell anyone but I find hunting dreadful too. I manage to hit the ball back in tennis, though.'

To her disappointment, Babs clapped her hands just then and ordered them all to change partners every time she rang a bell, starting then.

A young man in uniform took over from Alex as Olivia's partner and she plastered a smile to her face. This man was easy because he talked non-stop and hardly listened to her replies. There was something feverish about the way he was going on. Poor lad! She could guess why. What dreadful things must he have seen in the trenches?

And he'd have to face it all again when he went back.

An hour later, Olivia's feet were throbbing and she knew her face was flushed. To keep the dancing simple, they were doing mainly the one-step, which anyone could cope with, Babs said, but which could get quite tiring after a while.

Olivia wasn't so sure about it being easy to do, either. Some of these young men were rather tiddly by now and couldn't speak at all coherently, let alone dance well. Several had trodden heavily on her toes.

When the change partners bell rang again, she nerved herself to turn to a new man, but found herself looking at Alex instead. He put one finger to his lips and pulled her to the side of the room, then led her behind a group arguing cheerfully about something and up the stairs.

'You were looking a bit frazzled.'

'I was feeling it and I'm not sure my feet will ever recover.'

'We'll sit on the stairs near the top, where we're hidden by the bend, and your poor feet can have a nice long rest.'

There was another couple on a small couch on the landing but they had their heads together, whispering and smiling, with eyes only for one another. Alex and Olivia were alone on the stairs.

Music from the little band blared out and she took off one shoe at a time to rub her aching feet.

They didn't chat, just sat quietly, which felt good.

But it didn't last. A man with a very loud voice yelled, 'Five minutes to go to 1916. Charge your glasses, everyone.'

Before people could start speaking Babs shouted, 'Come down and join us all who are hiding up there.'

Two other couples appeared from around corners, looking sheepish, and the couple on the landing excused themselves as they made their way down.

Alex sighed and pulled Olivia to her feet. 'We'd better join them. But look. If you take my arm and gaze at me and only me, we might be thought a couple and left alone from now on.'

'Good idea. I've enjoyed your company.'

'And I yours.'

When they both had full glasses of the sickly red drink, he didn't join the mass of people in the centre of the room, but gestured to a quieter area in the bow window. He seemed to have a knack for finding peaceful oases.

'If you could make a wish for the coming year, what would it be?' he asked suddenly. 'Apart from peace, that is, which I'm sure we all wish for.'

'To build a new life and learn to stand on my own feet.'

He looked at her gravely, then nodded. 'I can understand that. Will you and I be able to stay friends while you're on this important quest?'

'I hope so.' She was impelled to be honest with him. 'But you should know that . . . Well, I'm not done with grieving yet, Alex.'

'I've come to understand that from the way you talk of Charles. If your quest makes you vanish for the whole year, will you meet me here at the same time next year? Babs always gives a party and she's sure to invite us both.'

'Yes. I'd like that very much. But I'm sure we'll meet several times before then. I'm not going to hie myself to a nunnery.'

'And as you're coming to tea tomorrow, you'll know where to find me if you need me before the year ends. You wouldn't hesitate to ask if you needed help with something, would you?'

'I wouldn't hesitate at all.'

He didn't say anything else, but she knew there had been

some sort of promise given between them. Nothing binding, nothing definite, but she'd allowed him to set up a possibility for the future.

When *she* was ready.

The following day, breakfast was brought to Olivia in bed by a maid. Shortly afterwards there was a knock on the door. 'May I come in?' Babs called.

'Yes, of course.'

She perched at the foot of the bed, her hands clasped round a delicate china cup of what smelt like Earl Grey tea. 'There are some cousins staying overnight, but they never get up till noon, so you and I can have a little chat, if that's all right. Don't worry, I'll get rid of them before it's time for us to visit Alex.' She took another sip and sighed with pleasure. 'I love my first cup of tea in the morning.'

She took another sip and added, 'You and he seemed to be getting on very well last night.'

'We were.'

'Is he courting you?'

Trust Babs to ask such a direct question. 'No. I told him I'm still grieving. And I am. But we've agreed to meet again at your next party, or before if we choose to.'

'If *you* choose to, you mean.'

'Yes.'

Babs surprised her by saying, 'Good. I was worried you might rush into something.'

'As I said, I'm not ready for that sort of thing yet.'

Babs patted her hand and changed the subject. 'Shall we set off on Monday and start our investigations into setting up Women's Institutes?'

'Yes. That'd be interesting, I should think.'

'And at the same time, you can start learning to drive.'

Olivia took a deep breath. 'I'm a little scared of that, I must admit, but I'll give it a try.'

'You'll do well, I'm sure. I watched you dancing. You have good coordination.'

She wasn't sure about anything, except that she was going to try new things, even ones which frightened her.

She heard the echo of a beloved voice in her head. 'Go for it, old girl.'

No, she definitely wasn't ready for another man yet. Charles was still with her.

At two o'clock the next day Babs and Olivia arrived at Alex's shop, which had double plate glass windows with an elegant cream and gold signboard above them. It had 'Seaton' painted in large gold letters and 'Antiques' painted in much smaller letters beneath it and slightly to the right.

It said 'Closed' but the door was slightly open. When they entered, Olivia stopped to stare in surprise. 'You were right. It's more like an elegant drawing room than a shop. Oh, look at those carved figures!'

'Japanese, I should think. Ah, Alex.'

'Welcome to my shop.' He locked the door again, then picked up one of the tiny figures and held it out to Olivia. 'They're called netsuke. This one is made of ivory. Hold it. It won't break. It's already lasted at least two hundred years.'

After she'd admired it, he set it back carefully in place and led them to some stairs halfway to the rear of the building. En route he stopped to switch on the electric lights and show his visitors a particularly fine watercolour of the Lake District and a little bronze horse from China.

Babs gestured to the lights. 'You're very modern for someone dealing in antiquities.'

'I love electric light. It's the way of the future, believe me. One day all homes will have it as a matter of course.'

The small sitting room upstairs was just as beautiful as the public rooms. Alex had set out a display of special pieces on a side table. He rang for tea and as they waited, he showed them the pieces one by one, holding them reverently, his love for them betrayed by every caress of his fingertips.

For once Babs stayed in the background, and although Alex addressed a few remarks to her, his main attention was on Olivia.

The tea was served in an exquisite china tea service, which was, he said, only fifty years old, but was a masterpiece of French porcelain.

In the end, Babs said they had to leave. 'We're setting off for Singleton on Monday, Alex, and then we'll drive across to Dorset. We'll be away for a week or so, I should think.'

'Are you visiting friends?'

'No. As I told you, I mean to get Olivia involved in the Women's Institute movement, so we're going to visit the women who have set up what are probably the first two groups in England, then we're visiting a friend of mine.'

She chuckled. 'Singleton WI was set up by the landlady of the local pub. How daring is that? Women meeting in a pub! The Dorset WI was set up by a titled lady and *they* meet at her house . . . or was it the church hall? I've forgotten.'

'Drive carefully.'

'I shall. But you should say that to Olivia as well, because I'm going to start teaching her how to drive during our little trip.'

His expression turned anxious and he opened his mouth to say something, but closed it again.

Olivia was touched by his obvious concern for her. 'I'm always careful, whatever I do.'

'Let me know how you get on. Please. If only an occasional postcard.'

She nodded.

He went out with them and hailed a taxi. As the vehicle set off, Olivia turned to look back at the shop. Alex was still standing in the doorway, watching them. He raised one hand and she waved back.

Babs nudged her. 'He's got it bad.'

Olivia didn't know what to say to that, so kept quiet. Anyway the motor taxi's engine was rather noisy so it wasn't easy to chat.

She had wanted new things to happen, but so much was happening at once, she felt almost breathless. She glanced sideways at Babs, but her friend was staring out of the window at the crowded pavements and looked lost in thought.

Was she letting herself be pushed into something by Babs? Olivia wondered. Maybe. But she could always say she'd changed her mind if she didn't like what she found.

The idea of Women's Institutes pleased her, though.

And the idea of learning to drive, too.

Chapter Eleven

Corin read the letter from Joe for about the tenth time, wishing he could be there to protect his wife.

Would Phoebe use the gun if she had to? He thought she would. She was courageous in many ways, large and small. But she was carrying his child and that made her so much more vulnerable.

Oh, damn this war! Damn the separations.

He hoped the fighting would end before the bright-eyed lad who'd written to him had to join the army. And if not, he prayed that Joe would survive. The mass killing which all-out war brought utterly sickened Corin. So many young men's lives cut off before they'd done more than sip the cup of life.

He hoped he would survive the war, too. He wanted to raise a fine family with Phoebe: sons who wouldn't have to go to war, because surely this would be 'The war that will end war', a phrase first used by the writer HG Wells, and now in common use. Corin heartily endorsed that hope. He also wanted daughters who wouldn't have to wait anxiously to see if their sons, husbands or brothers survived the fighting.

There was a knock on the door and a grey-haired woman came in, saying crisply, 'They're gathering in the east room now, sir.'

'Thank you, Miss Tucker. Look. I wonder if you'd have time to make a copy of this letter and send it immediately to Captain Turner at this address?'

'Certainly, sir. I'm here to help you in any way I can.'

'Thank you.'

He watched her leave. Her clothing was severe, a brown tailored suit styled rather like a uniform, and her bearing was quasi-military. She was old enough to be his mother and worked as a general secretary to the officers in this special unit. They'd have made much slower progress without her efficiency and brilliant organisational skills.

There might have been questions asked if an attractive young woman had been appointed, but although there were some disapproving glances cast in Miss Tucker's direction, no one actually suggested replacing her with a male secretary.

He smiled. They'd better not. His commanding officer would have their guts for garters if they tried, as the age-old saying went.

He knew there was agitation in various groups in society to allow women into the armed forces, but it was proving hard to convince politicians and the old guard military that this should happen.

They had a name for a women's force already, though: the Women's Army Auxiliary Corps. But efforts to set up a corps kept getting bogged down in red tape and sheer bloody-mindedness on the part of those who didn't want women involved with the military.

In spite of the resistance to their involvement, women were being employed in military units here and there, however, mostly in secretarial, nursing or catering jobs. So whether they liked it or not, the older, sour-faced top brass were getting used to seeing females around.

Thank goodness he wasn't working for one of those old fogeys. He'd been hard put to keep his mouth closed at some of the remarks he'd overheard in corridors and even at meetings.

He gathered his papers together and tried to focus on the job in hand, setting aside his worries about Phoebe. He'd done all he could to help her. She wasn't alone, at least.

He let out a little sniff of laughter. Not the least of her supporters were a benign ghost and the maid Ethel, with whom he'd had a quiet word before he left.

Ethel held the gun steady, trying to remember all the instructions Mrs Latimer had read out from the manual. Now or never. She fired the gun and waited to see how she'd done, feeling a bit shaky.

'Very good!' Olivia said. 'Better than I did the first time. Try again.' She stepped back from the target, out of the line of sight.

Ethel took a deep breath and fired again . . . and again. What would her hubby think of her doing this? She knew he hadn't approved of women doing men's work, but perhaps he'd have thought it important for her to be able to defend herself against cowardly attackers.

When she'd finished, she found she'd hit the target board nearly every time, and come close to the central bullseye with two of the bullets.

'That's excellent, far better than I did,' Mrs Latimer said.

Ethel couldn't prevent a smile.

They packed the things away, putting the gun in a big leather lady's handbag, and walked back to the kitchen together.

Cook looked at them sharply. 'Everything all right, ma'am?'

'Everything's fine. Ethel's going to be a good shot.'

'I'll stick to my rolling pin, thank you very much.' She brandished an imaginary one as she spoke.

Ethel dared to wink at her mistress.

'Are you still going to have the Steins round to spend the evening with you tonight, ma'am?' Cook asked. 'Only I heard as the internees weren't to be allowed out at night anymore.'

'They don't have to go *out* to spend an evening with me.'

Cook hesitated, then said, 'I like Mr and Mrs Stein, don't mistake me, ma'am. But people in the village seem to know everything that goes on at Greyladies, and I did wonder if it'd be better for you to have them round another time, once Captain Turner has found a way to prove the troubles are Hatterson's fault. We need to get rid of the nasty creature.'

'The Steins are coming this evening. I shan't give in to bullying and threats.'

'Very well, ma'am. Hope I haven't given offence. It's just . . . I'm worried about *you*.'

'We have a gun now, don't forget.'

'Yes, ma'am.' Cook turned back to stir a pan and only Ethel heard her mutter, 'One gun and a whole big house to defend.'

Ethel didn't say anything. She had her own plans for this evening. She was going to borrow a book from the library and have a good old read.

During the afternoon of the last day of the year, Phoebe visited Miss Bowers and asked her about the group of women Ethel had spoken of. 'She says they're trying to better themselves, learn to read and write or acquire whatever skills they need. Do you know anything about them?'

'I do. But I think you'd be better joining them one day rather than me trying to tell you about them. Let them *show* you what they're doing. As for your Ethel—' She broke off abruptly. 'Well, you must have realised by now that she's a treasure, far too clever to be a maid. She'd make a good schoolteacher.'

'I know I'm lucky to have her. Ethel was held back by her husband, who sounds to have been a despot – benevolent and loving, but a despot all the same. Did you know she once begged him to let her open a little sweet shop, because they hadn't been able to have any more children after their son Danny, and he refused? Married women find it very difficult to run businesses without their husband's approval and written permission. The law is an ass about that.'

She looked at Phoebe. 'Are you still having the Steins round this evening?'

'Yes. I'm not giving in to that bully.'

'I agree. But be very careful to keep the curtains drawn. Captain Turner suspects that someone at Greyladies is giving information to Hatterson and his cronies.'

'I know. But I've met all four soldiers who're stationed here and they're always very pleasant to me. And it can't be the nurse or doctor, surely? Which leaves only the orderly or servants.'

'Sadly, it can be any of them, my dear Phoebe. People do strange things when they're not happy about something. Now, let me send my neighbour's son home with you so that no one can waylay you. And please don't come here on your own again till things are safer. How did you escape Ethel and Cook, anyway?'

'I used the secret tunnel from the cellar to the crypt, then I detoured through the ruins of the abbey and walked into the village from the other side. If someone was keeping watch on the house, they'd not have seen me leave and they won't see me return, either.'

'They might be keeping watch on that side of the village if they saw you arrive. It was a dangerous thing to do on your own. You'll oblige me by bringing someone with you next time, preferably Ethel.'

Phoebe sighed in resignation. When Miss Bowers spoke in that tone of voice, it was tantamount to a royal decree.

'No, I've changed my mind, Phoebe. I shall walk back with you myself,' the old lady decided aloud. 'And we shall go into Greyladies openly, thank you very much, so that no one can trace the way you came. Besides, I'm too old to go crawling along tunnels.'

'You don't need to crawl along this one, just bend down at one part.'

But Miss Bowers was already putting on her coat and hat, and picking up her umbrella.

'It doesn't look like rain,' Phoebe said in surprise.

'I'm carrying it in case we're attacked, and you should carry one too from now on. Take your husband's umbrella. It'll be heavier, much more suited to the job. Hold it halfway down so that you can use the handle to hit with.'

She maintained a pleasant conversation during their walk and as they parted at the kitchen door, reminded Ethel to introduce her mistress to the women's group soon.

Phoebe spent a pleasant evening with her former employers, but the Steins said they were too old to stay up until midnight to greet 1916. She saw them to the door between the two parts of the house, hesitated, then locked it carefully with the huge key that Anne Latimer must have used.

If there was a traitor in the other side of the house, he or she wasn't getting free access to the old house from now on.

She wouldn't stay up till midnight, either, she decided. She was tired and worried. Her condition was beginning to show, just a little, and slow her down.

In the morning Phoebe suggested another practice session with the gun to Ethel and couldn't help feeling a trifle miffed when it produced similar results. The maid had taken to shooting as if born to it and was far better at it than her mistress.

'You learn quickly,' Phoebe told her. 'I'm going to give you a key to the gun cabinet and you have my permission to take out that gun if you ever feel it's needed. If you carry it in that handbag we're using or even in your skirt pocket, I don't think anyone will know it's there.'

'Thank you, ma'am, I'll do that.'

'I think the post has arrived. Could you please check whether there are any letters for me?'

There was a postcard from Corin saying he was well.

There was also a letter posted in London, in a handwriting she didn't recognise.

When she opened it, she let out a cry of dismay. It said, in crude, printed letters:

HUN LOVERS ARE TRATERS
GET OUT OF CHALLERTON MISSUS
IF YOU VALUE YORE LIFE

She held it out to Ethel, her hand shaking. It felt as if the paper itself was soaked in venom.

'Whoever it is must be stupid. Can't even spell.' Ethel looked at her mistress, her eyes troubled. 'You'd better be even more careful from now on, Mrs Latimer. I don't think you should come to tomorrow's meeting. It'll be dark by the time we break up.'

'I'll be with you, not on my own.'

'We'll take the gun, then.'

'No need for that.'

Ethel got a stubborn look on her face. 'We don't have to use it, do we? But if anyone attacks us, it might save our lives. Think of the baby.'

'Oh, very well. Do as you please.'

The meeting was held in the church hall, only a short walk from the gates of Greyladies. The vicar approved of self-help groups and his wife had joined this one, apparently.

'I still don't think you should have come out tonight,' Ethel worried as they left the grounds. 'There's a lady come to stay with Miss Bowers, who's going to speak about setting up reading groups, so we're bound to finish later than usual.'

'I won't let this villain stop me going out and about,' Phoebe repeated, wondering how many times they'd have to have this argument. 'I'm not stupid enough to go anywhere on my own, but I won't cower in the house like a rat in a trap. You wouldn't do that, either.'

Ethel gave her a wry look. 'No. I wouldn't. But then, I'm not important enough for anyone to go after me.' She patted the handbag. 'I brought it.'

'Well, I hope you made sure the safety catch was on the gun.'

'Of course I did.'

There were a dozen women standing chatting in the hall. Miss Bowers was at the front table with a stranger, a middle-aged lady wearing a ghastly hat and a dowdy grey frock and jacket. She was twirling a pair of pince-nez on the end of their cord as she made some point.

Phoebe waved to Miss Bowers, but when the former teacher didn't beckon her over, she let Ethel introduce her to the trio of women closest to them. She recognised them by sight, but didn't know the names of two of them, or their role in village life.

They seemed nervous at first, but relaxed as she asked them questions to find out what had brought them here tonight.

'I want to improve myself, Mrs Latimer,' the youngest woman said. 'I've got three children and I don't want them reading better than I do. How would that look? As if I'm stupid, that's what, and I'm not.' She broke off, looking a little scared, as if worried she'd spoken too strongly.

'Good for you,' Phoebe said.

Miss Bowers' quiet voice somehow seemed to cut through the crowd. 'If you'll come and sit down now, ladies, I'll introduce our visitor.'

'Most of them know her by sight already, because she's come to visit Miss Bowers before,' Ethel whispered.

Miss Cowley started her talk, telling them about the reading groups she had started in her own village, each with a skilled reader in charge of helping the others. They read aloud to one another for the first part of their meetings.

'It costs only the purchase price of the books and I'm happy to see to that. The same book can be used by each group in turn.'

By the end of the talk, Phoebe had to admit that it seemed a practical idea, and when there was talk about starting up reading groups in Challerton, she volunteered to pay for the books. That was what the money in the Latimer Trust was for, after all, helping women in large and small ways.

After a polite round of applause for the speaker, the tea urn was put into use.

A lad slipped into the hall the back way and edged across to Miss Bowers, who listened to him and frowned, then beckoned to Phoebe and Ethel.

'There's a man keeping watch on this hall. Joe here saw him follow you here.'

'How on earth would anyone know we'd gone out?' Phoebe exclaimed.

'They must have someone passing on information from the big house.'

'But we didn't see anyone following us and I doubt Captain Turner would let the people under him wander in and out as they please.'

After a short silence, Joe said thoughtfully, 'They could have signalled from the house, Mrs Latimer. A light in an upstairs window or something. I'll watch out for that next time.'

'Why were you watching the house, Joe?'

'Practising.'

Phoebe looked at him in puzzlement. 'For what?'

'For when I go in the army next year. Soldiers keep watch, don't they? I don't want any enemy creeping up on me and killing me.'

'How are we to get you home safely, Phoebe?' Miss Bowers thought for a moment or two. 'I know what we can do,' she said triumphantly.

She clapped her hands and everyone turned to her. 'A man followed Mrs Latimer here and has been watching the hall. You all know there have been incidents at the big house. I don't think she and Ethel should walk back to the big house on their own. How about some of you go with them? Make a lot of noise, keep them in the middle, and take them right round to the back door.'

Immediately everyone volunteered, which made Phoebe feel touched. 'I can't thank you enough.'

The speaker was watching them in surprise, so Miss Bowers quickly chose five women to go with Phoebe, then went back to her guest.

Joe slipped out of the kitchen door and it was carefully locked behind him this time.

When he'd had time to find a vantage point to watch from, he grinned as the group of seven women fairly erupted out of the front door, talking at the top of their voices.

Five minutes later they were at the kitchen door of the big house, standing in a semicircle round it as Phoebe and Ethel went inside.

'How kind of them!' Phoebe said.

'It's a nice place to live, this village,' Ethel said. 'I'll just go and put the gun away.'

Standing in the shadows behind a big tree, Joe watched the mystery man follow the group to the gates of Greyladies.

This fellow limped very slightly, but not nearly as much as Hatterson did, so it couldn't be him . . . could it?

The man stopped near the gates and watched the women go round to the back of the house, then hurled a stone at the nearest tree and cursed under his breath as he walked away.

Joe again followed him and saw him go into Hatterson's house.

Was it Hatterson or not? Whoever it was, what had he intended to do with the stone?

On that thought, Joe decided to come back in daylight and see if he could retrieve the stone. Perhaps he might be able to tell where it came from. That's what Sherlock Holmes would have done. He'd read those books again and again. Such a clever man, Mr Holmes.

In the meantime, Joe watched the group of chattering, excited women walk back to the village hall, where the meeting continued instead of breaking up. When he went to eavesdrop, they were talking about the danger to Mrs Latimer.

Joe's older cousin was one of them. Like him, she wanted to better herself, but it was harder for her because she was married and had to stay here. He was going to use the army to better himself – or the air force if they'd take him. That was a new sort of thing, warfare in the sky. He loved watching it on the newsreels at the cinema in Swindon, and he'd seen single planes flying past in the distance, sounding like huge angry wasps.

Perhaps he could get into the air force sooner than his call-up date if he volunteered and lied about his age. He didn't want to fly the planes, though. He wanted to work on their engines. He loved machinery of all sorts. His dad said he was a fair marvel at mending things.

The light went off in the church hall. Miss Bowers and her guest were the last two to leave, and they talked quietly as they walked back to her house.

He waited where he was till they were inside her house, just in case Hatterson – if it was him – came after them, but he didn't.

Joe checked all the way round Hatterson's cottage. There were no lights inside, no sounds of people talking and the door remained firmly closed.

In fact, no clues to be found.

He continued to patrol the village until the sky began to brighten then sought his own bed, yawning, but pleased with his night's work.

Chapter Twelve

Olivia listened carefully to Babs's instructions, then had a go at starting the car. She looked at her mentor in delight as the motor came to life. 'How much easier it is with a starter motor instead of having to swing a crank handle round. Even Charles had trouble starting our motor car sometimes, and I haven't dared try to get it going since he died. So it's just sitting there in our – *my* – garage, useless.'

'You should definitely sell it and use the money to buy another car that's easier to drive. Being able to get around would make a big difference to your life. No, wait. You'll probably have trouble finding another car to buy, though, because everything's geared to the war effort now and not many companies are producing new vehicles.' Her face brightened. 'I know! You can ask Alex's help.'

Olivia was well aware that it was no use being tactful with Babs, so asked straight out, 'Are you by any chance matchmaking?'

'Actually, no. I just think if anyone could find you another car, it'd be him. He's very quiet, but he's well thought of and knows everyone. He *likes* to help people.'

'Oh. Well. That's all right, then. I'll think about it.'

'Up to you. Now, let's see how you go at driving . . .'

The lesson reduced Babs to fits of the giggles because Olivia made every mistake possible and the car jerked along like a drunken kangaroo, as her friend didn't hesitate to tell her. Not that either of them had ever seen a kangaroo, except in books and on the newsreels at the cinema.

When they drew near the next small town, Olivia stopped the car and looked at her friend anxiously. 'I'm terrible at driving, aren't I? Perhaps I shouldn't bother trying to learn.'

'Oh, is that what's making you look so unhappy? No, no. Truly you aren't doing at all badly. It isn't easy to double-declutch. Took me ages to get the hang of that.' She saw Olivia's doubtful expression and gave her friend's arm a little shake. 'I'm telling you the simple truth. If you persevere and keep practising, you'll improve gradually.'

'Well, if you're sure. As long as I'm not a danger to other people. I'd hate to cause an accident. But I daren't drive into a town yet.' She got out of the car and changed places with Babs, relieved to have done with the strain of trying to drive for the time being.

They were made very welcome by the landlady of The Fox in Singleton, who was the main force behind the local Women's Institute. She insisted they stay at her pub for the night, rather than drive on in the dark after they'd finished chatting.

They talked to her for a long time, ate a late tea and daringly sat in the tiny ladies' room at the pub to sip a glass of port wine each. Some men gave them dirty looks but no one approached them or said anything out of place.

The next day, they stayed for longer than they'd expected because a special meeting had been arranged in the morning for those who could make it, so that the women members could also meet the visitors.

'We pride ourselves on being trailblazers,' the landlady told them proudly as she got a room in the pub ready.

The meeting was lively and, unusually, women of all backgrounds – labourers' wives, farmers' wives, the local clergyman's daughter and the widow of a baronet – sat together and spoke as equals.

Minutes of the meeting were kept by one lady, who turned out to be the schoolmistress. And afterwards, everyone had a cup of excellent tea and scones from the plates that had been brought by some women.

Mrs Fox whispered, 'We keep it to scones, because some of them can't afford to buy the materials for fancy cakes, but most women know how to whip up a batch of scones. We take it in turns to bring something.'

Afterwards they chatted to her for a few minutes then left.

As Babs drove away, Olivia mulled over what she had seen at Singleton. 'I think it's wonderful,' she said suddenly.

Babs didn't need to ask what she was referring to. 'So do I. You don't usually see women from all sorts of backgrounds coming together like that, do you?'

'No. I could never be a suffragette, but since the war began I've seen what women can do. They cope with men's jobs, lift heavy objects, drive buses, work in munitions factories, and drive ambulances at the front – in fact, they do whatever is needed and just as well as a man would. Those who don't go out to work get together to roll bandages or make comfort packs for the soldiers.'

Babs nodded agreement, 'They usually organise the part-time working groups themselves, too, and do it well. So I feel more strongly than ever that we women *ought* to have the vote.'

'I agree. And we shouldn't make such a fuss about class differences or differences between men and women. My cousin Donald *expects* women to defer to him, and I hate to say it of a relative of mine, but he's rather stupid, so why would anyone follow his advice?'

Babs slowed down to a stop and set the handbrake but didn't switch off the motor. 'Come on. Change places and have another go. There's a long stretch of country road coming up, just right for you to practise on.'

'How do you know your way around the country?' Olivia asked as she settled into the driving seat and tried to calm herself.

'One of Humfy's old relatives used to live near here. That husband of mine had relatives and friends all over England and Scotland, so we used to drive around a lot.'

'Can I . . . ask you something?' At her companion's nod, she said, 'Do you miss him still? It's been nearly a year now since you lost him, hasn't it?'

'Yes, of course I miss him. Dreadfully. But you can't change what's happened, can you, so you have to make the best of it. I'm a bit ahead of you on the widowhood stakes, so I can assure you that it does gradually get a bit easier.' She clapped Olivia on the shoulder. 'Now, we'll forget about unhappy things and practise some more, shall we?'

By the time they changed places again, Olivia was feeling a little more comfortable behind the wheel, at least in the quiet of the countryside.

'I've arranged somewhere nice to stay tonight,' Babs said as she took over.

Her idea of somewhere nice turned out to be a friend's

country residence. Not another widow this time but a woman whose husband was serving in France.

Since Charles's death Olivia felt her life was mainly lived in a world of women. Wonderful women, some of them. But she missed having a man to talk to.

She realised suddenly that she was missing Alex on this journey. She'd enjoyed her trips with him very much.

Of course, she didn't mention that to Babs, but hugged the thought to herself that Alex was her friend now and perhaps could become more.

Was that wrong of her?

The other Women's Institute they were to visit was in Wallisdown in Dorset. Lady Wimborne and her daughter Lady Chelmsford had started it, with the help of Madge Watt, using the latter's experience with Women's Institutes in Canada. Indeed, Mrs Watt was helping to raise interest in the idea all over England.

The two local ladies were enthusiastic about what they were doing and had a lively conversation with their guests about the best way to set about the task.

'Find someone who is respected locally,' Lady Wimborne said firmly. 'But not someone who wants to rule the roost. In a Women's Institute the meetings are run democratically.'

They all talked about equality and democracy, Olivia thought, whoever they were. But what did ladies like these do in practice? Still, she approved wholeheartedly of any progress.

Her Ladyship said thoughtfully, 'You know, after you've seen our group tomorrow, I think you should go and visit my friend Miss Cowley.'

Babs smiled. 'We've already arranged to do that. She's a friend of my aunt.'

'Oh, good. She runs a self-help group in her own village and she was telling me about another village nearby – I think it's called Challerton, yes, that's it – where they also have a self-help group. Those might be good places for you to make a start. Can you spend several days in the area?'

Babs frowned. 'I can spend a few, but I have to allow time to drive back to London, where I have appointments.'

Olivia said, 'I can stay longer, if necessary, and come back by train. I don't have any engagements.'

'Jolly good,' said their hostess. 'The lady at the big house in Challerton is a Mrs Latimer, who is particularly interested in helping women. And Miss Cowley's friend there is a retired schoolteacher, a Miss Bowers?'

Lady Wimborne looked questioningly at Olivia. 'I'll telephone Vivian Cowley, then, and see whether she'll be at home the day after tomorrow. If so, you must stay another night here.'

One thing seemed to be leading to another, Olivia thought as she got ready for bed that evening in a very comfortable bedroom with a small fire burning in the grate.

It was good to be out in the world again doing things – useful things, she hoped. She had felt stifled at Donald's house.

Perhaps if Alex could help her find a car that was easier to start, she would continue learning to drive, so that she could go anywhere she wanted. Well, she could if she could get the petrol. The war had made that more difficult.

Always the war. She'd almost forgotten what it felt like

to live in peacetime. How long would it be before they could live normally again? She didn't doubt that Britain would defeat Germany, of course she didn't, but it wasn't going to be easy – or quick.

As she lay there, she realised suddenly that she didn't want to settle down again in the house where she'd lived with Charles. A new start in every way seemed the best path to take.

And her late husband's voice in her head sounded fainter than before as she seemed to hear the words, 'You go for it, old girl.'

When Phoebe woke the morning following the meeting in the village, it was early and still dark, so she decided to stay in bed for a while longer.

Her first thought was of Corin and she mentally sent him her love and prayed for him to stay safe, as she did morning and evening. Then she mulled over yesterday's meeting and what she could do to help the local women in their quest to improve themselves.

She wasn't the sort to lie in bed, so decided to get up, even though it was too early for Ethel or Cook to be about.

The minute she thought of that, she began to feel uneasy, as if something was wrong. What had caused that feeling? She didn't usually worry about nothing.

She lit her oil lamp with a Swan Vesta safety match and washed quickly in the icy cold water in her jug, not wanting to wait for Ethel to bring her some hot water. Something was definitely wrong in her house, because she couldn't shake off that sense of foreboding, and she intended to find out what.

Everything was still and silent as she made her way down to the kitchen to get a cup of tea. She took the shortcut down the back stairs, but as she reached the first turn, a bar of light flashed into existence and barred her way. Something told her to stand still and as she could sense Anne Latimer's familiar presence, she obeyed the impulse, sure the family ghost would have a good reason for barring her way.

She held up her lamp and looked round carefully. Her heart seemed to stutter in her chest as she saw the rope stretched across the stairs about a foot from the floor. It was tied to the banisters on either side, just where the stairs started to go straight down again after the turn.

If she'd continued, if Anne hadn't barred her way, she'd have fallen and hurt herself badly, might even have lost her baby or set fire to the house if she'd dropped her oil lamp!

Dear heaven, who could have done this? And how? The house was locked up every night.

She heard footsteps clattering down behind her and called out, 'Is that you, Ethel?'

'Yes, ma'am.'

'Stop behind me. Don't try to get past. Look. Someone's set a trap.'

Ethel stared downwards and gasped. 'I'm always the first to get up, so it must have been set for me.' She clutched Phoebe's arm. 'Only it nearly got you. What stopped you? Did you see it?'

'No. Our ghost warned me.'

'Oh.'

'Leave the rope where it is. We'll go back and use the

main stairs. I want to show this to Captain Turner before we dismantle the trap.' She had a thought. Why not show it to a few people from the village as well? Someone might recognise the type of rope, which was thin and rough, cheap stuff of a type she hadn't seen around here before.

Cook came slowly down the attic stairs in her voluminous flannel nightgown and they called out to her to stay on the landing.

'Someone's set a trap,' Ethel explained. 'They've tied a rope across the stairs.'

'Oh, my giddy aunt! What a wicked thing to do! I'd not believe it if I hadn't seen it with my own eyes.' Cook gasped. 'That means someone was creeping round inside the house while we lay helpless in our beds. We could have had our throats cut! Or worse.'

Phoebe wondered what was worse than being killed. 'We have to make sure it doesn't happen again. We should all use the front stairs till Captain Turner has seen the trap.'

'Show it to old Walter as well,' Cook said. 'I know he's only acting as village policeman while Sam Telby is in the army, but he's a knowing sort of man, worth listening to.'

'We can show it to anyone from the village who wants to come here,' Phoebe said rashly.

'I don't think we should do that, ma'am,' Ethel said at once. 'Just show it to the ones Walter approves of. Otherwise anyone can come into Greyladies and spy out the ground, even that Hatterson man.'

'You're right. I wasn't thinking straight. Let's go down and see how they got in.'

But there was no sign of a forced entry at any of the

outside doors or at the connecting door to the new house.

When they got back to the kitchen Phoebe thought through it aloud. 'They either have a key or they picked a lock to get in. Then they found a way to lock up again after they went out. What *is* going on?'

'We'll have to make sure we use the bolts on all the outside doors,' Ethel said. 'You can't get past good strong bolts.'

'There aren't any bolts on the inside of the connecting door. There used to be. You can see the marks, but someone took them off years ago.'

'Then you should have more bolts put on, ma'am. And before the day is through.'

Ethel nodded, then asked again, 'Why would anyone want to trip *me* up? It's not likely to have killed me if I fell.'

'To get rid of you for a while?'

Ethel clapped one hand to her mouth. 'Oh! So *you* would be without protection.'

In spite of the seriousness of the situation, Phoebe couldn't help smiling. 'Is that what you're doing? Protecting me?'

'Yes, ma'am. Major Latimer asked me to keep an eye on you before he left.' She took a deep breath. 'I think, if you don't mind, I should move into a bedroom near yours for the time being. That connecting one, perhaps. So that I can come and help you if you're attacked.'

Phoebe could see no fault in this. She realised she had her hand on her stomach again, as if instinctively protecting her baby. She'd been doing that quite a bit lately. 'Good idea.'

'And we should take the gun to bed with us.'

'I suppose so. What about you, Cook? Do you want to sleep downstairs as well?'

'No, ma'am. I like my own bed. But I'm taking my rolling

pin upstairs with me every night and I'd be grateful if you'd have bolts fitted to the inside of my bedroom door while you're at it.'

'Of course.' Phoebe took a last look at the rope, shivering slightly at the thought that someone had been walking round her house while she was asleep.

Well, they wouldn't do it again!

Ethel informed the soldier on guard outside the house of what had happened and he reported it to Captain Turner, who came to the kitchen door immediately, together with the doctor, since they didn't have a key to the connecting door, there being only one in existence.

The two men examined the rope but were unable to figure out who could have done this, or why. As to how they'd got into the house, they must have had a key.

'Excuse me, sir, but can you send someone down to the village to fetch Walter? He *is* the policeman here and he ought to know about this, so that he can keep an eye on certain people.'

'Good thinking, Ethel.' He looked at Phoebe. 'Will you be all right at night from now on or would you like me to station one of the men inside your house?'

She shook her head. 'Thank you, but no. I'd prefer to keep everyone who doesn't live here out.'

Walter came up to the house as soon as he heard. He might walk stiffly, but he was dressed smartly in the old-fashioned police uniform he'd worn when he was the village bobby. He was well liked because he was always ready to help if there was trouble, either in his official capacity or unofficially.

Joe was trailing along behind him.

'Couldn't stop the lad following me,' Walter grumbled to Phoebe. 'What's the world coming to when people have to rely on old codgers like me and young lads like him to defend the village?'

He was shown into the kitchen and with a jerk of his head, he invited Joe to follow. 'Keep quiet, though, unless you have something important to say.'

Joe nodded, looking round eagerly.

Walter also had to admit that he was baffled as to how anyone could have got in, or why they would have wanted to hurt Ethel.

Joe put up his hand, as if he was still in school.

'Well?' Walter asked.

'If Ethel was hurt, it'd be easier for them to get into the house and attack Mrs Latimer. Can I keep watch here at night? Can I? I won't go to sleep.'

Walter opened his mouth to answer, then shut it again and frowned. 'Might be a good idea, Mrs Latimer. It's up to you, of course.'

'Did my husband ask you to keep an eye on me?' Phoebe asked.

He wriggled uncomfortably, then nodded. 'Keep an eye on the house at night, the major said. He's paying me to do it, too. So I sleep in the mornings and go out after dark. But this morning my mum woke me up and said she'd heard there'd been a break-in here, so I got up again straight away and came to see.'

'That Hatterson did it,' Ethel said suddenly. 'I know it's him.'

Joe shook his head. 'I didn't see him or anyone else come out of his cottage last night, and I was nearby all the time because I wanted to see if there was a signal to him from the big house. But I didn't see anyone go in or out.'

Walter was still frowning. 'Could I see the other side of the connecting door, sir? Before you open it, though.'

'I'd like to see it too,' Phoebe said.

They all walked round the outside of the house, leaving Cook, properly dressed now, muttering over the kettle and clattering her pots around.

Captain Turner had a soldier keeping guard on the connecting door, so gestured to him to move aside.

An elderly internee came to the door of one of the big common rooms to watch them, but he stayed at a distance and no one told him to move away.

Phoebe joined the commandant at the door and together they examined the lock. She tried desperately hard to remember exactly what the big old-fashioned lock and the woodwork round it had looked like. 'I think some of those scratches weren't here when I last went through it.'

Joe sidled hesitantly up to join them, as if expecting to be sent away. Ethel followed him more confidently.

'A few of them look like new scratches to me,' the boy said.

'They are new scratches,' a voice with a heavy German accent said from the other side of the entrance hall. 'I don't sleep well, so I get up before the others. The rug was out of place and one corner folded under, so I came across to straighten it.' He shrugged. 'We are old, don't want to fall. I see the scratches near the lock and wonder who has been tampering with it.'

'Do you know about locks, sir?' Ethel asked.

'Yes. I was a jeweller and sometimes people brought locks

to me to unfasten on their trinket boxes. Over the years I learn a lot about how to mend simple locks. Why is the wood scratched, do you think?'

'Someone broke into the old house last night,' Ethel said before anyone could stop her. 'We're trying to find out how, but they locked up after themselves, so we weren't sure how they did it, whether they came through here.'

'I can look inside the lock for scratches if I fetch my magnifying glass,' he offered. 'If you want me to, that is. Or if you want me to go away and not say anything, I can do that too. I don't want to cause trouble.'

'The trouble has already been caused, Herr Brauchman,' Captain Turner said. 'Please fetch your magnifying glass and see what you can tell us about the lock.'

The old man inclined his head and walked slowly up the stairs.

'He's a nice old fellow,' the commandant said. 'He plays the violin sometimes, and very well too, and he's been of great help with information about certain matters.'

'Why does that Hatterson say Germans are evil?' Joe asked suddenly. 'That old man don't look evil to me. He looks like my granddad's brother, Uncle Ralph. Got the same kind smile.'

'Out of the mouths of babes . . .' Phoebe said.

Herr Brauchman came stiffly back, with a bundle wrapped in felt. 'Please excuse me,' he said to Phoebe, and she stepped back from the door.

He set the felt bundle on a nearby chair and unrolled it, taking out a large magnifying glass and a small one. First he examined the area round the lock, making a little grunting noise as he found something.

'Please look through this at the scratch, Herr Commandant,' he said. 'It is a new one but someone has tried to disguise it.'

Captain Turner took the magnifying glass from him and studied the wood. 'By Jove, yes.'

When Phoebe looked, she could see the marks quite distinctly, as well as traces of something that had been rubbed into the slight depressions. She passed the glass to Ethel and Joe.

Herr Brauchman took it back and looked inside the hole. 'For this I need more light.'

'I have one of the new handheld electric torches.' Captain Turner hurried to his office at the rear of the hall and came back shortly, waving the metal tube.

He showed Herr Brauchman how to switch it on and off, and the old man shone it into the keyhole. He made more faint sounds of excitement as he examined the interior, then put down the big magnifying glass and used the small one. 'This is very strong magnifier for small things. Ah! There are several scratches inside, where they forced the lock. Please check them, Herr Commandant, ladies.'

Again, everyone looked in turn into the old lock and it was quite obvious that something had scratched the metal inside it recently because the marks were shiny, as if newly made.

'This is how they get in,' Herr Brauchman said. He looked from one to the other. 'This lock is old and easy to force. You should put in a better one. I cannot do that, but a good locksmith could and without changing its appearance much.'

'Thank you, Herr Brauchman,' Phoebe said. 'But my family has never changed the old lock, not for centuries. I think I'd prefer to have bolts put on the other side of the door, where there used to be some. I don't know why they were removed.'

'Well. Thank you for your help, Herr Brauchman,' Captain Turner said. 'Please don't discuss this with anyone.'

The old man nodded, rolled up his pack of tools and walked away. Everyone else turned back to study the door.

'Do you still have the old bolts, Mrs Latimer?' the commandant asked.

'I think we do. Somewhere in the attic.'

'If you get them out, I'll find someone to fit them today. We can't have people breaking into your part of the house from here. What I want to know is how they got into the new part, and I can think of only one way.'

Silence greeted his words, then Joe blurted out, 'Someone must have let them in.'

'Yes. That's what I'm afraid of, lad. There's no other explanation. I thought all our people were loyal but there must be one who isn't. Some people get paranoid where Germans and Austrians are concerned, even those who have lived here so long they're loyal to Britain.'

He stood for a moment lost in thought, then turned to Phoebe and repeated, 'So . . . if you can find the bolts, I'll see that they're fixed on to the door before nightfall.'

'Thank you. I think it's safe to go home this way now, don't you?' She took out the only key, a huge iron piece, and inserted it in the lock.

Joe followed her and Ethel into the old house. 'I hope you don't mind me coming through this way, Mrs Latimer, only I get a bit nervous when there's just me and the commandant.'

'Any lad your age would. He's used to ordering people round, isn't he?'

'Yes. He's worse than my dad.'

'Thank you for keeping an eye on things, Joe.'

'That's all right, Mrs Latimer. The major pays me and I like doing it. It's good practice for when I'm called up.'

'Don't be in a hurry to go,' Ethel said sharply. 'Your mother will be terrified every day you're away.'

Phoebe knew the maid was thinking of her own son.

The two women escorted Joe to the back door and he nodded politely to Cook as he went out through the kitchen. Phoebe closed and locked the door immediately after him, then stood staring out of the window, feeling rather numb.

Corin was right. She had to take great care. A fall today could have made her lose the baby.

'Shall I get your breakfast now, ma'am?' Cook asked.

'I don't feel hungry.'

'You have to eat for two now.'

'Do I? Well, a piece of dry toast is all I can face.'

'With an egg on it?'

She shuddered. 'No. The mere thought of an egg makes me feel sick. Dry toast, Cook, and only one piece. Is the fire hot enough? If you tell me where the toasting fork is, I'll toast the bread myself.'

Cook looked as if she would object, then shrugged. 'Life's topsy-turvy these days, isn't it? I never thought I'd eat my meals with the mistress.'

'If it upsets you, I can go back to eating on my own.'

'Bless you, no, ma'am. The major wouldn't want you to be lonely and if you're with us, we can make sure you're safe.'

Phoebe found herself nodding off as she slowly forced down the toast, and when Ethel shooed her upstairs for a lie down 'for the baby', she went meekly.

She felt warmed by the kindness of her two servants and the people in the village.

She lay down on the bed without undressing and didn't wake till someone started hammering downstairs.

Ethel opened the kitchen door to a man whose horse and cart were standing in the stable yard.

'I've come to put the bolts back on the old connecting door. Walter sent me a message. He knows I only come out now for jobs I enjoy doing. I mended that old door once, years ago that was, when Agnes Latimer looked after the house. Beautiful wood that door is, even after all this time. Oak.' He paused, head on one side. 'Aren't you going to let me in, girl?'

Ethel laughed. 'Girl? I'll have you know I'm fifty.'

'You seem like a girl to me. I'm past seventy but I can still do a good day's work, mind.'

She let him in and he nodded to Cook, who clearly knew him.

'Got any cups of tea handy, missus?' he asked.

'You always were a cheeky one, John Mullard,' she said.

'And you always make a good cup of tea.' He turned to Ethel. 'Where are these bolts?'

'Oh dear. I don't know. I'd better go and wake the mistress. She'll know.'

But when Ethel got to the landing, there was a light glowing at the foot of the attic stairs. She stopped, but didn't feel afraid. 'Did you want something?' she asked the ghost.

The light glowed more brightly for a moment or two then began to move up the stairs.

Ethel hesitated, then decided to follow it. She hoped she was right about what it wanted her to do.

In the attic the light drifted across to one corner and she followed it.

The glow shone on a jumble of pieces of black iron with little holes in them here and there. It took her a moment to realise these were the bolts and fittings. 'My goodness! Aren't they big? I'll have to fetch Mr Mullard up to check that these are the right ones and help me carry them down.'

The light began to fade and she felt impelled to call, 'Goodbye. Thank you.'

What next? she wondered as she went downstairs. Had she been talking to thin air, imagining all this, or had a friendly ghost really helped her?

What a strange house this was. But she loved living here. The work kept her mind off what Danny was doing – well, most of the time.

When she woke up, Phoebe lay for a moment trying to remember the details of the vivid dream she'd just had. In it, the war was over and she'd been leaving Greyladies, one arm linked in Corin's, the other waving goodbye to a misty woman's figure standing in the doorway. She had been feeling sad and yet happy at the same time.

Did that mean she was one of the chatelaines who only stayed for a short time at Greyladies? If so, it also meant that Corin would survive the war. Well, she hoped it did.

But perhaps it had only been a dream and she was reading more into it than was meant.

She realised suddenly that someone was hammering loudly downstairs. She tidied herself up and as the noise was still going on, she followed it down the main stairs to the connecting door.

There she found an elderly man she'd seen occasionally in the village. He was hard at work attaching the old bolts. As she watched, he stopped to stroke the wood, then continued to drill out the holes for them. There were holes in the door already, which had been plugged with tiny round pieces of wood. She'd noticed them before and wondered why the bolts had been removed.

Ethel came across to her. 'I hope you don't mind, ma'am, but I found the old bolts in the attic and gave them to Mr Mullard. He said Walter had sent for him, and Cook knows him, so I thought it was all right to let him into the house.'

'Yes, of course. How did you find the bolts?'

After a moment's gaze down at her feet, Ethel explained about following the light up to the attic. 'I don't think I was imagining it.'

'No, I don't either. You've seen Anne Latimer before. She must approve of you.'

She looked across to Mr Mullard. 'We'll all feel safer tonight if we're able to bolt this door.'

'And the bedroom doors,' Ethel said. 'Mr Mullard says he can fit bolts on Cook's bedroom door and check those on our doors, too.'

'Good.'

'Are you hungry now, ma'am?'

'Ravenous.'

'I was just the same with my first. Queasy of a morning, then it'd pass and I'd be hungry.'

Phoebe followed her to the kitchen, feeling that the day might not have started well, but what had come out of it was good. She felt even closer to the people she was living with now.

Chapter Thirteen

Olivia and Babs enjoyed meeting the Wallisdown WI members, and also enjoyed the company of their hostess for a further evening. After their two-night stay, they left Wallisdown and drove to meet Miss Cowley. She was a brusque woman of about seventy, and spoke in the loud tones of a slightly deaf person. She dressed appallingly badly, too, but Olivia and Babs soon realised that behind the thorny exterior was a woman who cared deeply about others. She had found ways to help the poorer women in her village, even though she didn't have much money to spare – as she admitted quite frankly.

'Stay and meet my village ladies,' she boomed at her visitors. 'If I send word round, some of them will come here tonight. We use my front parlour because West Fittonby is too small a village to have its own church hall. Indeed, we only have half a clergyman for our little church.' She laughed heartily at her own joke. 'Because we share a clergyman with another village,' she added.

Forewarned by their previous hostess, they'd stopped to purchase some food on the way. When Miss Cowley asked them what she should buy from the village store for their tea, and wondered whether the baker would have a spare loaf, Babs produced the bag of food from the car.

'Oh, how kind. I don't keep much food in, you see,' the old lady explained. 'Well, there's only me and a daily help. But I *can* offer you a bed for the night.'

'We wouldn't dream of troubling you,' Olivia protested. 'I'm sure we can find somewhere nearby to stay.'

'No trouble. The only things I have plenty of here are bedrooms and furniture. This was my family's home for over a century, but there's only me left now, last of the Wiltshire Cowleys, so there are seven bedrooms standing empty.' She sighed, then jerked into action again to take the food to the kitchen.

That evening they made an excellent tea of ham, pickled vegetables and chutney, with fresh crusty bread, followed by apple pie and clotted cream.

Afterwards, they got ready for the visitors.

One by one, women arrived at the house, greeting the strangers shyly but seeming quite at home with Miss Cowley. They teased her as they set out home-made biscuits and one had brought a bunch of flowers from her garden which she'd dried herself at the end of autumn.

Miss Cowley blinked her eyes rapidly when they were given to her. 'So kind. So very kind. And you do the drying so well, Mrs Wotton. I do miss my flowers in winter.'

'I saw your last lot of dried flowers had fallen to pieces,' her guest said complacently.

They held their usual reading session for an hour or so, and Olivia was touched at how hard they worked to improve their halting words. After that they chatted over tea and biscuits before going home.

As the door closed after the last one, Babs took Miss Cowley's hand and shook it vigorously. 'Congratulations. You're doing an excellent job here.'

Miss Cowley turned bright pink and lost herself in a jumble of broken phrases.

'Now,' Babs said. 'We need to talk to you about founding a Women's Institute in West Fittonby. You're the perfect person to start things going.'

'I've heard of them but I wouldn't know enough to start one, I'm afraid.'

'A lot of people say that. If we gather information and come back with it to help you, will you try?'

Their hostess took a deep breath and said, 'Yes, I'd love to. I like to keep busy. Will it . . . um, be expensive?'

'No. Definitely not. Your main contribution would be to let the women meet in your front parlour. But I believe each member pays the organisation about two shillings per year to cover the costs of postage and other expenses, so you would all have to pay that.'

The worried expression vanished from Miss Cowley's face. 'Oh, that's all right, then. I'd be very happy to let them meet here.'

'Now.' Babs produced three small bars of chocolate and waved them at her companions. 'I think we all deserve a little treat.'

'Chocolate!' whispered their hostess. 'Oh, my. How wonderful!'

In the morning, Miss Cowley gave them instructions for getting to her friend Miss Bowers' house in Challerton.

At the last moment she suggested they visit the abbey

ruins while they were there. 'It was a small foundation, but must have been pretty once, judging by the stonework in the crypt. The abbey itself was destroyed at the orders of Henry VIII during the Dissolution of the Monasteries, but the former guest house wasn't touched and it became the home of Anne Latimer, the former abbess. I'm not boring you, am I? Not everyone enjoys history.'

'No, do go on.'

'Well, the old house is still standing but a new house was built at the front and it's that which has been requisitioned by the War Office. The family still lives at the rear, though I gather Mrs Latimer's husband is in the army at present. She has a key to the crypt and takes people to see it from time to time. She allows Miss Bowers to show people round, too. That's how I was able to see it.'

'We must definitely ask about it, then,' Olivia said.

As they drove away, Babs said feelingly. 'Helping run a Women's Institute is going to make Miss Cowley a very happy woman in her declining years.'

'Poor thing. Reading between the lines, she's short of money and has been very lonely.'

'Well, she didn't sit and weep after her mother died, did she? She started helping other women in the only way she could find. I admire that.'

Miss Bowers heard the sound of a motor car and looked out of the window of her small house. She smiled approvingly as she saw a lady driving the car, which had just pulled to a halt further along the street. Two ladies got out and started looking for house numbers – only there weren't any, because everyone here knew who lived in which house.

Before she could go out to them, they asked a passer-by, who pointed to her house. These must definitely be the two ladies Lady Wimborne had phoned her about. Now, what were their names again? Oh yes. Mrs Horner-Jevons and Mrs Harbury.

If she'd been younger, Miss Bowers would have learnt to drive a car too. The era of motor cars had come too late for her, though, and these days she couldn't have afforded to buy one, as she had to be a bit careful with her money. The old age pension helped a lot, but she was slowly using up her savings.

You were never too old to dream, though.

The knocker sounded and she went to open the front door. 'Mrs Horner-Jevons and Mrs Harbury? I guessed who you were. Do come in.' Then she looked along to where the car was parked. 'No, wait. I think your car might be safer if you put it in front of my house.'

They looked at her in surprise.

'We have a newcomer to the village who is causing trouble. If he knows you're visiting me and then going on to Greyladies, I wouldn't put it past him to damage your car if you leave it outside his house.'

'Goodness me. How terrible!'

'You must have noticed his untidy garden. He lost a leg in the war and does nothing to keep his home nice. Indeed, I don't know what he does do with himself all day except complain and shout at his wife. You can hear him yelling at her from the street. I pity that poor woman.'

Babs went to move the car, after which Miss Bowers took them into a small parlour crowded with bookcases. 'My besetting sin is books, and now that I've retired I spend a lot of time reading. But you didn't come here to talk about me. Do sit down, please.'

They sat on the comfortable sofa indicated by their smiling hostess, feeling truly welcome.

'Let me put the kettle on the hob, then you can tell me about these Women's Institutes. They're not something I've come across before.' She bustled out again.

Olivia couldn't resist reading the book titles in the nearest bookcase and smiled when she realised Babs was doing the same thing with some at the other side of the small room.

Then their hostess came back and soon they were telling her about the new Women's Institute movement. With two short interruptions for her to finish making and serve the pot of tea, they went through some of the activities that were going on all over the country to found institutes.

'That sounds to be a wonderful thing for rural women!' Miss Bowers said.

'Some urban women too,' Babs amended.

When Miss Bowers had finished asking questions, she fell silent for a few moments, looking thoughtful. 'I wonder . . . do you have time to come and tell Mrs Latimer about it? She lives at Greyladies, the big house for this village, and she manages a family trust fund set up to help women in need. I'm sure that if you helped us, she and I could set up an institute in Challerton.'

'We'd be happy to do that, but will she have time to see us today? She might be busy, and I have to get back to London tomorrow,' Babs said.

'Unfortunately, someone is threatening Mrs Latimer's safety, because of the Germans interned in part of her house.' Miss Bowers lowered her voice unnecessarily, 'Possibly that dreadful man two doors along. As her husband is away serving in the war, she daren't go out and about as she used to until we find a way to catch the villain in the act.'

They made appropriate sounds of disapproval.

'When you've finished your tea, we'll walk across to Greyladies and see if she's at home. It's not far. No, no. What am I thinking of? We should go in your car to keep it safe.'

Miss Bowers asked Babs to stop the car just inside some large iron gates. The gravel drive had deep wheel ruts in it from some heavy vehicles. She indicated a large house at the far end. 'I thought you'd like to look at Greyladies. This is the best view of the front part.'

They could hear the pride in her voice and obediently studied the house. It was built of grey stone with steep roofs tiled by large slabs of another sort of grey stone. Several gables lent it character.

Olivia's breath caught in her throat. 'It's beautiful.' There was something about it, something almost magic. How lucky the people were who lived here!

'The front part has been requisitioned by the government as a convalescent home for German and Austrian internees. Fortunately, the family have been allowed to stay in the rear part, which was the original house.'

'Miss Cowley mentioned something about that.'

'We who have grown up in Challerton are very proud of Greyladies. I myself have written a small book about its history.'

A truck with two soldiers sitting in the open back tooted its horn and Babs pulled the car further to the side to let it pass.

'Such a pity they have to be here.' Miss Bowers shook her head in disapproval, then indicated the way to the rear of the house.

The old part was even more beautiful and picturesque

than the front and Olivia felt so moved by the sight of it she couldn't speak. It was as if she'd come home.

Their guide got nimbly out of the car and knocked on a door at the rear. They got out to join her.

'Miss Bowers, how lovely to see you!' The lady who had opened it had reddish hair, and was possibly in the family way. She had a sweet expression and seemed fond of her visitor, giving her a hug rather than shaking hands.

'Phoebe, my dear, I knew you'd be at home today, so I've taken the liberty of bringing some visitors to meet you.' She made the introductions.

Phoebe smiled at them. 'I'm so glad to meet you. I was feeling like a long walk and I know I mustn't go out alone till this trouble is sorted out. So frustrating! You couldn't have come at a better time to cheer me up.'

'Could I ask what sort of trouble?' Babs inquired.

Their hostess explained briefly about the various attacks and break-ins at Greyladies. 'But you didn't come here to talk about my troubles. Let me ring for Ethel and get her to bring us a tea tray.'

'Perhaps we could do that later? We've just had some tea,' Miss Bowers said tactfully.

Olivia hadn't said a word since she'd come into the house, she felt struck dumb by its beauty. Something seemed to be tugging at her, urging her to explore and the words were out before she could stop them. 'May I look round this room, Mrs Latimer? It's such a beautiful old place. I take it this was the old hall.'

To their surprise, she stood up without waiting for permission and began to walk towards the narrow, old-fashioned staircase that led to the minstrel's gallery.

Before anyone could speak, Phoebe gasped and whispered, 'Oh! She's the one! Miss Bowers, she's going to be the next lady.' She clapped her hand to her mouth and watched her guest, who was moving slowly, like someone in a dream.

'My goodness!' Miss Bowers looked from Phoebe to the guest, who was now at the other end of the large room. Like her hostess, like all the true Latimers, their visitor was a redhead, but Phoebe had foxy-coloured hair while Olivia's was a rich red in shade. And when you looked closely, there was a resemblance, too, something about the eyes and cheekbones, the straight nose.

Babs opened her mouth to speak and Miss Bowers made a quick shushing sound, putting one finger to her lips.

They watched Olivia stop at the foot of the stairs and stare up them as if she could see something. Unfortunately the ornately carved woodwork of the banisters and landing rail hid whatever it was from the others' view.

But then a light began to shine in the minstrel's gallery itself, and they could see that. It gradually grew brighter till it lit up the whole of the gallery.

Miss Bowers reached out and took Phoebe's hand, holding it, offering unspoken comfort as they watched the scene play out. She knew that this was a poignant moment for her young friend.

Olivia stared at the shaft of soft golden light pulsating gently in the gallery above her. It was only a couple of paces away from the top step. She knew she shouldn't wander around someone else's house but she was drawn to that light, so strongly attracted that she didn't even try to resist its pull.

She couldn't speak . . . couldn't turn away . . . just had

to go up to it, knowing instinctively there was nothing to be afraid of.

She set one foot on the lowest step and walked steadily up them, moving ever closer to the beautiful radiance.

Just before the top step, she paused and watched the light shimmer and form itself into the figure of a woman in old-fashioned clothing – late Tudor garments, if she remembered her history correctly. The figure slowly gained form and colour, now appearing as solid as herself.

The apparition was dressed in grey robes, with a white chemise showing above her bodice and white undersleeves, gathered at the wrist with the resulting frill edged in narrow lace. She had a half-moon headdress of grey velvet on her russet hair, from which a veil hung down her back.

Olivia suddenly realised the significance of the grey clothing. Of course! The house was called Greyladies. Was this . . . could it possibly be the ghost of one of the original occupants, a former grey nun?

She'd sensed ghosts before. All her family did. But she'd never seen one so clearly. She wasn't afraid, couldn't possibly be afraid of a woman with such a kindly expression.

The lady held the folds of her skirt in slender, elegant hands as she dipped into a sweeping curtsey to Olivia, who managed an awkward bob in return.

The ghost spoke then, in a soft, melodious voice, the words echoing slightly as if coming from a great distance. 'Welcome to Greyladies, my dear Olivia. One day, quite soon, you will live here as chatelaine. And you will be very happy here.'

'I will?'

'You loved this house at first sight, I could tell. We who look after it all do.'

'Yes, I did. I think it's not only beautiful but welcoming.'

Olivia still felt no fear. How could she when the ghost's eyes shone with love? She had never seen that emotion show so clearly in anyone before.

'I will come back to help you whenever I can,' Anne Latimer said. 'I can help . . . sometimes . . .'

The light began to fade and with it the figure until only a few drifts of bright sparks remained, winking out one by one.

Olivia wished the ghost had stayed because Anne had brought a serenity with her, a serenity that had been lacking in Olivia's life since Charles's death.

It took her a while to realise where she was. How shocking! She'd come into a stranger's house and ignored her hostess to walk up the stairs and speak to a ghost.

But anyone who lived in this house must surely have seen the Tudor lady as well. She was such a vivid apparition.

With a sigh, Olivia turned and went back down the stairs, to where her hostess was waiting for her. She was still finding it difficult to speak coherently because her mind was full of the wonder of what had just happened, but she ought at least to try to apologise.

Another gentle voice spoke to her and when she gathered her wandering wits, she found that Mrs Latimer had come across to her, leaving the other two women standing further away.

'Are you all right, Mrs Harbury?'

'Yes. Thank you. I'm sorry if I seemed . . . rude.'

'No. You were doing what was necessary.'

'Necessary?'

'It happens with us all.'

That was puzzling and Olivia had so many questions

she didn't know what to ask first. 'Who was the lady?' she managed at last.

'She was and still is, I suppose, Anne Latimer, the founder of the Latimer family who built and still own this house. She always appears to greet the women who are going to live here as chatelaines. It happens when they first visit Greyladies. That's how we recognise them. And sometimes she appears to warn us of danger or to comfort us as best she can.'

Olivia stared at her, amazed at what she was saying. 'Me, live here?'

'Yes. And if Anne appeared to you, that means you and I must be related. Do you have any Latimers among your ancestors?'

'Well, yes. It was my maternal grandmother's maiden name.'

'Ah. Then you and I are distant cousins, as I'd guessed. Come and sit down and we'll talk. You must be feeling a little disoriented still.'

'I am. More than a little. But I knew she was real, I just knew it.'

'Of course she is.'

'She has the most wonderfully kind eyes.'

'I think so too. She must have been a strong woman to save the family legacy in such troubled times. I'll tell you her full story one day. Here. Take this chair.'

Miss Bowers was smiling gently at her from a sofa and Babs was sitting next to the old lady, looking ready to burst with curiosity. Olivia sank down on the chair, unable even to raise the energy to reassure her friend that she was all right.

Mrs Latimer rang the bell and asked the maid to bring them a tea tray, then told the two visitors a little more about Anne Latimer.

'But what exactly does her appearance *mean*?' Babs asked.

'That Olivia will one day become chatelaine of Greyladies and I will leave. We Latimers only hold the house in trust. We can't sell it or leave it to someone else. It passes down the female line, but *we* don't choose to whom. Either Anne chooses her successor or fate brings the right person here. Who knows how that happens?'

'Aren't you upset about it, Mrs Latimer?' Olivia asked. 'If it means I'm going to take over this beautiful house, that will mean you leaving. How can you bear to do that?'

'Do call me Phoebe and I'll call you Olivia, shall I? And to answer your question, no, I'm not upset – well, only a little. I do love this house and shall be sad to leave it, but as soon as I became pregnant, I began to feel . . . distanced from Greyladies, less of a Latimer chatelaine somehow, more Corin's wife.'

'What will your husband say?'

'Corin agreed to give up his own family home, which he loves dearly, to marry me and live here. He even changed his name to Latimer. It's my guess that when the war ends and he leaves the army, we'll both move into his home, because it's what fate intended.'

'Good heavens!' Babs said. 'I've never believed in ghosts before. Only, well, I saw the light and I couldn't think where it came from.' She stared at the others. 'I can tell that you all believe in ghosts.'

Miss Bowers smiled. 'That's because we've all seen Anne Latimer.'

'I've seen other ghosts as well,' Olivia admitted. 'Only I don't tell people about that because they'll think I'm mad. My husband came to say goodbye to me after he was killed.

I've heard his voice several times since then, and I'm quite sure it wasn't my imagination. But his voice is fading now, growing fainter each time I hear it.'

'As is only right,' Miss Bowers told her gently. 'He's allowing you to make a new life and he is moving on, too.'

Olivia saw Babs shake her head in bafflement but she wasn't in the mood to argue with her friend. She needed time to think about it.

'Can you both stay here for a day or two?' Phoebe asked Olivia. 'I think you should get to know Greyladies and we have plenty of room.'

Olivia turned to look at Babs.

'I can't, I'm afraid. I have to get back to London.' Then Babs brightened. 'But you can stay, Olivia, and I can send Alex down to pick you up whenever you're ready. He'll be quite happy to do that.'

'I said no matchmaking!' Olivia snapped, but when Babs pulled a cheeky face at her, she stopped scowling. 'Oh well, I do enjoy his company, so I don't mind too much.'

She turned back to Phoebe. 'I'd be happy to stay for a while, then. If that's what you really want.'

'I do. It's good to have time to hand over the house, and there is a trust to deal with as well, so we'll need to introduce you to the family lawyer.'

'I think,' Babs said suddenly, 'I'll set off for London this afternoon, if you don't mind. You'll be able to tell our new friends more about Women's Institutes, Olivia, and I can start making some practical arrangements to help found them. Well, if you're still interested in spreading the word, that is.' She paused, head on one side, waiting.

Olivia didn't hesitate. 'Of course I'm still interested. It

seems I'll not be taking over Greyladies yet.'

Babs outlined the present situation of the WI movement to the other two. 'The Committee is thinking of employing Voluntary County Organisers, but you know how long committees take to arrange anything. I shall pay your expenses in the meantime, Olivia, to help you make a start in Wiltshire. No, I insist. You're not rich and I'm comfortably circumstanced. But you must sell your husband's car and buy one you can drive, because you'll need to travel around.'

Since she was aware that Babs was more than 'comfortably circumstanced' and indeed, had more money than she knew what to do with, Olivia didn't protest. 'Very well.'

'It'll work out quite nicely, I'm sure. Unfortunately I can't become a Voluntary County Organiser myself, because I still have other duties in connection with the war.'

'Do you think I'm doing the right thing staying here?'

'Only you can tell that.'

Olivia glanced over her shoulder, looking across the huge room to the minstrels' gallery. 'I think it's already been decided for me.'

'Won't you find life in a village rather quiet?'

'I've discovered that I enjoy village life. Though not when I'm forced to live with my cousin Donald. I even enjoyed working in the village shop. That experience will help me understand the women we want to attract to the WIs. And I do need something different to do with my life until . . .' She shrugged and glanced at Phoebe.

'Until you take over here,' her hostess said with a smile.

'And Alex?' Babs prompted. 'What about him?'

'Stop bringing him into this.'

'Well, it's obvious that the two of you are attracted. Anyone can see that.'

'If anything happens between us, it'll happen without your help. He and I are both quite capable of working out how to manage our lives. Besides, I don't have to rush into anything. The ghost said the changeover wouldn't happen quite yet. So I can carry on with the work on WIs, see if I can help a few get started, see if that feels worthwhile.'

Babs smiled at her. 'I'll leave you to it, then. I'd better set off for London. I don't want to be driving after dark.'

She said goodbye to Phoebe and Miss Bowers. 'Don't bother to come out with us. Olivia can get her suitcase then I'll be on my way.'

As Olivia stepped away from the car, Babs said urgently, 'If you need help, any sort of help, don't hesitate to phone me.'

'I won't.'

'Will you be going back to your own home after you leave here?'

'I don't know.' She didn't even like the thought of leaving Greyladies.

Olivia waved goodbye to her then frowned. She felt suddenly uneasy, as if someone was watching her, sending waves of hatred her way, not from the house but from the side of the gardens nearest the village.

How silly could you get?

She turned resolutely to face her future and once she was inside the house, the strange feeling faded and joy filled her again.

Chapter Fourteen

Sidney Hatterson sat in his usual armchair and watched the car stop outside his house, wondering who it could be. Then two ladies got out, spoke to a passer-by and went to the old hag's cottage. Soon afterwards the driver came back and moved the car, so Sidney knew the visitors must be more damned Hun-lovers, like the old hag.

He'd taken a dislike to Miss Bowers the minute he saw her and avoided speaking to her. People might say she was a kind old lady, but he didn't agree at all. How dare she look at him as if he was a naughty boy? Typical schoolmistress. She'd probably caned her pupils as hard as his teacher had caned him.

It made him even angrier that a woman had been driving the car. Women shouldn't be driving vehicles at all. They weren't capable of doing it properly, weren't safe on the roads. Look how she'd parked it the first time! Nowhere near Miss Bloody Bowers' cottage.

He kept watching. Well, what else had he to do with himself with only one leg?

Then all three women came out and got into the car.

Out of sheer curiosity he slipped out of the back door and went down the narrow lane between the cottages to a slight rise from which he could see which direction they'd taken.

They left the village and went towards the only house on that road – Greyladies. He should have guessed they'd be going there. That Latimer woman was another who needed teaching a lesson, a female who'd let Huns live in her house. He couldn't bear to see the same villains who'd shot off his leg walking freely round his village.

Ha! They weren't walking about at the moment, were they? He and his friends had put a stop to that, made them afraid to poke their snouts outside the trough.

He wished the women had left their car outside the hag's house and walked to Greyladies, as Miss Bowers usually did. If they'd done that, he'd have given the driver something to think about. He fingered his penknife regretfully. He could have ruined one of her tyres easily. Just bend down as if to pick something up and give it a couple of slashes. That'd have shown her she couldn't look after a car, let alone drive one properly.

The Pocock family, who ran the village store, were sharp-eyed and would notice if he walked openly towards the big house. And there were always females in the village church, fiddling around with flowers or pretending to be useful. So he had to stay out of sight of that, too. He didn't let *his* wife waste her time on that sort of thing. She had enough to do at home.

He walked in another direction and once he was out of sight, he took a little-used footpath across the fields to the ruins of the old abbey. He didn't like it there. The place made him shiver. But cutting across the back was a useful way to get out of the village to Greyladies without being seen, so he ignored his discomfort.

As he walked past the entrance to the crypt, with its wrought iron gates, he scowled at the big lock on the door. If it was part of a church, it should be open to everyone. He stopped on a sudden thought. He had an old padlock, might be able to use it here to cause them more trouble.

Then he heard sounds, and from behind a tree he watched the two women come out to the car.

It was damned cold, but he lingered to watch. You had to know what your enemy was doing.

The chubby woman got into the car. The other one, the skinny redhead, took a suitcase out of the vehicle, waved goodbye and went back into the big house with it.

So she was staying, was she? Well, she'd regret that decision when she got caught up in the next stage of his plan.

He grinned at the thought. He and his friends were going to deal with that whole bunch of traitors and enemies. He might not be able to fight for England now, but he could still kill England's enemies. Oh yes.

When he went home, he would find the old padlock and put it into his overcoat pocket, just in case.

In London Alex sighed and looked at his pocket watch. Seven o'clock. He should have gone home an hour ago, but who would know whether he was there or not?

Since his staff left for the day, he'd been wandering around his shop like a moonstruck idiot, wondering how Olivia was getting on, feeling as if something unpleasant was happening to her. Strange, that, but then he'd always had a vivid imagination and sometimes the things he pictured in his mind actually happened.

It ran in his family. He'd been sternly warned as a child not to tell people about that, because they'd think him mad. As an adult he'd seen the sense of that and continued to keep his hunches to himself.

It surprised him how much he missed Olivia, when he'd only met her a few times. But he did miss her . . . very much.

Just as he was about to leave for home, the telephone in his office rang. He hesitated, decided not to pick it up, then curiosity got the better of him and he rushed to snatch the receiver off the hook, nearly sending the stand off the edge of his desk as he did so. You had to wonder whether there might not be some better design of telephone apparatus than this glorified candlestick.

He leant forward to speak into the mouthpiece at the top of the stand. 'Seaton Antiques.'

'Babs here, Alex. Look, I've just got back from our trip to the country and I've a few things to tell you. Also, Olivia is going to need picking up from Wiltshire in a day or two, so of course I thought of you. If you're free, that is. If you're interested . . .'

'You're a meddling woman, Babs, as I've told you many times. But if your meddling gives me a genuine reason to spend time with Olivia, go ahead and meddle any time. Of course I'll pick her up.'

'You've fallen for her, haven't you?'

'Yes. But I'm not going to discuss that any further with you. It's between her and me.'

'That's what she says, too. But I'll need to tell you about where she's staying and what she's going to be doing there, and it's quite complicated, so why don't you come to supper at my house tonight? It won't be a fancy affair, so don't get dressed up. You and I will have a simple meal and a chat. I didn't want to come to your shop tomorrow, because we can get interrupted there. How about eight o'clock?'

'I haven't eaten yet so that would be delightful. I'll come to you instead of going home.'

He hung the receiver up, pleased at the prospect of company tonight. It would be easy enough to leave his business for a few days and drive Olivia anywhere she needed. He'd been lucky and found some very capable employees who could be trusted to keep things going as he'd have wished. He didn't believe in breathing down people's necks and checking their every action and none of his staff had abused his trust. On the contrary. They surprised him sometimes.

He drove to Babs's house and was shown straight into her personal sitting room where a small table in one corner was set for two.

Babs bounced over to greet him in her usual ebullient way and asked the maid to have the food sent in as soon as it was ready. 'I hope you don't mind eating straight away, Alex dear, but I'm ravenous.'

'I'm hungry too.' He hadn't been till he got her call.

'Let's sit at the table. I don't think the food will be long.'

He seated her and took his own place. 'Tell me how your trip went.'

'Oh, it was excellent.' She launched into a tale of all their doings, making him smile. Then, after their soup had been taken away and the main course brought in, she looked at him more seriously. 'But what you really want to know is what has happened to Olivia.'

'Yes.'

'I'll just have a few mouthfuls of this, then I'll tell you.'

He barely touched his own food as he listened to her. When it came to the scene with the ghost he could hardly breathe, he was so enmeshed in what she was saying. It was almost as if he could see it for himself.

'She wasn't afraid of this ghost?'

'No. Apparently, it's a very benign spirit. Even I saw the light, such a soft, beautiful glow. And now Olivia is staying at Greyladies for a few days to get to know the place and, well, it sounds as if she'll be living there one day. If it's all right with you, she'll phone you when she wants to leave. Unless you're too busy . . . ?'

'You know I'm not. I'll never be too busy to help her.'

'I wanted to explain and give you time to think about it – you know, about how you and Olivia could manage lives so far apart.'

He surprised himself. 'I'd sell my business in an instant, if necessary, to be with her.'

'You *are* badly smitten.'

'Yes. But she's still grieving so I have to be patient.'

'I think this new turn of events has jerked her out of her mourning. She said herself that her husband's voice is getting fainter in her head.'

Alex hoped she was right. He changed the subject. 'You were talking about setting up Women's Institutes. If I can help in any way with that, money or time or whatever, I'd be happy to do so, Babs, and not just because of how I feel about Olivia. I see women all the time who are downtrodden, hardly allowed to breathe for themselves, let alone think. And then I meet women like you who are busy and fulfilled. It doesn't seem fair.'

'Most men don't care about the details of women's lives.'

'Perhaps I have some fellow feeling. I've always suffered from being the family weakling. People used to treat me as if my brain was affected as well as my body, my mother always spoke about me as "poor Alexander" when I was little and left me almost completely in the hands of my nursemaid. As I grew older and looked like surviving, my father tried to dictate everything I did. He'd have kept check on how I breathed in and out if he could.'

'More fools they!'

'Yes. But I'm financially independent now, in spite of everything, and have been able to manage my life as I please for many years.'

'You're one of the shrewdest businessmen I know.'

They finished the meal, chatting amicably about mutual friends and the latest developments in the war. He left around ten, seeing how tired Babs was.

He would now have to wait till Olivia telephoned him to say she was ready to be picked up. That couldn't happen too soon.

After Babs had left Greyladies, Miss Bowers soon followed. 'I need a rest in the afternoons now. So annoying when a body grows older and weaker, and a mind still thinks it's young.'

'Just a minute.' Phoebe rang for Ethel. 'Could you please walk back with Miss Bowers? We don't want any more incidents and she can't run away as you or I could.'

Miss Bowers scowled at that. She hated needing to use a walking stick.

'And then, when you get back, Ethel, could you please

prepare a bedroom for Mrs Harbury. She's a distant cousin of mine and will be staying here for a few days.'

'Yes, ma'am.'

After Miss Bowers had left, Phoebe turned to her guest. 'Would you like me to show you round the older part of Greyladies now or do you want to rest?'

'I'd love to see more.'

'Unfortunately, the War Office has requisitioned the front part, though I'm sure the commandant, Captain Turner, will let me show you round the downstairs rooms. The internees are a very pleasant group of people, mainly elderly gentlemen, but a few women live here as well. My former employers, the Steins, are among them.'

'How strange that they've ended up interned here!'

'Yes. But it was a piece of good luck for the house. Mrs Stein is enjoying herself, mending and altering curtains. She says if I buy her a sewing machine and find some material, she'll make new ones where needed. These particular Germans are *not* our enemies, I promise you.'

'I've witnessed the odd act of violence against Germans, some of whom have been living in this country for decades. I detest that. You don't need to worry. I'm not likely to be rude to the internees.'

'Good. So let's do a quick tour, then you can wander round on your own at will.'

'I'd love that. Oh, and Miss Cowley said I should visit the crypt. Would that be possible one day?' Olivia looked round with a smile. 'You know, I feel very much at home here already.'

'I was the same when I first came into the house. As for the crypt, of course I'll show it to you. It's a very peaceful place, with some lovely stonework, but we keep the entrance barred, because we don't want anything damaged. There's a passage from the crypt into the cellars. There are one or two surprises like that in the house. I'll show you them gradually. It'd be too much to take in all at once.'

'How fascinating! I'm honoured that you trust me enough to tell me these secrets.'

Phoebe laughed gently. 'The grey lady has chosen you. She always knows. And how could I not trust the next chatelaine who will be caring for this house after me? Now, let's start with the ground floor.'

There was a knock on the door and Ethel poked her head round it. 'I took Miss Bowers back. That Hatterson is keeping watch on this house again. I saw him hiding near the crypt and thought I should warn you.'

'Oh dear! I have such a bad feeling whenever I think of him.'

'Miss Bowers seems to distrust him, too,' Olivia said. 'She warned us not to leave the car where he could get at it. Is he really that bad?'

'I must admit I don't like him. I'll be interested to see what you say after you've met him.' She shuddered. 'And *he* makes no bones about wanting "the Huns", as he calls them, to leave Greyladies. I think he'd kill them if he could.'

Olivia was shocked. There was going to be a lot to think about and learn here. But oh, she loved the old house already.

Phoebe left Olivia to explore the attics on her own the following day, because she'd been asked to speak to Joe's mother, who was worried about him. Joe came to fetch her in the pony trap, looking sulky. Usually he chatted as they drove out to the farm but today he was silent.

'You're very quiet. Have I done something to upset you?' Phoebe asked as the silence continued.

He shrugged. 'No. Sorry. It's Mum. She's going on at me because I want to join the air force. I think I can do that earlier than I'd get called up for the army, if she and Dad will only give me permission.'

'Well, you can't blame her. There are still a few months to go before you'll be called up, aren't there?'

'Yes, but she's got it wrong about the air force. She says I'll be flying planes before you know it and get killed. Pilots don't live all that long, compared to others.'

'I know. They're very brave men.'

He reined in the pony and looked at her earnestly. 'I don't want to fly planes; I want to work on the engines. I'm good with machinery.'

'Have you told her that?'

'I've told her again and again, but she says they won't listen to me and they'll have me flying before you can say Jack Robinson, and then I'll be killed.'

'She must love you very much.'

They arrived just then and Joe made a chirruping noise to the pony, which obediently came to a halt in front of the door. He jumped down and came round to help Phoebe down from the trap. 'Will you help me convince her?'

'I'll see what your mother says first.'

But it was just as Joe had said. His mother was determined to keep him out of the military forces as long as possible, and she wept so piteously as she talked to Phoebe, that it was impossible to discuss it with the poor woman logically.

As Joe was driving her back, he sighed. 'No need to tell

me, Mrs Latimer. I know what she said to you. Same as she says to me. Every day, she says it. Stay out till you have to go in.'

His expression was so stubborn, Phoebe was sure he'd get his way in the end. Or even forge the necessary signatures, as many lads did.

'I'm not going to work on the farm, anyway,' he added suddenly. 'It's machinery I love, not cows. Dad thinks I'll change, but I won't. My younger brother can have it.'

After that he kept silent and soon was dropping her off at Greyladies.

As she walked inside, she thought of the many young men who had gone off to war eagerly in the early days – looking forward to travel and seeing a bit of the world and expecting to be home again in a few months' time.

She had seen them come back looking years older or suffering from bad injuries, and some had not come back at all.

They were calling it the Great War. It ought to be called the dreadful war, the worst there had ever been, she was sure. Casualties were high and most young men weren't as eager to enlist nowadays. But some, like Joe, still saw it as a way to build a more interesting future than their fathers had, a way to escape their mundane lives.

And who was to say Joe was wrong? He was an intelligent lad and very determined.

She prayed he and the other lads from round here would survive.

When she got back, Phoebe felt restless. After their midday meal she suggested showing Olivia the crypt, and they both put on their winter coats and wrapped scarves round their heads to cross the garden, because a chilly wind was howling through the village today and the crypt would be cold.

Phoebe unlocked the metal grille with a huge old key. The metalwork was beautiful and Olivia stopped for a moment to admire it.

When they went inside, Phoebe locked the metal grille carefully behind them. She saw Olivia's surprise. 'We don't want anyone following us inside, do we?' she said.

'I suppose not.'

They went down a short corridor to one side and that took them out of the icy wind, at least. The light was dimmer here, so Phoebe lit two of the candles standing ready in candlesticks on a stone shelf. There was now enough light to see clearly the stonework near the door and the two stone box tombs in the middle, each marked by a woman's name, age and the words *Sister in God*.

'They were two of the first group of nuns,' Phoebe said. 'No others were ever buried here. I think the abbey was destroyed before anyone else could grow old enough to die.'

'Isn't Anne Latimer's tomb in here?' Olivia asked, lifting her own candle high and staring round.

'No, she's buried in the village church, under the floor halfway down the right-hand side as you go in, and her husband with her. Women sometimes sit in the pew next to her grave to pray for all sorts of things. They say they feel as if someone is listening.

'One woman was distraught and spent the night weeping there after her husband was killed. She swears that as dawn was breaking she felt a hand on her shoulder, and it comforted her as nothing else had. She said she heard a voice, too, and Anne told her she'd find love again. You can choose whether to believe that or not.'

'I saw Anne Latimer, remember. I can picture her comforting someone in such distress. What's the woman doing now?'

'She did find love and is married again, to a former soldier who'd been discharged after a leg injury. He limps badly but as he has a job in an office, that doesn't matter. They live in Swindon.'

'It's a lovely story.'

'Now, we should—'

There was the sound of something metallic clicking loudly and a man called in a high, false voice, 'Get out of that, if you can, you rotten bitches!'

'He might have disguised his voice,' Phoebe said, 'but that's Hatterson. He has an unusual way of pronouncing the letter R. Let's go and see what he's done now.'

They went back to the entrance, checking that he was no longer there before they examined the door.

There was another big padlock and chain on the door, so it was now double-locked.

Olivia looked at her companion in shock. 'We're trapped.'

'No. We can go through the hidden tunnel to the cellar, then send someone to saw off the padlock. Surely Hatterson knows there's a secret passage? Most of the people in the village do.'

'Perhaps he doesn't talk to them – or they don't talk to him.'

'Could be. This is a nuisance and we shall get dirty in the passage, but that's all. Before we leave, I'll show you the little shrine. It's such a pretty one.'

Olivia admired the little carved stone figures. When her new-found cousin bowed her head in prayer, she guessed Phoebe was praying for the safety of her husband and waited quietly for her to finish.

'We get out this way,' Phoebe said. She twisted a stone rose and there was a grating sound as a hole opened to one side of the shrine. 'The passage is a bit cramped at times, but at least we won't have to crawl. Are you all right about enclosed spaces?'

'Yes. I don't like being shut in but I won't panic, I promise you.'

The two women edged inside the hole, still carrying their candles.

'The first time I came this way, I was escaping a madman and I had no light,' Phoebe said. 'I just had to trust that Anne really had shown me a way out.'

'You were very brave.'

'Sometimes you do what you have to and it doesn't occur to you that you're being brave at the time. Anyway, let me close the panel and we'll start moving.'

Olivia didn't like the feeling of being shut in by the heavy stone panel, but she controlled her fear, trusting her companion to lead her out through the tunnel.

Hatterson waited outside, and sure enough, he saw the two women discover the padlock. He grinned, waiting for them to panic and start screaming for help.

The padlock he'd brought might be old but it was a strong one and would have to be sawn off. He was glad he'd thought of this possibility and been ready for it. He'd been lucky today; he had come out for a walk and so seen them.

He loved making trouble for rich sods who didn't appreciate how lucky they were. Making big trouble would have been better, but you couldn't always do something big, so in the meantime you could annoy them in smaller ways.

But these women didn't panic, damn them. The one who owned the big house said something quietly to her companion and they vanished inside the crypt again.

They'd have to come and yell for help eventually and he'd enjoy listening to that, so he waited, keeping his ears open for anyone else approaching this area. It was damned cold today and he wished he'd dressed more warmly.

After a while he began to wonder whether he should go home and leave them to it. Someone would find them eventually, he was sure . . . unfortunately. And he didn't want anyone to find him here as well.

So violently was he shivering by then that he nearly missed the sound of people approaching. Cursing his damned artificial leg, he limped away as quickly as he could, crouching awkwardly behind some of the low ruined walls from the old abbey just in time to see two soldiers turn up.

They examined the padlock then started searching nearby, so he slipped away as fast as he could, wincing as his stump protested against the speed with which he was forcing his artificial leg to move.

The two women must have got out of the crypt and sent the soldiers after him.

How the hell had they escaped?

It took only a moment or two's thought for him to realise there must be another entrance. He'd walked round the area under which the crypt lay during the day and seen nothing. Perhaps there was an underground passage from inside it, linking it to the house? Yes, that would be it. Why had no one in the village told him about that? Miserable sods. Most of them didn't even bother to say good morning to him.

What a waste of a day's effort!

Well, the big operation was nearly planned out now, and the others were ready to act. These rich snobs were about to get a shock. He wasn't the only one who didn't want Huns being housed in luxury. He didn't want Huns in England at all.

It was his patriotic duty to deal with the enemies on the home front.

Chapter Fifteen

After two days of her newly discovered cousin's company, Olivia felt she had made a good friend as well as found a relative. But she could see that Phoebe was looking a little tired and wondered if she was trying to do too much in her condition.

'I think I'd better leave you for a while,' she said that evening. 'You need to rest more and I need to make a start on gathering together the information for the WIs and planning my talks.'

'Perhaps a quiet day or two would be good for me,' Phoebe agreed. 'I get tired much more easily at the moment.' She looked down at her stomach and grimaced. 'It seems to be growing more quickly than I'd expected.'

'What do you want, a boy or a girl?'

'Either. Just a healthy child.' She patted her stomach fondly, then smiled at her companion. 'Not that I haven't enjoyed your company, because I have, and you must certainly come back soon for another visit. Or if you're working nearby, you could stay here overnight any time. Don't hesitate.'

'I'd like that.'

'Why don't you telephone your friend and ask him if tomorrow would be convenient for him to pick you up?'

Olivia hesitated to call Alex, waiting for her husband's voice to echo in her mind, as it sometimes did when she was doubtful about doing something. But that jolly voice had been quiet the whole time she'd been at Greyladies and she was beginning to wonder if she'd ever again hear it echoing so clearly in her mind. 'Very well. May I use your telephone?'

'Of course.'

She lifted up the earpiece and listened for the operator's voice.

'Exchange and number, please.'

She told the woman the details Alex had given her and waited. Within a couple of minutes they had been connected and she heard his voice. It sounded a bit tinny and echoed slightly, but no man she'd ever met had a deep, soft voice as beautiful as his. She'd recognise it anywhere.

'Alex, it's me, Olivia.'

'How lovely to hear from you! Are you all right?'

'I'm fine. Did Babs tell you what happened to me?'

'Yes. That must have been a big shock, however pleasant.'

'It was.' She hesitated. It wasn't a small favour to ask.

He said it for her. 'Babs told me you'd need picking up, since there isn't a railway station in Challerton.'

'Is that convenient?'

'It will always be convenient to fetch you, Olivia. You know that.'

There was a silence, then she said quietly, 'Yes, I do know it. Thank you, Alex. I appreciate your helpfulness.'

She felt as if some other message had passed between them, words of encouragement from her, even. She knew something inside her had changed greatly during the few days she'd been at Greyladies. Could a house do that to you?

She realised she was wasting the phone call and he was politely waiting for her to continue. 'Can you come for me tomorrow?'

'Oh, yes. I'd set off right now, if you needed me.'

She chuckled. 'I think I can allow you to sleep in peace tonight. Phoebe, who turns out to be a distant cousin of mine, has invited you to take luncheon here before we leave.'

'That will be a pleasure. I'll arrive about twelve o'clock, shall I?'

'Yes. You'll need to drive round to the back of the house. The front part has been requisitioned.'

'Yes, Babs told me.'

'Well . . . Goodbye for now, then.'

She hung up the earpiece, thus cutting the connection, and smiled at her own face in a nearby mirror. Or was she smiling at the thought of Alex?

She was looking forward more than she'd expected to seeing him. She waited, expecting to feel guilty about that. But she didn't.

'Forgive me, Charles,' she murmured and thought she heard him laughing gently.

Nothing to forgive, old girl. Be happy.

Something told her it'd be the last time she heard him in her mind.

When he put down the telephone, Alex smiled and didn't move for a few minutes, going over their brief conversation two or three times. Olivia had asked his for help and had sounded glad to speak to him. Was he wrong to think that promising?

At length he realised he'd been sitting there for a while,

smiling like a fool, so went to find his assistant and ask him to take over the shop. Then he tried to get on with the rest of his day's work. But he had no valuations to go out to that day, or even that week, a rare lull in that sort of business, and he couldn't concentrate on paperwork or even on designing a new display of some rather beautiful Georgian furniture he'd acquired recently.

For once he went home early, stopping on the way at a pie shop he patronised when he didn't want the bother of preparing an evening meal.

People kept telling him he ought to find himself a cook–housekeeper, but he didn't want anyone in the house when he got home. And he wasn't a hearty eater, anyway. He had a system for running the house: he left messages for his daily help, who did some shopping for him. Madge had been working for him for long enough to know what he needed almost as well as he did.

After he'd eaten the steak pie while it was still warm, he finished off with a nice, crisp apple and washed his plate and cutlery. Then he went upstairs to pack an overnight bag. He could get to Challerton and back in one day, but something might go wrong and then he'd have to stay away overnight.

That had happened to him once when he first started driving around the countryside, and though he'd found a mechanic and somewhere to spend the night, he'd had no clean clothes for the next day, no toothbrush or washing things, which he'd hated. He always took a change of clothing with him now when going on longer drives, just in case.

Olivia was waiting for Alex in the library area of the medieval hall. She looked fondly across at Phoebe, who had sat down with a book but had promptly dozed off. She had that look some women got when they were expecting, like a luscious ripening fruit.

When a car engine sounded and Alex's sleek vehicle turned into the stable yard, Phoebe jerked awake and Olivia went to open the door. No need to disturb the two maids in the kitchen.

Yesterday's biting wind seemed to have dropped but it was so cold her breath clouded the air around her and she wished she had a shawl to throw round her shoulders.

'Go inside. You'll catch your death of cold!' he scolded.

When she didn't move, he put an arm round her in a companionable way and they walked to the door together. 'I'm so very glad to see you again,' he said softly and planted a quick, shy kiss on her cheek.

'Oh.'

He raised one eyebrow as if asking whether she was upset at this familiarity and she smiled. 'I'd forgotten how nice a kiss of greeting can be.'

But his kiss had been more than that, they both knew.

She opened the door. 'Quick! Don't let the warm air out.'

Laughing, they almost tumbled inside, by which time her cousin was wide awake. 'Phoebe, this is Alex. Alex, meet Phoebe.'

He went across to shake his hostess's hand. 'I can see the resemblance between you two.' But his eyes lingered on Olivia.

She was only too aware of that and tried to speak lightly. 'Both of us are carrot tops, you mean.' But she felt herself blushing at the warmth of his smile.

'It would be more accurate to say that both of you have beautiful red hair,' he corrected.

'Please sit down, Mr Seaton,' Phoebe said.

'Do call me Alex. Since I'm a good friend of Babs and Olivia, surely you and I needn't be so formal.' He stopped, frowned slightly and looked behind him. 'What a beautiful room! Is that a minstrel's gallery?'

'Yes. It has some beautiful carved woodwork.'

'There's a light up there.' Without asking anyone's leave, he walked down the long room and looked up the stairs. 'Do you mind if I go up?' But he didn't wait for permission; he started climbing the stairs.

The two women exchanged startled glances.

'She doesn't usually appear to men,' Phoebe whispered. 'Go and see what's happening.'

Olivia hurried across to the foot of the stairs and saw the figure of Anne Latimer at the top, fainter this time and transparent, but still clearly delineated.

From part way up the stairs Alex glanced down at her, then continued upwards. He stopped and waited for the ghost to speak, looking calm and almost happy. She could hear their conversation clearly.

'Welcome to Greyladies, Alex Seaton. One day you will live here.'

'With Olivia, I hope?'

'Yes, of course. And you'll both be very happy here, in ways you never expected.'

'I'd be happy anywhere with Olivia, but this is a beautiful house.'

'It's getting shabby. You will do a lot to restore it.'

'That would be a great pleasure.'

'But first you must look after my two ladies. They are both in danger. Find a gun and make sure you can use it. You'll need it.'

The figure shimmered out of existence abruptly.

Alex stood near the top of the stairs with his head bent, then Olivia heard him blow out his tension in a long, slow breath.

When he turned to come down again, Olivia said quietly, 'Take your time. It leaves one feeling rather disoriented. Have you ever seen a ghost before?'

'Several times.'

'Then you must be sensitive to them.'

'Yes. It runs in my family.' He began to move slowly down the stairs and at the bottom he took Olivia's hand and gazed at her lovingly. 'It seems she approves of us being together.'

'Yes. I'm . . .' the words which came out weren't what she'd expected, 'happy about that.'

He didn't let go of her hand. And she didn't pull away from him as they walked to the other end of the long room to join Phoebe.

'I don't remember ever hearing about a man seeing her before,' she said.

'She's lovely. Warm and kind. What's her name?'

'Anne Latimer. She was the founder of this house and set up the legacy that goes with it, to help women in trouble. May I ask what she said to you? I couldn't make out the words from here.'

'She told me you and Olivia are both in danger and said I must protect you. What sort of danger could that be?'

'Ah. There's a man in the village, Sidney Hatterson. He lost a leg in the war and he's leading a hate campaign against the Germans interned here, and also against me because I'm the chatelaine. I'm rather worried about what he'll do next.'

'Your ghost said I would need a gun. Do you mind if I bring mine in?'

'You have a gun with you?' Olivia was astonished at that.

'I felt if the war went badly, even civilians should be able to defend themselves, so I learnt to shoot. And as I visit some very remote places, I carry the gun with me in the car. I haven't had to use it, though.'

'I'd never have thought it of you.' Olivia flushed again. 'I didn't mean to sound insulting. It's just that you seem so gentle.'

'I'm not a violent person but I hope I would defend myself if I had to . . . or try to protect those I care about.'

'My maid is carrying a gun around with her too.' Phoebe swallowed hard and glanced down at herself. 'My husband said I should keep it nearby but I'm not in the best fighting form at the moment.'

'Carrying twins must be even more wearing than carrying one baby.'

Both women gaped at him.

'Oh, hell. I'm sorry if I've shocked you. I don't usually blurt things out. It's just, I can sometimes sense things like that.'

'Twins?' Phoebe asked faintly. 'You think I'm carrying twins?'

'I'm fairly sure of it. Sensing that is a gift that runs in my family. I don't usually mention it to strangers because people get upset. They tell me I'm lying, or when I turn out to be correct, they say it was just a lucky guess. Do you want to know whether they're boys or girls? I can sense that too.'

She thought for a moment, then nodded. 'Yes. I'd like that. It'll be easier to make the right sort of clothing.'

'You're carrying two boys.'

'Ah. That explains it.' She spoke slowly, looking sad.

The others waited for her to explain what she meant.

'That's the reason I'm leaving. The women who act as chatelaines at Greyladies rarely have children and if they do, it's usually girls. I've never heard of anyone having more than one baby at a time, let alone two boys.' She saw they were still looking puzzled. 'With two babies to look after, I'd not be able to give the Greyladies legacy the attention it deserves. There's quite a lot of work involved, especially when we're not at war.' She brushed away a tear. 'I can't help feeling sad about leaving, but it's the right thing to do. We chatelaines have helped a lot of women over the years. That must go on.'

Olivia went to sit on the arm of her cousin's chair and hold her hand, patting it to offer comfort.

Phoebe smiled suddenly. 'It seems Corin has inadvertently reclaimed his birthright. Anne wouldn't take a woman away from her children, I'm sure. She had two daughters, you know, but five years apart. And regretted that she couldn't spend more time with them.'

Unexpectedly Olivia felt tears rise in her own eyes. Of course Alex didn't miss that.

'What's wrong?'

She stood up and shrugged. 'Jealousy, really. I envy you, Phoebe. I've never been able to have a child. Charles and I tried very hard, consulted a couple of doctors, but nothing helped.'

He put one arm round her shoulders. 'I can understand how you feel. I never expected to meet someone to love, let alone have children.'

After a few moments, Phoebe said firmly. 'We might as well eat now. We'll have plenty of time to think about the future.' She rang for Ethel to serve the meal.

'There's trouble in the village,' Ethel announced the

minute she came through the door from the kitchen.

Cook followed her, standing by the door.

'What's happened?'

'Someone's thrown stones at Miss Bowers' windows. Broken three of them, they have. Woke her up in the middle of the night. Of course the neighbours came running so she wasn't left alone in case the rascals came back.'

Phoebe looked at her in shock. 'Who would do that?'

'Same fellows who threw the stones here.' She looked at Alex and Olivia. 'Me and Cook don't like to think of Mrs Latimer being here on her own till he's been stopped.'

'Perhaps I shouldn't leave you yet,' Olivia said.

'Perhaps I should stay as well, just for a day or two,' Alex offered. 'I do carry an overnight bag with me and I have my gun.'

Ethel produced a gun from her skirt pocket underneath the apron, making Cook jump and bless herself. 'I'm carrying this with me all the time till he's stopped.' She looked at Alex approvingly. 'Mrs Latimer won't carry it, and anyway, I'm a better shooter than she is. I think you should stay, sir. You *and* your gun.'

He looked at Phoebe, who threw up her hands. 'You're more than welcome to stay, but we do have soldiers on guard at night and other men next door as well who will come running if we shout for help.'

'One soldier patrolling the grounds and the other sitting in the kitchen *protecting the house*,' Ethel said scornfully. 'Excuse me if I'm going beyond what I'm supposed to do, ma'am, but your husband asked me to look after you and I'll do it, whatever it takes. The same way *you* looked after me when I first came here.' She took out her handkerchief and blew her nose loudly.

'It seems I'm surrounded by protectors,' Phoebe said. 'Thank you, Ethel. I really appreciate you caring about my welfare. Now it's all decided, could we have our luncheon, please, Cook? I'm sure Mr Seaton is hungry after driving down from London. And afterwards, could you please prepare a room for him, Ethel?'

'I'll put him within screaming distance of you and Mrs Harbury.'

When the maid had gone, they exchanged smiles.

'Screaming distance! How loudly can you scream?'

'I don't know and I'm not intending to practise.'

Alex chuckled. 'I wouldn't like to face Ethel if she was protecting you. She's an amazing woman.'

In a big old house near London, Corin felt uneasy all day. He didn't know why, he just . . . kept worrying about Phoebe.

In the end, his commanding officer asked him bluntly, 'What's wrong, Latimer? And don't pretend there's nothing. I wasn't born yesterday.'

'I'm not sure, sir, but I'm worried about my wife. There's a man in the village who's been trying to harm her, and harm the internees living in our house. Others are keeping an eye on the situation but . . . I keep feeling I should go to her. She's . . . that is, *we* are expecting a child.'

'Congratulations.' He leant back in his chair. 'Well, you're not a fool and we've almost finished this stage of the planning. How about you take one of the staff cars and a driver, and go down to Wiltshire the day after tomorrow. You can stay overnight, check for yourself that she's all right, then come straight back. Two days maximum, mind.'

'Thank you, sir. I appreciate that. But I can drive myself down.'

'No, take a driver and an official car. That way you'll have his help if you need it. Also, you'll be able to sleep on the way back, if necessary.'

'I'd rather drive down late tomorrow.'

'Arrange it as you please, but now it's me who has a feeling you shouldn't go alone. Humour me in this.'

'Very well, sir. And thank you.'

'You're contributing a lot. You come up with some interesting ideas, as if you're looking at a situation from a different angle. We need that, which is why you haven't been sent back to the front. What this boils down to is, you'll work better if your mind is at rest. Stands to reason.'

It was the best he could hope for, Corin knew. But he wished he could go immediately.

Chapter Sixteen

As darkness fell, the occupants of the rear house started to feel uneasy. In the kitchen Cook muttered over the stock she was preparing from a chicken carcass for the following day's soup, while Ethel patted the gun in her pocket several times, to make sure it was there, ready. She felt comforted by its presence.

Things were no better in the long hall. All the curtains had been drawn as soon as it began to get dark, but even several lamps and a cheerful wood fire didn't seem to dispel the darkness that hugged the corners of the rooms and alcoves this night.

At times conversation flagged and one of them would look uneasily in the direction of the rear stable yard.

Alex suddenly jerked upright. 'I've been worrying that my car will be all right and I've just had a thought. I might go and set a little trap. I have a gadget that will make a noise if anyone messes around with the car.'

He looked at the two ladies with a wry smile. 'It's another little item I carry round with me when I'm travelling. I don't know why I didn't think of fitting it before.'

'But it's dark outside.'

'I'll get a lantern from the kitchen. They're bound to have one. I'll only be out there a minute or two.' He left the room as quietly as ever.

'I like your Alex,' Phoebe murmured.

But Olivia wasn't listening. She was feeling even more uneasy and wondering whether to go after Alex.

In the kitchen Ethel frowned at his request for a candle lantern. 'One small light won't do much good out there, sir. It's a cloudy night and I shouldn't be surprised if it doesn't rain tomorrow. Someone could easily be lurking outside. Plenty of shadows to hide in.'

'I only need the lantern to see where my gadget is and then it won't take me more than a minute to set my little trap, which makes a noise if anyone touches the car.'

'You wouldn't hear it from the bedrooms.'

'I've been considering sleeping downstairs. I have a feeling something's brewing.'

She sighed. 'I have the same feeling, sir.'

He went out, setting the lantern on the ground. He unlocked his car boot and took out his little apparatus. As he bent to pick up the lantern again to set it on the running board and illuminate his task, he thought he heard something and tensed, turning his head slightly.

The blow intended to smash his skull missed hitting him full on, but it did knock him senseless.

The attacker bent over to check him, then stepped back and raised his arm again.

Joe had been out in the village *patrolling*, as he liked to think of it, checking that everything was quiet. He did this a couple of times a night, with a big scarf his mother had knitted for him wrapped round his neck, the ends crossed over his chest to keep him warm.

Mostly he saw no one. People in Challerton had better things to do than linger outside on nights like this

He shivered. It felt very cold tonight. He even wondered about popping into his friend's house for a warm drink. His friend's mother wouldn't mind, he was sure.

But then he saw something moving and slipped sideways into concealment as one of the shadows a short distance ahead of him moved into the open and turned into a man. The person had a knitted balaclava on his head that showed only his eyes, so Joe couldn't make out who it was.

Excitement ran through him and he forgot about feeling cold as he followed the man carefully through the village.

Who was it? Where had he come from?

When another shadow slipped out of the darkness and began to walk along beside the first one, Joe could hardly breathe for excitement.

The two men went towards Greyladies, stopping every now and then, seeming to be listening, checking they weren't being followed.

But Joe had been practising moving quietly ever since he was a lad playing soldiers with his pals. He smirked as he stopped and waited for them to move on. He was much better at moving quietly than they were.

They must have known about the sentry patrolling round the big house. Great clumping fellow, he was, making so much noise you could hear him coming a mile off.

When the sentry had passed, the two figures set off again, making their way towards the rear of the house. Joe had good eyesight and had no trouble seeing where they were going.

Neither of them limped, so Hatterson couldn't be one of them. Pity! Joe would have liked to get Mr Nasty in trouble for trespassing. Hatterson had caught him practising keeping watch one evening and now mocked him loudly about it every time they passed one another in the village. One day Joe was going to shut his mouth for him.

At the rear of the house, the men vanished into the shadows and Joe couldn't be certain where they were or if they'd moved on. He wasn't going round the narrower part of the drive at the corner of the house until he was sure they wouldn't see him coming. The trouble was, if he made a detour, he might lose them.

So he waited. You had to wait patiently sometimes. But it was hard when you were itching to act.

Then the kitchen door of the old house opened and a man came out carrying a small candle lantern. Those old-fashioned things weren't much use. Joe was saving up for a modern electric torch, but it'd take him a while and his mother kept saying he would be a fool to waste good money on a toy like that.

Perhaps Major Latimer could speak to her about it and assure her some of the newer gadgets were very helpful. *He* had an electric torch, Joe knew, because the major had let him try it.

The man who'd come out of the house set the lantern down and bent over the boot of the car, unlocking it. He took something out of the boot and slung it over his arm. As he bent to pick up the lantern one of the intruders stepped out of the shadows and hit him over the head, sending him tumbling to the ground. He swiped him really hard and if the man from the house hadn't moved at the last minute, he might have been killed.

The attacker bent to check him, then stood up and raised his hand to strike again. Joe wasn't having that. He yelled 'Stop!' at the top of his voice. The man paused, but his hand didn't drop and Joe wasn't close enough to get there in time to stop him hitting out again.

Joe was shocked. Was he about to watch a *murder*?

The kitchen door had just opened and a woman yelled, 'Halt or I fire!' She had a gun and was holding it as if she knew what to do with it.

The intruder let his arm drop and darted off into the shadows, keeping the car between himself and the woman.

Joe rushed forward to see how the man on the ground was. Surely he wasn't dead?

Ethel moved further out of the kitchen at the same time, lifting the gun to aim it.

'Don't shoot! It's me, Joe,' he called.

'What on earth are you doing here?'

'Following two men. I think they've gone now, but you keep that gun handy in case they come back. I'll get this man inside out of harm's way.'

'Hurry up, then!'

Joe found that the injured man was quite light, so was able to pick him up. The poor fellow was groaning now but he wasn't fully conscious. As the lad hefted him to get comfortable, he stared down at the row of bells on wires strung over the man's arm and shoulder. What was that thing for?

'Will you hurry up!' Ethel yelled.

So Joe carried both man and string of bells inside, hearing them jingling loudly as he walked.

As they went inside, the house door at the other side of the kitchen burst open and a lady came running across to help him.

'What happened to Alex?'

It was Mrs Harbury, a friend of Mrs Latimer. Joe always kept note of visitors to the village.

The man was groaning and trying to move, so Joe sat him down on a chair, squatting to hold him in place.

Behind him, Ethel locked the back door and leant against it, letting out her breath in loud relief.

'I was watching and saw this man jump out from nowhere and attack Mr Seaton, so I went outside with my gun, ma'am. I yelled that I'd shoot him and he ran away. If he'd hit Mr Seaton again, he might have killed him. What a coward, to attack an unconscious man!'

'I think he meant to kill your friend, Mrs Latimer,' Joe said. 'He tried to hit him really hard the first time. Luckily your friend moved his head. But then the attacker raised his hand again. It's a good thing you came out with the gun, Mrs Kiddall.'

'That's what it's for,' Ethel said grimly. 'I *knew* I'd need it, I just knew.'

Joe stepped back a little as Mrs Harbury knelt down beside the injured man.

'Do you have some warm, boiled water to bathe his head, Cook?'

'Yes, ma'am.'

'I'm all right, Olivia.'

But the gentleman's voice was thick and he didn't sound all right, Joe thought, watching the two of them with interest. This woman loved him, he could tell. His friend's sister got that sort of soppy look on her face when she was with the man she was going to marry. But she was only nineteen. Fancy old people like these two falling in love, though! Still, stranger things happened in wartime.

'Should we fetch Captain Turner?' Phoebe wondered aloud.

'What can *he* do?' Ethel muttered. 'His men can't even keep away intruders.'

'We'll be awake all night if you tell the commandant now,' Cook said. 'Pardon me for saying it, ma'am, but he does like to make a fuss.'

Olivia looked down at Alex. 'Why did you insist on going outside on your own after dark?' she scolded softly.

'I wanted to set a booby trap on the car to keep it safe. I thought I'd be safe enough, because it wouldn't take a minute to fix it on and I'd see anyone coming. He must have already been behind the car.'

'Tell me how it works, mister, and I'll set it for you now,' Joe offered.

Alex blinked at him and turned his head slightly, wincing.

'I'm good with mechanical things,' Joe assured him. 'Ethel can come outside with her gun and make sure they don't attack me. And I could stay here overnight to keep an eye on the car, if you like. Major Latimer is paying me to keep watch on what's going on in the village and the big house, so he'd approve of it, I know he would, especially now you've had intruders here.'

'That's the best idea anyone has had so far,' Cook said. 'As long as young Joe doesn't fall asleep.'

'I won't. I'm training to keep watch, ready for when I'm called up. You can't fall asleep when you're on night duty.'

* * *

His young voice sounded grim and determined. In spite of his throbbing head, Alex smiled at the eager lad. 'I think it'd be an excellent idea for you to stay here in the kitchen and keep an eye on the back yard. As long as you promise us you won't go outside on your own.'

'I promise I won't, sir. I saw what happened to you.'

'*Touché.*' That'd also keep the lad safe if the attackers returned, Alex thought, but didn't say that. He explained how to fix the simple alarm on the car and Ethel took out her gun again to keep an eye on him.

'It's fixed,' Joe said when they returned five minutes later. 'It's clever, that is. I've never seen one before.'

'I met a lad trying to sell them, so I bought one.'

By that time Cook had brought across a bowl of tepid water and some clean rags. 'Do you want me to do this, Mrs Harbury? I've bathed the heads of my nephews many a time. If they've no one else to fight with, that lot fight one another.'

'That's all right, thank you. I've some experience in this area as well.'

Alex watched her study his wound, then she murmured, 'I'll try to be gentle, but I'm afraid this will hurt.'

It was almost worth being bashed to have her caring for him, standing so close, even though they were not exactly alone, with three other women and a lad watching her every move. How gentle her hands were. He was sure it'd have hurt much more if anyone else had done it.

When she'd finished cleaning the wound, Olivia frowned. 'I don't know whether I should bandage it or leave it to dry.'

'Leave it to dry, Mrs Harbury,' Cook said. 'But I don't think he should be left on his own. When my oldest nephew knocked himself out and took a while to come to himself again, like Mr Seaton did, the doctor said we had to keep an eye on him all night.'

'There's no need for Mrs Harbury to lose her sleep,' Alex protested at once.

'I think I'd rather be careful, Alex. I'd not sleep for worrying about you, anyway. Why don't you lie down on the sofa in the sitting area and I'll sit on an armchair nearby?'

'I've got an alarm clock you can borrow, Mrs Harbury. You can set it for every hour in case you drop off,' Ethel said. 'Or I could keep watch on Mr Seaton for you.'

To Alex's relief, Olivia said, 'No, thank you. I prefer to do it myself.'

He'd prefer to have her with him, too. He decided to distract the maid. 'Ethel, perhaps you could go round the house before you retire to your bedroom and double-check that every door and window is locked, and they haven't tried to force their way in anywhere?'

'Good idea, sir. Joe, you can come round with me,' Ethel said. 'Then you'll know your way round the inside in future.'

'Yes, Mrs Kiddall.'

At last they all left and Alex was alone with Olivia. Unfortunately, not in romantic circumstances, but he valued every second spent with her.

He let her make him comfortable, then suggested she pull the smaller armchair closer.

She did that and settled down in it.

Without thinking he reached out for her hand.

Without protesting, she let him take it.

A few minutes later, she said. 'What a strange day!'

'Yes. It seems a long time since I left London . . . you have a beautiful ghost here, by the way. I do hope her prophecy comes true.'

It was such a long time before Olivia replied that he began to feel anxious. Perhaps she didn't share that hope. But she hadn't taken her hand away, so perhaps there was hope.

Then she said it. 'So do I.'

His heart felt as if it would burst for joy.

As their eyes met, he raised her hand to his lips. He couldn't think of anything to say, but from the way she was smiling back at him, words weren't necessary. Happiness filled him, making him forget his aching head, making him forget everything but her.

In the morning Alex woke first and had the pleasure of seeing Olivia sleeping as soundly and sweetly as a child in the light of a nearby lamp burning low. He didn't wake her, because she looked comfortable in the chair, but she stirred of her own accord soon after, then sat up and stretched.

'Is it morning already?'

'Yes. After the best day of my life.'

'Best day! But you got hurt, Alex.'

'That doesn't matter. I was also given a glorious hope for the future. You won't change your mind, will you, Olivia? I'm not a big strong fellow like your husband, but I love you more than anyone else ever could.'

'You're strong in other ways, Alex, morally and mentally.'

'So are you – and the other three women here are as well, come to think of it. No hysterics from any of them last night, and Ethel probably saved my life.'

'Ethel and Joe combined.'

'I must thank them properly today.' He swung his feet to the ground. 'I'd better use the bathroom and tidy myself up a bit.'

As he was coming back someone hammered on the connecting door. 'Mrs Latimer! Mrs Latimer! Are you all right in there?'

Joe peeped in from the kitchen. 'That's Captain Turner. Shall I let him in, Mrs Harbury?'

Ethel pushed past him. 'That's my job, young fellow.' She went to open the door and the commandant came straight in.

He didn't pause for polite greetings. 'As soon as it got light, one of my soldiers found a mess of new footprints in the mud at the edge of the stable yard. We were worried that someone had broken in and—' He saw Alex's face and gasped. 'What happened?'

So they explained about the attack.

'Why didn't you call for our help?'

'We managed to drive them away ourselves – Ethel had a gun – and afterwards we were busy looking after Mr Seaton. Besides, Joe stayed here all night keeping watch. He was under orders to call on you for help if he saw the intruders again.'

'Oh. Right. No idea what they wanted?'

'To do some damage, probably. Or else they were reconnoitring for future reference. It's all part of a well-organised campaign against our Germans, isn't it? It's not just people from our village, but other people who are involved.'

'Unfortunately, yes. There's apparently quite a nest of troublemakers in Swindon. I'm sorry our being here has brought danger to you and your beautiful house.'

'So am I. And I think what's happened so far is only the start.'

'Yes.'

A man yelled from inside the new house, 'There's a car coming along the drive, Captain Turner.'

He swung round and started to return, but the voice yelled, 'It's going round the back.'

'Mind if I stay and see who it is, Mrs Latimer?'

'Be my guest.' She ran through to the kitchen and looked out. 'It's Corin!' she shouted and ran outside to fling herself into her husband's arms.

Corin kissed her, then held her at arm's length to study her face. 'Something's wrong. I could sense it. I'm not mistaken, am I?'

'No. There has been an incident.'

'We set off at two o'clock so that we could get here as early as possible. Unfortunately I only have two days' leave approved, so if we can't sort this trouble out quickly, you're coming back to London with me, and I'm not taking no for an answer.'

'Am I, indeed?'

'Yes. There isn't just you involved.' He laid one hand briefly on her stomach.

'I'm all right, darling. Everyone here is looking after me. Come inside and we'll tell you what happened last night.'

They took seats in the library area of the long hall and Phoebe whispered to Ethel to join them, then explained what had happened the previous evening.

'Well done, young Joe,' Corin said warmly, then frowned. 'Hatterson *must* be involved!'

'Neither of them was limping, sir,' Joe said. 'I always keep my eyes open for that. My ma says he's a real bad 'un.'

'Your mother's right,' Ethel said grimly. 'He's downright rude to me and Cook if we run into him when we're out shopping.'

'He just looks at me, mostly,' Phoebe said. 'But he seems

so filled with hatred, even that makes me shiver. Most other people in the village are so friendly and helpful. Well, one or two avoid me, but they don't say anything or glare at me. They just turn away.'

'I think we need to do something about him and those he's bringing into the village,' Corin said slowly. 'I'm not quite sure what yet. Let me get something to eat and take time to consider the situation, then I'll see what I can come up with. Joe, go and get some sleep, but come back here this afternoon.'

'Yes sir!' He saluted and ran out.

'That boy!' Ethel said fondly. 'He's a lively one. Reminds me of my son.'

'He's the sort of lad who makes Britain great,' Corin said.

'Joe's itching to join the forces,' Ethel said. 'His ma is desperately worried. He wants to go into the air force and become a mechanic.'

'That'd be safer than the trenches,' Corin said, shuddering at his own dark memories. 'Maybe I'll see if I can help. He could even be officer material. Anyway, that's for another time. Where's that breakfast? I'm famished. Alex, are you sure you're all right now?'

'I'm fine. I hope you don't mind me staying here.'

'I'm delighted. I hope you'll stay on for a while. I hate leaving my wife unprotected. I have a few ideas about that, which I'll tell you about later. Maybe we can flush those would-be murderers out.'

Chapter Seventeen

Hatterson pushed his breakfast away and stood up abruptly, wincing as his stump throbbed in protest. He'd seen better artificial limbs than this one, but only the officers and rich folk got those. Cannon fodder, that's all he'd been, thrown away once he was no use. Well, he'd show them what a one-legged man could do. Then see what fools they'd look.

'I'll be busy this morning,' he told his wife. 'I don't want disturbing, so don't come into the front room. If I need a cuppa I'll come out and get it myself.'

'All right, Sidney. I have to go out to the shop anyway. What do you want for tea?'

'Some ham – decent stuff, not that gristly cat meat you brought back last time.'

'I'll do my best, but I can only buy what they've got in the shop and there are shortages of some items, so they can only do their best, too.'

'It's up to you to make sure we get our share of the good stuff. And remember when you get back, no disturbing me.'

She nodded.

He went into the front room and sat down. His friends

had called in last night after the fiasco at Greyladies. A chap had come out of the old house to fiddle with a car, offering himself on a plate for a good bashing, and they'd still missed making an example of him, damn them.

Well, they'd make up for that failure tonight. They'd checked everything out and made their plans about where to attack from. It'd be the big one tonight, the offensive to destroy the Huns and give the rich traitors their comeuppance.

He liked to use the word 'offensive'. It showed he and his friends were professional about what they were doing, not just hooligans. Some of them were ex-soldiers, invalided out like him; others had been denied the chance to fight for their country for silly medical reasons; a few had even been told they were too old to serve. Well, the doctors were wrong. All of the people who'd be involved were capable of acting, and so people would see before too long.

He waited till he heard Pearl go out, then settled his stick with the knitted hat on top in the chair to make it appear he was sitting there reading. Crouching to avoid being seen from the street, he left the room. While Pearl was out, he had to get the attic ready for tonight. A few chaps would be trickling in during the rest of the day and could hide up there. Some might spend the rest of the night there after the offensive.

He was going to send Pearl to visit her cousin at the farm this afternoon and tell her to stay there overnight, since they always asked her to. That'd keep her out of the way nicely. Those two women never stopped nattering once they were together. He hadn't stopped her visiting the farm every now and then, even though it was a waste of time, because it was a useful way of getting rid of her.

He went up to the attic and got out some old bedding and a slop bucket.

As he went down again, he heard the back door open and close.

He hurried to the kitchen and saw Ted standing there.

'Had to come early, Hatty, lad. Someone I don't want to see came looking for me.'

Hatterson glanced through the rear window. No sign of Pearl, thank goodness. 'Come upstairs quickly, and keep quiet once you're there. The wife will be back soon from the shops. I'm sending her away while we're doing this.'

'Good idea. Got a newspaper I can read?'

'Only yesterday's. She uses them to light the fire.'

'Yesterday's will do.'

Hatterson went back downstairs, decided he was thirsty and made himself a cup of tea. Then he took it into the front room, bending low again to get across to his chair. To make sure the old witch or one of the other nosy parkers in this street saw him, he put the hat on, stood up to look out of the bay window, pretending to stretch and yawn. That should do it.

As he sat down he glanced at the clock on the mantelpiece, wondering where his wife was. She was taking long enough at the shop. Gossiping probably. Well, he wouldn't chastise her about that today.

Pearl queued up at the shop, feeling exhausted and in despair. Sidney was getting worse not better, treating her like a slave, working her to death, and who knew what he was planning. Something bad, that was sure.

Just before she got to the counter everything began to

spin and she cried out as she felt herself falling. When she came to, she found herself lying on a sofa, with a neighbour fanning her face.

'Ah, you're awake again, Mrs Hatterson. You went and fainted on us. Did you miss your breakfast today?'

Pearl couldn't seem to think straight at first, then remembered they'd run out of bread because Sidney had treated himself to a few slices of toast last night. To save him complaining and perhaps thumping her, she'd given him what was left this morning. 'I wasn't hungry.'

The woman crouched in front of her. 'You're thinner than you used to be. Are you getting enough to eat? He's working you too hard.'

Pearl tried not to show that this had hit the mark, but tears welled in her eyes. 'I do my best – he has been injured you know – but I can't keep up with everything the way he likes.'

Mrs Pocock came out from the kitchen and shoved a cup of tea at her. 'Here you are. It's nice and sweet. You get it down.'

'Thank you. That's very kind.'

She saw the two women look at one another. 'Look. We all know what's going on,' Mrs Pocock said. 'If you ever need to get away from him, you come here to me and I'll hide you, then tell Mrs Latimer. She knows a place for women who aren't happy at home and she helps them make new lives.'

Pearl was so horrified at the bits and pieces she'd overheard at home that she said without thinking, 'It's Mrs Latimer he's going after!'

'*What?* Why would anyone go after her? She's a really kind lady.'

'Because of the Huns.'

'Them being at the house is nothing to do with her. It was requisitioned by the War Office. Has your husband gone mad?'

There was silence and Pearl didn't know what to say. Sidney did seem a bit . . . strange at times. 'He's changed a lot since the war.'

'Look, dear, I think it's time you let us in on what's going on. He's planning something nasty, isn't he?'

'If Sidney hears I've told you anything, he'll beat me black and blue.' Then she clapped one hand to her mouth. She hadn't meant to tell anyone that, either. She had her pride, after all. She glanced quickly over her shoulder, but no one else was close enough to overhear.

Mrs Pocock kept her voice down too. 'Everyone in the village knows he beats you, love. You can't hide all the bruises.'

She burst into tears and couldn't stop crying from shame till she remembered he'd see her red eyes when she went home and want to know what she'd been crying about.

'Stay here, Pearl. Don't go back. I'll tell him you're leaving him, if you want,' Mrs Pocock said. 'He won't beat *me*, I promise you.'

'No, no! I must go home. He mustn't know. I *daren't* cross him. He'll kill me.'

And in spite of their attempts to persuade her to stay, she pulled herself together, splashed cold water on her face and bought what she needed, before making her way slowly home. She nearly turned round halfway, but then she stiffened her spine and continued. *For better, for worse*, that's what she'd promised.

When she got home, she heard Sidney talking to someone in the attic. What was that about? Who had he got hidden up there? She'd better not let him know she'd heard them.

He started down the stairs and she glanced round in panic, then darted into the wash house. He came into the kitchen, so she stayed where she was till he'd made himself a cup of tea.

She saw him carry it towards the front room. Strange. He usually took a good slurp before he moved, because carrying full cups of tea around with his limp made him spill it sometimes. But today the cup wasn't rattling in the saucer as much as usual. And he wasn't limping as much, either.

When she heard him set the cup down, she left the pantry and stood for a moment staring at herself in the mirror. She was chalk white, but the latest bruises didn't show, thank goodness. She opened the back door quietly and pretended to come in again but the wind blew it out of her hand and it banged loudly shut.

That brought him straight out into the kitchen, mouth open to scold her for another imaginary fault. But he stopped and stared at her instead. 'You've been crying.'

'Sort of.'

'What the hell does that mean?'

'I fainted in the shop and I was upset afterwards. Mrs Pocock gave me a cup of tea, but I still feel a bit dizzy.' She fumbled for a kitchen chair and dropped down into it at the table.

'Did you get the shopping?'

'Most of it. At least, I think I did. It's in the shopping bag. I don't feel well. Perhaps I should go and have a lie-down.'

'Nonsense. You've been working too hard. Lying down

won't help. What you need is to get out in the open air. That'll freshen you up. Why don't you go and spend the afternoon nattering to that cousin of yours who lives just outside Challerton? In fact, why don't you stay overnight at the farm? Jen's always asking you.'

She stared at him, trying to work out what was going on. Obviously he wanted to get rid of her, but why? It must be to do with his hidden friend. What were they up to?

'Well?' he prompted. 'Cat got your tongue?'

'I was surprised. You don't usually want me to go out.'

'You don't usually faint all over people.'

There was a thump upstairs as if someone had knocked over a piece of furniture.

'What's that?' she asked, because it'd have looked strange if she hadn't asked.

'Ah. Well, to tell you the truth a friend of mine has come to visit me and he didn't get much sleep last night so he's having a lie-down in the attic.'

'Why didn't you put him in one of the spare bedrooms?'

'I – um, thought he'd be quieter up there. I've invited another couple of mates to visit me later, so it'd suit me if you went out today.'

'It would be nice to see Jen.'

'There you are, then. We'd both be suited.'

'But it's a long way to walk and I'm still not feeling right.' She held her breath. Would he get upset at this and hit her? He'd locked her bike away a few months ago, saying she didn't need it. She missed the freedom of being able to go further afield. Five miles was too far to walk.

'Why don't I get your bike out? The light's not working properly, but if you stay overnight, you won't need to ride back after dark. Me and my mates will be able to have a few beers in peace and make as much noise as we please.'

'Oh. Well, all right. If you're sure.'

'Of course I'm sure. Why don't you pack an overnight bag and go straight away?'

'Before I've made your lunch?' Again she held her breath as she waited for an answer.

'I can make myself a damned sandwich. I'm not helpless, you know. It's my leg that's gone, not my hands.'

'I will, then. And thank you very much. I shall enjoy a break.'

He patted her shoulder and she couldn't help flinching away from him, thinking he was going to hit her. He smiled at that. He liked her to show she was afraid of him.

'I'll go and check your bicycle, oil it a bit. You can leave as soon as it's ready. Get that bag packed.' He walked out whistling cheerfully.

She wondered who was hiding upstairs, what had made Sidney so cheerful all of a sudden. It probably meant someone was going to get hurt. She ought to tell someone. Did she dare do it, though?

As she put her hand over her mouth, she caught sight of herself in the dressing table mirror, looking like a timid child. That made her feel angry. She was twenty-five years old, not five. And *she* had done nothing wrong and didn't deserve to be hurt.

Slowly she let her hand fall. She'd do it! Leave him. And it'd serve him right. She'd call in to see Mrs Pocock again before she went out to Jen's farm and warn the shopkeeper that strangers were coming to the house. That never normally happened, well, not openly in the daytime.

Only, this person wasn't here openly. Sidney had looked annoyed at the noise he'd made. Someone should keep watch and see who else turned up, find out what was going on. She'd suggest that to Mrs Pocock. The shopkeeper knew everyone in the village.

From the things Sidney had said about the foreigners at the big house, he was intending to cause trouble there. That was bad enough, because Mrs Latimer was a lovely person. But Pearl also hated to think of those gentle old people getting hurt. She didn't want to be part of hurting anyone.

She'd had enough. Mrs Pocock was right. She shouldn't put up with it. She was definitely not coming back and if Jen wouldn't help her, she'd go to Mrs Pocock.

On that thought she began cramming as many of her clothes as she could in the shabby little suitcase. She didn't dare take the big one, so she quickly put on two or three of every undergarment possible and stuffed her pockets with handkerchiefs, gloves, anything small she could find.

She jumped like a startled rabbit when he called from the bottom of the stairs. 'Your bike's ready, Pearl.'

'Thank you, Sidney. I'll be down in a minute.'

With some difficulty she forced a half-smile as she passed him in the kitchen. He didn't follow her out, but her fingers were shaking as she strapped the little suitcase to the rack on the bicycle. She kept expecting him to call her back and say it had all been a joke, and she couldn't go.

But he didn't. He didn't even stand in the garden to watch her leave.

She had no trouble smiling as she parked her bicycle round the back of the shop and went in to see Mrs Pocock.

She was with people now. He couldn't drag her back, even if he came after her.

On the way to her cousin's she threw back her head and laughed aloud, which set the bicycle wobbling wildly across the country lane and nearly landed her in the ditch.

Still laughing, she managed to control the bicycle and carry on . . . pedalling her way to freedom.

Once that poor cowed creature had left, Mrs Pocock called in her husband and after an earnest discussion, he set off for Greyladies, taking a roundabout route.

To his shock, someone grabbed him as he was passing the crypt and before he could do more than let out one yell, he found himself on the ground, with one arm twisted behind his back.

He heard Major Latimer's voice and sagged in relief.

'I'm going to let you get up, but if you try to run away, I'll really hurt you.'

Mr Pocock heaved himself to his feet, one hand to his chest. 'You've got the wrong end of the stick. I was coming to see Mrs Latimer, to warn her.'

The major's expression was grim. 'About what?'

'We've heard Hatterson and his cronies are gathering at his house today. We think they're going to stage a big attack tonight, perhaps try to capture the big house. There's someone at his house already, and one of my customers saw a stranger in their street.'

'How do you know this?'

'Mrs Hatterson fainted in the shop today and my wife told her if she left her husband we'd help her, or Mrs Latimer would. Well, he's been beating the poor little thing for years, as well as making her do all the work. She can't be more than five foot high and she's as thin as a lath. My wife doesn't think she's even eating properly.'

'Go on.'

'Mrs Hatterson came back to see us later, riding her bicycle, which he'd taken off her but he's given it her back so that she can go and visit her cousin, who lives on a farm outside the village. Mrs Hatterson was told to stay the night there.'

'That's ominous.'

'She said she couldn't stand it any longer and she's decided to leave him. She told us he was expecting some of his friends, and he'd got *that look* to him.'

'What look is that?'

'Wild-eyed. I know what she means. I've seen him in a rage a couple of times. She thinks he's gone mad and is planning to do something terrible, but she doesn't know what.'

The silence seemed to go on for ever, then the major spoke in a normal, friendly tone and Mr Pocock sagged in relief.

'You'd better come to the house and talk to my wife about it. We're making plans to protect ourselves, which is why I was checking the crypt. But if we get an attack by a mob, there may too few of us to defend Greyladies properly. Most of the internees are too old and feeble to help. Look. You know everyone in the village. You'll know who we can rely on, who's strong and ready to fight for his country.'

'I do indeed. And I don't believe in mob rule, sir.'

'Good. To set the record straight, our Germans are helping the British government with information about all sorts of things. They're making a significant contribution to the war effort on our side.'

'We'd heard rumours about that.'

'Had you? By Jove! It's not supposed to be known.'

Mr Pocock shrugged. 'It's a small village. You know how things get talked about.'

'If everyone knows about it, why is that fellow trying to stir up trouble?'

'He's an incomer, and what's more he isn't liked. No one would tell him anything. There are a few others who don't join in much, as well, and we don't discuss it with them, either. Two or three of them have been seen going into Hatterson's house lately or leaving the village after dark. There have been motor cars stopping nearby during the night, too. Hatterson's uncle must be spinning in his grave about what's being done with his old home.'

'Yes. Funny how things turn out sometimes. I didn't realise I was coming home today to lead an unofficial battle against hoodlums, but that's what it'll amount to. There isn't time to get more soldiers here and in place before nightfall, and anyway, we have no real proof of what's being planned, so I'd have trouble getting any sent.'

But he was going to phone the nearest unit and set up certain arrangements with them.

'Well, as I said, I'm ready to help out, because it's *my* village, and I can name a few others who'll help as well. I hope you get Hatterson locked up in prison for the rest of his life, then he won't be able to beat up that poor woman . . . or betray his country.'

He was looking forward to helping sort this out, had been itching to get hold of Hatterson and give him some of his own medicine. He couldn't be doing with people who beat up their wives and caused trouble in the village.

As for traitors who attacked British houses and soldiers, he'd stand the sods up against a wall and shoot them himself, by hell he would.

In some amusement, Corin watched Gilbert Pocock, in his sixties and distinctly plump, stride beside him into the house with an attempt at a military bearing.

People like him and Joe were the salt of the earth, were what had made Britain the great nation she was.

Chapter Eighteen

Joe had been set to keep watch on Hatterson's house, with strict instructions not to show himself or do anything except watch.

He carried out his instructions to the letter, but when two burly men grabbed him from behind, he had no time to do anything except yelp in shock before a gag was shoved into his mouth and he was bound tightly.

Laughing and joking, they carried him towards Hatterson's cottage, dumping him in the coalhouse.

He lay in the muck, bitterly aware that he had failed Major Latimer, failed everyone. Tears of shame leaked from his eyes, though he tried hard not to give in to despair.

He dreaded to think what those men would do to Greyladies.

The door opened again and a light was shone on him. He blinked and turned his head away.

'Yes, it is him. Think you're clever, don't you, you little sod,' Hatterson said, and aimed a kick at him, laughing as it connected with his ribs.

A gurgle of pain escaped Joe, but he managed not to make a noise when the second blow slammed into him.

'Aw, come on, Hatty. He's not worth it. Just lock him up till we've carried out our plan, then we'll let him go.'

One more kick came Joe's way, then the shadow looming over him fluttered backwards and the door was slammed shut. This time he heard a padlock click shut on the outside.

There was no way he was going to get out of here, even if he got free of his bonds.

He lay in the darkness, waiting for the pain to ebb. His ribs hurt, but his pride hurt far more.

He had failed, failed all those people depending on him. More tears fell.

Men filtered into the village and it wasn't possible now to keep their arrival secret. They gathered at prearranged points and no one came out of any of the houses to challenge them.

They laughed as they waited, boasted about what they would do to the Huns, and to the cowards guarding them if they resisted at all.

People who overheard them from the nearby houses grew angry, but they had their instructions: they were to do nothing until the signal was given unless their very lives were threatened.

And for that signal, they depended on Joe.

Miss Bowers sat in the darkness of her unlit house, watching the back lane and listening through a half-open window to the men passing along it, going into and out of Hatterson's house. She shivered in the cold air that was coming in, but huddled her shawl more closely round her neck and continued to keep watch.

But it was no use sitting there. She could only catch

snatches of the various conversations and it was hard to make sense of anything. The invaders, as she thought of them, were too confident and there were more of them than had been expected.

Perhaps she could hear something useful if she went outside, not right into the back lane, but staying in her own garden. She opened the door cautiously, listened, then tiptoed out and stationed herself near the gate in the middle of the high back wall of her garden. From here she would be able to hear a lot more.

But to her disappointment the men all seemed to have gone past. She was about to open the gate to peep out and check that when she heard another gate bang shut close by. She froze.

More footsteps approached and she recognised one voice immediately: Hatterson. He was boasting about what he'd do to the lad they'd got locked in the coalhouse after they got back. It was obvious from what he was saying that it was Joe they'd caught.

When they'd gone she waited a bit longer, but no one else came. Taking a deep breath, she opened her back gate and peered out, ready to duck back and lock the gate. No sign of anyone else and the footsteps were fading into the distance.

The next gate opened and old Mr Diggan peered out from his house between hers and Hatterson's. She hurried along to him.

'They've captured Joe and have him locked up. We have to rescue him.'

'I thought he was too good at surveillance to be caught.'

'No one is perfect. I think they've got him locked in the coalhouse. Come on. We have to hurry.'

'That Hatterson has a padlock on the coalhouse door. He doesn't even trust his neighbours not to pinch his coal. He's a sick soul, that one is. Let me get something to break the lock with.'

He came back hefting a sledgehammer.

'Are you able to swing it hard enough?'

He let out a dry cackle of laughter. 'You start it swinging and its own weight carries it down. And if I damage the door because I miss the lock a time or two, who'll care by the time this night is over? You look after that. If they've tied him up we'll need it.'

He thrust a knife handle into her hand and she jumped in shock as she took it from him. He grabbed her other arm and then kept hold of it as they went into Hatterson's back garden.

From the coalhouse they heard the sound of agonised, muffled sobbing.

'He's just a lad,' whispered Miss Bowers. 'They forgot that. He's such a clever boy.'

'We'll back off a bit and come along making a noise,' Thad said. 'He won't want us to hear him crying.'

When they got to the door for a second time, he called out. 'Is someone in there?'

'Who's that?'

'Thad Diggan and Miss Bowers.'

'Can you get me out? I have to go to Greyladies. I have to tell them what I heard. I got the gag out of my mouth, but I can't untie myself.'

'Aye. I've brought my sledgehammer.'

It took four blows to break the wood around the padlock and another two to knock the hasp of the padlocked bar from the door frame. 'I'd ha' done that in one when I was younger,' Diggan muttered as he tugged the door open.

The moonlight showed the lad on the floor, propped up on a heap of coal.

Miss Bowers didn't need telling to cut the ropes binding Joe. 'Can you move about all right? Good. Then get going and spread the word. But take more care how you go this time.'

'They must have been expecting me, lying in wait, but they won't catch me again.' And he was off, hurrying along the back lane to the street, then slowing down to move along the verge from shadow to shadow, stopping to tap on the windows of some of the houses he passed.

The two old people followed him to the end of the lane to make sure he got away.

'We can't do any more,' Thad said.

'Oh yes we can. He's rousing the men who can fight. You and I are going to rouse the whole village. Those attackers are about to find out they're not only facing soldiers; they're facing the loyal people of Britain: men *and* women. They're going to know we're ashamed of their wickedness.'

'How many do you think will come with us?'

'Except for the traitors, everyone who can walk or hasn't got small children to look after. You'll see. You go that way, Thad, and I'll go this. Knock on every single door. Call people out. Tell them we must *all* go to Greyladies to stand up for what's right. See how those – those *fiends* like that!'

One of the soldiers Corin had set to keep watch on the perimeter of the grounds grunted as he was hit from behind. He fell to the ground and the man who'd hit him laughed.

'Tie him up and gag him, you fool!' Hatterson said in a low voice. 'Do you want him to make a noise and give warning?'

'What about his rifle?'

'Leave it where it fell. We're not thieves.'

'But it might come in useful.'

'We – are – not – *stealing*, and especially not from our fellow soldiers.'

They walked slowly and carefully across the soft grass of the abbey ruins, moving in ones and twos and gathering near the crypt.

'Not yet,' Hatterson muttered. 'Spread the word not to start till we're all here. Nev is going to send a message round when they're all in place at the other side.'

Corin marshalled his men, making sure they were all armed.

Ethel came to join them. 'You don't need to leave anyone inside the kitchen, Major, because I have your gun and I know how to use it. I'll not let anyone come in that way.'

'I thought I'd given it to my wife.'

'I'm a much better shot than she is and she hates even touching it.'

Cook came to stand beside her. 'I'll be there too, sir. With this.' She brandished a wicked-looking meat mallet.

'Good. Go and take your places.'

When he went back into the new house, a group of the more able internees met him.

'We want to help as well, Major.'

'I'm sorry, but I can't allow that.' He hesitated. 'Though if they get through and try to hurt you, I'd be more than happy to see you defend yourselves with whatever you can find.'

Since Phoebe refused point-blank to leave the old house, he stationed the doctor with her and her two visitors inside the old hall.

'I'm worried about my wife's condition,' he whispered to the doctor.

'I'll keep an eye on her. But she doesn't seem the sort to panic.'

'No. But I'm worried because she's more vulnerable at the moment and who knows what they will do to her if they get inside? I can't spare any more men, but you have a gun. Be prepared to use it.'

'I have a gun too,' Alex said.

Corin studied him, then looked at the weapon, which was well cared for. Seaton seemed a sensible fellow and very fond of Olivia. *She* wasn't the sort of woman who panicked and screamed either. At least, he didn't think she was. Well, if she was going to be the next chatelaine, she'd have to be a strong, steady sort of person.

But even though he'd placed his forces carefully, the ones who could actually fight were few on the ground for defending such a big house. If a big mob came in from the surrounding area, they'd be overcome eventually, and who knew what a mob might do then?

When he'd done everything he could, it was a question of waiting.

To his relief, four of the younger men from the village turned up a short time later, one armed with an old shotgun.

'I can only pepper them with bird pellets, sir,' its owner said. 'But that's not pleasant and it ought to slow them down, at least.'

'*If* we're attacked,' Corin reminded them. 'Don't fire unless they attack.'

'They'll attack, and soon. They're gathering in the village now,' another man said. 'I heard a car drive round to the other side of the abbey grounds too, so they must be gathering there as well. There have been people passing through the village for the past hour or more, trying not to make any noise. Ha! Proper townies, they are! You could hear most of them a mile off.'

'They didn't see you leaving?'

'No, sir. We were careful.'

There was a tap on the door of the kitchen in the new part of the house and the army cook peered out of the window. 'It's the lad. I can't see anyone else.'

He opened the door and shut it quickly once Joe was inside. After making sure the door was bolted behind him, he said sharply. 'Stand still, you, until we tell you it's all right to move. What are you doing here?'

'I need to see the major. I've come from the village and I've got information for him.'

'What the hell happened to you? You're filthy.'

'The troublemakers caught me and locked me in the coalhouse. Miss Bowers got me out.'

'Shall I take him to the major?' his assistant whispered.

'Yes.'

Corin wanted to know more details and Joe tried not to wince as he stood there, but his arm hurt every time he moved it. 'I've warned the men waiting in the village that it's nearly time.'

'Good. How did you get hurt?'

'After Hatterson tied me up, he gave me a kicking.'

'Damned coward! Better let the doctor look at that arm. Someone fetch him.'

'I'll go for him, Major. That at least I can do for you.' Mr Stein, who had been standing nearby listening, set off before anyone could stop him.

Corin continued questioning Joe about what he had seen and who he'd recognised, becoming grimmer when he heard that most of the men gathering in the village were outsiders.

'What the hell are they doing here, then?'

'There'll be some who're only interested in looting,' the commandant said. 'There always are. And some who enjoy violence and destruction. But there will be others going after our internees.'

'Unfortunately, yes. And there sound to be more of them than we'd expected. There have been some shocking incidents with mobs attacking Germans and other aliens living in Britain. And since we incarcerated them here at Greyladies, it's our bounden duty to protect them.'

He decided to stick to his original plan. 'We'll wait for them to start it. If they're anything like other hotheads, they'll not be able to hold back for long.' He looked at the commandant. 'You know what to do when I give the signal?'

Captain Turner nodded.

Then they all went back to waiting.

When told what had happened, the doctor frowned. 'If he's been badly beaten, I'd better have a look at that lad and check him for broken ribs or fractures. It'd make things worse if they bound up broken ribs.'

'I'll stay here in case I can be of use,' Mr Stein said. 'I may be too old to fight, but I can take messages or tell the major if they break in.'

'Good man. Find yourself somewhere out of sight near

the connecting door, because if they do break in, you'll want to leave before they have a chance to stop you. And it'd be better if they didn't see you go.'

The doctor left, and after examining Joe, he decided the boy didn't have any broken bones, though he was badly bruised, especially on the arm. He saw the tracks of tears on the boy's face and touched Joe's cheek lightly. 'Is the pain bad somewhere I haven't examined? If so, get the rest of your clothes off and show me.'

'No, sir. It's not that. I was . . . upset at myself for getting caught.'

'Well, you've wiped that mistake out now, because you got here without getting caught a second time and you alerted the people who're going to come up on our attackers from behind. Anyone can make a mistake. The thing is to learn from it. All in all, you've done very well indeed.'

'Can I go back and help fight them?'

'No. You'll be a hindrance rather than a help because your injuries will hold you back. But we'll ask the major if he needs a lookout anywhere. Youngsters have sharper eyes than us old fellows, especially in the dark, so you can still make yourself useful.'

Joe nodded, squaring his shoulders and standing very upright.

When he was assigned an upstairs bedroom at the side, he proudly took his position there, ready to continue doing his bit.

The messenger arrived from Nev to say the other big group of attackers had gathered and were ready to start. As agreed, they were going to split up into smaller groups to attack the various windows at Greyladies and break into the house from front and rear.

'Are you all sure of what you'll be doing?' Hatterson asked. 'You'll need to—'

'Of course we're sure. And we don't need you ordering us around. You aren't in the army now, you know.'

'But I have been.'

'So have I. Where do you think I got this?' The messenger held up one hand that had lost most of its fingers, with only parts of two digits remaining. He thrust it close to Hatterson's face, making the other man flinch back. '*This* is what the Huns did to me and it's why I'm here.'

He waited a minute, but there was no response, so he pulled back his hand. 'Come on, Group D. Get yourselves into place. We're all going to have some fun tonight and maybe pick up a few things we can sell,' he called.

In consternation Hatterson watched them go and turned to his friend. 'They're intending to loot the place!'

'Of course they are. No use letting useful things go to waste.'

'It's still thieving. I don't like associating with criminal types.'

'Get away with you. Those men will do what we want and he was right about one thing: We're *not* in the army and *you* aren't going to get the best cooperation tonight by using that tone of voice. The chaps are here because they *want* to get a crack at the Huns, not because they want to play soldiers.'

'We're not *playing* at soldiers. We *are* soldiers, unofficially. And soldiers don't loot their own countrymen.'

'Ah, what harm does it do to take things which are going

to be burnt anyway when we set fire to the house? You should look after yourself tonight and grab a few bits and pieces. I intend to see what I can find. As well as getting rid of a few Huns.'

From a bedroom window at the side of the house, Joe saw the group at the rear split up into three smaller groups. He rushed downstairs to where the major was directing operations. 'The big group at the rear has split up, sir.'

'The group at the front has separated into smaller groups, Major,' someone yelled. 'I can't keep track of them in the dark.'

At that moment a horn blared outside. 'Hoy! You inside,' someone yelled.

Corin went to peer cautiously out of a front window. 'What do you want?' he yelled.

'*The Huns. We don't want to hurt any British people, so if you send the Huns out, we'll leave you in peace.*'

'Do they honestly think we'd do that after they've been heard boasting about burning down the house? It's just an excuse to get the doors open,' Corin muttered. 'I shan't even answer.'

When no response was made, the offer was repeated.

Still Corin kept silent.

'Right. Since you refuse, we'll come in and get them! Death to the enemies of Britain.' It was easily recognisable as Hatterson.

Corin signalled to Captain Turner, who rushed off to his office to telephone for help.

Suddenly stones were hurled at the house from every vantage point and someone with a gun began firing it.

'Mobs don't usually have guns. What the hell are they doing?' Corin muttered.

There was the sound of smashing glass.

'Damnation! There goes another window. Thank goodness for stone window frames. We have to stop them breaking in until help comes.'

He didn't add *if* it comes. He had to trust that the local commander would believe Captain Turner about the urgency of the matter and the size of the mob.

Chapter Nineteen

Hatterson had insisted on organising one particular job himself, even though most of the strangers were cynical about the information it was based on.

Well, he knew better. He'd overheard more than the villagers realised recently, because there was nothing wrong with his hearing. A couple of people had talked about a secret passage from the crypt to the big house, not as a legend but a fact, because that Latimer bitch had actually been through it.

So he'd insisted on two men armed with a bolt cutter being sent to cut off the padlock that was used to keep it locked. They were to open up the door into the crypt as soon as the fighting started. Then they were to look for the passage and enter the house when they heard him break in. The crypt wasn't all that big. They were bound to find it.

The two men did as he'd told them and the padlock was quickly disposed of. They pushed open the grille, laughing.

'Fat lot of good a door like this is,' the older one muttered. 'Anyone could break in.'

The other one shivered and stood still for a moment. 'Is it my imagination or is it colder in here?'

'Well, it's underground, isn't it? Bound to be. Where's that electric torch you were given? Switch it on. The sooner we find that passage, the better. I want to be one of the first into the house, so that I can get my choice of the pickings.'

'Ah, it's a big house. There'll be enough stuff to go round before we burn it down.'

'Do you know what we're looking for in here?'

The younger fellow nodded. 'Yes, I do and Hatterson agrees with me. You have to find something to twist, like a bit of carving or a knob of wood, then a panel in a wall opens up. I read a book about secret passages when I was a lad, and that's the way most of them work.'

They slowed down as they left the short passage and entered the main chamber of the crypt. Even the light of a modern electric torch didn't seem to illuminate the big underground space very well. Shadows danced on the walls around them, shadows that looked like menacing figures shaking their fists. Of course they couldn't be, but still, the two men moved closer to one another.

'I don't like this place,' the younger one said suddenly. 'It smells of death. I hadn't thought of that.'

'You're not here to like it; you're here to do a job.'

Just then they heard something move inside the crypt.

'That wasn't a ghost. Quick, switch that torch off and get down behind this tomb.'

There was a grating sound and a thin shaft of light shone out from the wall in a corner at the rear of the crypt.

'Told you so,' the younger man said. 'It's a secret panel. And they're showing us the way.' He laughed softly.

The older man took a hasty step back. 'We'd better go and tell the others there's a group from the house coming this way.'

But as they turned to leave, a light began to glow between them and the way out.

'What the hell is that?'

As the light shimmered into the outline of a figure, the younger man wailed and yelled, 'It's the devil, come to get us! No, no! Go away!' He crouched down, pressed against the box tomb, hands over his head as if protecting himself from blows.

When he wouldn't get up, his companion tried to drag him towards the door.

But the first man from the house had got through from the tunnel by that time and he was from the village, so knew exactly who the glowing figure was. The light around it grew brighter, illuminating the two intruders nearby.

Bobbing his head quickly to the figure in a gesture of respect, the villager rushed across to grab the nearest man and yelled, 'Someone get the other chap.'

Within seconds both men had been captured, and although the older one put up a half-hearted struggle, the other continued to wail and beg to be saved from the devil.

All the time Anne Latimer's figure glowed steadily, giving them light to see by.

'The devil is welcome to you, as far as I'm concerned,' the group leader said, shaking the younger man good and hard. 'Tie them up and stick them in a corner. We have a job to do.'

He bobbed his head again to the ghost. 'Thank you, My Lady.'

The final men were out of the tunnel by then and once the intruders had been secured, the men from the big house made their way out of the crypt.

Behind them the light faded slowly, leaving the big echoing space in total darkness.

The younger intruder began crying for his mother.

The older one kept silent, shivering, wishing he'd never come, wondering what the authorities would do with him.

Several of the windows at Greyladies were smashed by now.

'Time to take them by surprise,' Hatterson said as his friend came across to join him. 'Are you going to create that other diversion, Nev?'

'Aye. I've got the fireworks ready. With a bit of luck one of them will set fire to the roof.'

'It's made of stone. We have to get *into* the house to set it on fire.'

'Well, I hope you really do have a way to get in. You do your bit and I'll do mine with the fireworks, like we planned.'

As the assault on the front of the house increased in intensity, Hatterson smiled in anticipation. He had a key to the rarely used back door of the laundry in the old part. It'd cost him a pound to buy it off one of the men in the village who had worked at Greyladies for a while, but been sacked for drunkenness. If it worked, it'd be well worth the money.

With some of his group creating an extra diversion by lighting a bonfire in one corner, he crept round to the laundry door. The key was a bit stiff but it worked. The door opened with a brief squeak. He doubted anyone would hear that with all the racket going on near the old stables and the first of the fireworks zipping into the air.

As soon as the bonfire started burning outside, he moved quietly into the house, not bothering to exaggerate his limp now. No one would notice in the dim light how he was walking.

He beckoned to his companion to join him and they moved forward, avoiding the kitchen, which his informant had told him how to do.

He grinned as he peeped into the long hall and saw her. *Yes, you bitch,* he thought. *You're going to pay dearly for housing those Huns.*

He wondered who the short fellow standing near her was. He hoped it was a new Hun. And who was the other woman? She wasn't bad looking. He giggled softly as he wondered if she'd ever been taken by a one-legged man. If he got the chance later . . .

He and his companion crept round the side of the room, taking advantage of the occupants' attention being diverted by the bonfire. As he'd planned.

Suddenly light began to shine on them. He cursed. What the hell was that?

It resolved itself into a woman's figure. He didn't believe in ghosts. They'd probably found some way of shining lights to fool the attackers, like they did in the theatre when they projected 'ghosts' on to a stage. He'd seen that done a couple of times now. It made the lasses scream.

But when he tried to raise the hand containing a club to thump whatever it was out of the way, he could only move slowly. Bewildered, he tried to act more quickly, but it was like stirring up treacle.

By then someone was calling out in a clear, bell-like voice. '*Beware of intruders, Phoebe and Olivia. Beware of intruders.*'

Ethel heard the noise and voices in the main room and looked at Cook. 'They must have got in another way.' She took out the gun. 'You stay here. If anyone tries to get through a window, bash them good and hard.'

She slipped through the kitchen door and glanced round the room. She saw Mr Stein leave through the connecting door. He'd be going for help. But would it come in time? She'd spotted Hatterson now and the expression on his face was that of a man in a dangerous mood.

She'd seen men in pubs drunk and spoiling for a fight. He looked drunk on something else, hatred perhaps, from the bitterness she'd seen on his face when she met him in the village.

Well, he wasn't going to hurt her mistress or those precious unborn children.

Neither of the men with him noticed her because they were gaping at the ghost.

As Ethel reached the group, the ghost began to fade.

'Hands up or I fire!' she shouted as loudly as she could.

Hatterson spun round and gaped at her then lunged towards Phoebe, hand outstretched to grab her. At the same time the man with him waved a knife at Olivia.

Ethel didn't waste any time. She raised the gun and took careful aim.

Hatterson laughed at her. 'Go on! I dare you. You'll miss me by a mile and hit her. You probably won't even dare fire that gun. You women are all cowards at heart.' He'd got hold of Phoebe's arm now.

At the same time his companion slashed his knife at Olivia. Alex stepped between her and her attacker, pushing her behind him, so Ethel left him to it.

'Last warning, Hatterson,' she said. 'I know how to use this gun.'

'Ooh, I'm scared.' He tried to pull Phoebe in front of him and the wickedness in his eyes as he looked at her belly was the final straw.

As calmly as if she'd been firing at a target, Ethel aimed at him. She yelled, 'Duck, ma'am!' just before she squeezed the trigger.

Phoebe threw herself sideways, even though he still had hold of her arm.

The shot sounded so loud Ethel's ears were ringing and she couldn't hear for a moment or two. Then she stared at what she'd done. There was no mistaking what she saw.

Phoebe was free of him now and was also staring down at him, while rubbing the arm he'd been gripping.

'I've killed a man!' Ethel said, feeling sick.

'*No, you've killed a madman and saved the lives of a woman and two children*,' a voice said in her head. Anne Latimer. '*You had no choice*.'

Ethel turned to see Major Latimer striding across the room, also with a gun in his hand.

Only then did she allow herself to drop the gun and plump down on the nearest chair, trying to control her nausea.

To Olivia's relief, the major moved towards the man threatening them with a knife.

'Get back, soldier, or I'll hurt them!' the man yelled, still waving the knife about wildly. 'You're not capturing me.'

'Drop that knife,' Corin said quietly but firmly.

'If you come any closer, I'll hurt your friends. If you let us all out, I'll release them and not hurt them.'

'You're going nowhere.'

'Then neither will they!' He surprised them by slashing out again with the knife.

Alex couldn't duck out of the way of that blade, and though he protected Olivia, he earned a long cut on his left cheek before Corin could pounce on his attacker.

Even then, the man clung to his knife and was big enough to make it difficult to subdue him.

None of them noticed Mr Stein creeping across the room. He picked up a vase and darted forward to smash it over the knife wielder's head. The knife fell from the man's hand and as he stumbled to his knees, groaning in pain, Corin grabbed one of his arms and twisted it behind his back.

By then two of the men from the village had followed the major in from the front of the house to help them and they took charge of the man.

'Are you all right, Seaton?'

Alex's voice was muffled by the handkerchief Olivia was using to staunch the blood.

'I think he'll need it stitching,' she said quietly. 'Hold still, Alex darling.'

He looked at her with such love that her breath caught in her throat and for a moment or two they both forgot the danger they were in.

Then Corin reminded them. 'I think we'd better regroup in the new part of the house.' He raised one hand to salute

Ethel. 'Well done, lass! I'd not have been in time to stop that madman. Are you all right now?'

She stood up a little shakily, nodding and picking up the gun.

Corin looked at Phoebe and she moved towards him, knowing what his glance was asking.

'I'm all right, darling. Hatterson only bruised my wrist.'

Corin took charge again, speaking crisply. 'He'll never hurt anyone else.'

As they began to leave the old part of the house, another noise was heard outside above the yells and the sound of stones smacking against the walls of the big house.

'What's that?' Corin asked. 'Shh!'

They stopped and listened.

'It sounds to be coming from further away,' Olivia said. 'And there are women's voices as well as men's.'

'What now?' Ethel muttered. 'Have they brought the whole of Swindon to attack us?'

Joe ran down the stairs to join them. 'Go and look at them, Major! You'll never believe it.' He danced round excitedly. 'Hurrah! We're saved,' he yelled.

Everyone ran towards the windows and in the moonlight they could see a line of people behind the figures of the attackers. Men, women and even older children came to a halt, standing there till they'd formed a human wall. They were banging saucepans and yelling.

'That's Miss Bowers at the front,' Phoebe said. 'And old Mr Diggan too.'

'Get out of our village!' a woman yelled at the top of her voice.

The cry was taken up by others and in a short time had

turned into a chant punctuated by banging spoons and other rhythmic noises.

Get – out of – our – village. Get – out of – our – village.

The noise increased steadily and as the solid line of villagers began to step forward to the rhythm of their words, the attackers fell back step by step, edging closer to one another at the same time.

Then, as the line moved inexorably forward, with people brandishing all sorts of kitchen and garden implements as weapons, one man broke from the mob and ran away towards the back of the house, followed by another, and then another, until all of them were fleeing.

The villagers let them go, though a few of the men followed to check that they weren't regrouping. The people stopped chanting suddenly and stood in front of the house.

Corin unlocked the front door and yelled, 'Well done, everyone. Well done!'

They began to cheer and clap one another on the shoulders. Women hugged, children danced up and down yelling, men roared in triumph.

Then that noise died down too as sanity returned in a wave of murmurs. They were smiling, nodding, bearing themselves like the victors they were.

'What wonderful people!' Olivia whispered to Alex. 'I feel honoured to be coming to live among them.'

'This is a wonderful place. Will you marry me and let me live here with you?'

She smiled. 'What a time to propose!'

'I couldn't wait. And where better to propose than here at Greyladies?'

'Yes. Where better?' Then she noticed the blood seeping from beneath the handkerchief. 'Come on! We've got to get you to the doctor. I'm sure that will need stitching up.'

By the time two lorries full of soldiers arrived, the danger was past and people from the village were dispersing.

'So you managed to quell the riot without help, sir?' the captain in charge said.

'I didn't quell it. The whole village turned out, armed with saucepans, hammers and even damned rolling pins. Must have been two or three hundred of them, shouting to the mob to get out of their village. I've never seen anything like it.'

But then, he thought, he'd never seen anything like Greyladies, either. Its legacy was strange in many ways, but full of loving kindness, bringing out the best in people. He'd miss the old house in many ways, much as he was longing to return to his own home.

Before he could do that, however, Britain still had a war to win and the internees here were a part of some less well-known initiatives that would contribute to that.

'No trouble from the internees?' the captain asked.

'Trouble? These lot are on our side. They were ready to fight the mob by our side, too. Not all Germans want war, believe me, and the government is benefitting greatly from that.'

'Jolly good show, sir. Um – do you think you'll need any more help?'

'There are one or two prisoners you could take away. Apart from that, we'll look after ourselves.'

It was full daylight before he could take the opportunity to rest. He found Phoebe in bed fast asleep and lay down beside her with a sigh.

Once the doctor had sewed up Alex's cheek and warned him not to bang it or try to shave until the stitches had been taken out, Olivia and Alex returned to the old house and took possession of a sofa in the long room.

They cuddled close to one another, talking or falling silent, discussing what they would do next.

'How soon can we marry?' he asked.

'As soon as you like. There's no reason to wait.'

'Good. We'll buy a special licence.'

'Where shall we live?' she asked.

'Until Phoebe and her husband move out, we can either take over your house in Swindon—' He broke off as she grimaced. 'Too many memories?'

'Yes. I want to make a new start with you, darling.'

'Then I'll buy my mother's house from my cousin and we'll live there until Phoebe and Corin are ready to leave. I just want to say . . . I've never been as happy in my whole life, Olivia. Never. Even in my wildest dreams, I couldn't have believed I'd find someone like you, someone who would want me, love me, marry me.'

'I didn't think I'd find someone else to love.'

'Do you think your Charles would have approved of me?'

'I'm sure he would. He was never mean about anything and he'd want me to remarry. But I don't think you realise what a lovely man you are.' Her voice became teasing. 'What if I'm only marrying you for your money?'

'Then I'll give it all to you. Every penny. But I know you're not.'

They broke off to smile at one another in the soft light of a single oil lamp, the way only lovers can smile. She nestled down against his right shoulder, made a soft, happy sound and fell asleep between one breath and the next.

He felt like a king.

Tired though he was, he didn't fall asleep, but sat and smiled down at her lovely sleeping face.

He didn't need Anne Latimer's ghost to tell him he'd be happy married to Olivia. She was the most wonderful woman in the whole world and he was the luckiest man to have won her love.

Epilogue

Challerton parish church was so full some people had to stand outside, and though it was a chilly day, the sun was shining brightly.

The groom arrived first, as was only proper, driven by a chauffeur and more nervous than he'd ever been in his life. When Alex got out of the car, he found a lady he didn't recognise waiting for him near the church door.

She stepped forward, smiling. 'Allow me to introduce myself. I'm Harriet Latimer, a former chatelaine of Greyladies. Joseph and I didn't arrive until late yesterday evening, so there was no opportunity to meet you before, as you were staying with Miss Bowers.'

'Phoebe told us about you. She wasn't sure whether you could get here in time, given wartime travelling conditions. I'm delighted to meet you.'

'My husband is waiting for the bride, since he's giving her away today.'

Alex's nervousness began to dissipate at the warmth of her smile. It seemed he'd be acquiring several new relatives through his marriage.

'It'll be lovely to see our newest chatelaine start her life here by getting married,' Harriet said. 'You can't have too many joyful occasions in the middle of a war. I don't think any chatelaine has started her life here by getting married before. I'm sure Miss Bowers will know whether that's true.' She took Alex's arm. 'I've been asked to escort you down the aisle and show you where to stand.'

'Can't Corin get here? Do I need to find another best man?'

'He's here, but he only arrived a few minutes ago, so he has to change his clothes. I came on ahead and he'll be with us soon.'

'Have you seen Olivia this morning? How is she?'

'Happy. And she'll make the loveliest bride with such a beautiful wedding dress.'

'It won't be nearly as beautiful as its wearer. Phoebe told me they'd found the perfect dress in the attic at Greyladies and Olivia knew someone in Swindon who could alter it to fit her. I'm not allowed to see it till she walks down the aisle, though.'

The verger cleared his throat. 'Excuse me interrupting, but it would be helpful to get the bridegroom seated, Mrs Latimer. And may I say how lovely it is to see you again.'

'It's lovely to be here. Come along, Alex.'

As they turned to go into the church, Corin and Phoebe came through the churchyard to join them, having taken a shortcut through the gardens of the big house. He held out a perfect white rose. 'Look what I found blooming. A miracle winter rose. Put it in your buttonhole, Alex. It's a gift from Greyladies.'

Alex did as he was told, then allowed Corin to escort him

down the aisle, while the two ladies followed them. People called out good wishes again and again as he passed – some of them he knew and others were complete strangers. The whole village seemed happy today, he thought in wonder.

He paused by Mildred and Edwin, sitting in the second pew on his side of the church, not saying anything, his heart was too full.

Mildred beamed at him and he inclined his head, then noticed Babs sitting on the other side of them.

'I don't need to wish you happy,' she said, 'because I'm sure you will be. It shines out of you.'

No one in the whole world had ever been as happy as he was today, he thought, taking his place in the front pew.

As they waited for the bride to arrive, he only half-heard Corin's remarks because he was listening for her, wouldn't feel this was real till he saw his beloved Olivia. He couldn't help fingering his scar. The stitches had been taken out, but it was still red and raw.

A badge of honour, people said. He didn't care what they called it. He'd got it saving his future wife's life.

Olivia stared at herself in the mirror, twisting and turning in front of it. She was delighted with her wedding dress, made from a gown of the 1830s that had been found in one of the attic trunks. As a concession to the fact that she was a widow marrying for the second time, she'd deliberately chosen to wear a cream-coloured day dress, not a long white wedding gown. She wanted everything to be different about this wedding.

The skirt was a full four yards round the hem and ended in a lace trim about six inches above the ground. The seamstress doing the alterations had assured her that this was the very latest fashion, as well as being practical for walking. She had a slender belt in pale-pink satin and a little lace over-jacket, also in pink.

She wasn't wearing a veil but a wide-brimmed hat with pale-pink and cream silk roses around the crown. It was, she thought, the most flattering hat she'd ever owned, though if she wore it to church on Sundays she'd block the view of the people behind her.

It'd be hard to give her new husband the traditional wedding kiss while wearing it, but she was quite sure they'd manage.

There was a knock on the door and she heard a man call out, 'Nearly ready, Olivia?'

'Absolutely ready.' She picked up her little mother-of-pearl purse on its silver chain. It was designed to be carried to balls but it suited her very well today, because it held a lace handkerchief and a small silver comb.

Joseph was waiting for her outside, beaming. His mouth went into an O shape at the sight of her.

'You make a beautiful bride, my dear.'

'Thank you. And you look very elegant, Joseph.' She felt as if she'd known him all her life, though she'd only met him once before today. But it was like that with the chatelaines who'd preceded her at Greyladies as well. Both of them and their husbands had immediately felt like close family.

Joseph's car was waiting outside, though it was only a short walk to the church and there was no sign of rain. He had a bad hip, which made him limp and move slowly, and she didn't want to arrive looking windblown.

As she got out of the car outside the church, she found

herself facing a crowd of women. They swayed forward as if they wanted to rush towards her, but didn't. Such a row of smiling faces. They called out best wishes in the lovely rolling Wiltshire accent she loved and she called back her thanks.

And then she was in church, music was playing and she was walking down the aisle to Alex, walking slowly when she wanted to run into his arms.

The wedding itself seemed to be taking place at a great distance until the reality of the vicar's words made her look at her new husband with eyes brimming with happy tears.

'You may kiss the bride.'

Alex had to bend his head sideways to get past the hat and they both smiled involuntarily as their lips met.

Then he stepped back, offered her his arm and they went to sign the church register.

Alex had even found a photographer to record this happy day, so she posed and moved as told, growing more impatient by the minute.

When they got into the car, she sighed in relief. 'Such a lot of fuss when *you* are the most important part of my day, darling Alex, not the dress or even the reception at Greyladies.'

'I feel the same. But we'll allow them to fete us and share our happiness.'

As they entered through the new part of the house, they passed between two lines of internees, more smiling faces and congratulations.

Once they were inside the old part of the house, time itself seemed suddenly to pause as the familiar light glowed at the top of the stairs.

This time Anne Latimer came slowly down to greet them and welcome them to their new home. '*You will be happy here*,' she promised as she had before.

No one else seemed to notice that they'd stopped or that the family ghost had appeared, and when Anne stepped back and faded from sight, they continued walking.

With her welcome ringing sweetly in their ears, they went into the old hall to receive their wedding guests and start their new life.